STEVE JACKSON & IAN LIVINGSTONE

FIGHTING FANTASY

Fighting Fantasy: new Wizard editions

1. The Warlock of Firetop Mountain
2. The Citadel of Chaos
3. Deathtrap Dungeon
4. Stormslayer
5. Creature of Havoc
6. City of Thieves
7. Bloodbones
8. Night of the Necromancer

Also available in the original Wizard editions

6. Crypt of the Sorcerer
7. House of Hell
8. Forest of Doom
9. Sorcery! 1: The Shamutanti Hills
10. Caverns of the Snow Witch
11. Sorcery! 2: Kharé – Cityport of Traps
12. Trial of Champions
13. Sorcery! 3: The Seven Serpents
14. Armies of Death
15. Sorcery! 4: The Crown of Kings
16. Return to Firetop Mountain
17. Island of the Lizard King
18. Appointment with F.E.A.R.
19. Temple of Terror
20. Legend of Zagor
21. Eye of the Dragon
22. Starship Traveller
23. Freeway Fighter
24. Talisman of Death
25. Sword of the Samurai
27. Curse of the Mummy
28. Spellbreaker
29. Howl of the Werewolf

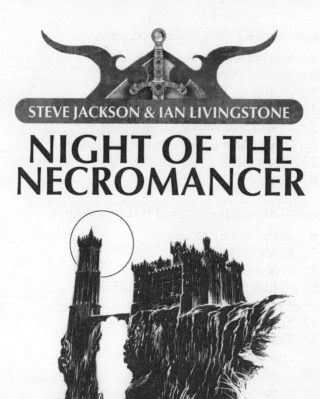

STEVE JACKSON & IAN LIVINGSTONE

NIGHT OF THE NECROMANCER

By Jonathan Green

Illustrated by Martin McKenna

Published in the UK in 2010 by Wizard Books,
an imprint of Icon Books Ltd., Omnibus Business Centre
39–41 North Road, London N7 9DP
email: info@iconbooks.co.uk
www.iconbooks.co.uk/wizard

Sold in the UK, Europe, South Africa and Asia
by Faber & Faber Ltd., Bloomsbury House
74–77 Great Russell Street, London WC1B 3DA or their agents

Distributed in the UK, Europe, South Africa and Asia
by TBS Ltd., TBS Distribution Centre, Colchester Road,
Frating Green, Colchester CO7 7DW

Published in Australia in 2010 by Allen & Unwin Pty. Ltd.,
PO Box 8500, 83 Alexander Street, Crows Nest, NSW 2065

Distributed in Canada by Penguin Books Canada,
90 Eglington Avenue East, Suite 700, Toronto,
Ontario M4P 2Y3

ISBN: 978-1-84831-118-3

Typesetting by Hands Fotoset, Mapperley, Nottingham

Printed and bound in the UK by
Clays of Bungay

For Martin McKenna – thank you

CONTENTS

HOW WILL YOU START
YOUR ADVENTURE?

The book you hold in your hands is a gateway to another world – a world of dark magic, terrifying monsters, brooding castles, treacherous dungeons and untold danger, where a noble few defend against the myriad schemes of the forces of evil. Welcome to the world of **Fighting Fantasy**!

You are about to embark upon a thrilling fantasy adventure in which **YOU** are the hero! **YOU** decide which route to take, which dangers to risk and which creatures to fight. But be warned – it will also be **YOU** who has to live or die by the consequences of your actions.

Take heed, for success is by no means certain, and you may well fail in your mission on your first attempt. But have no fear, for with experience, skill and luck, each new attempt should bring you a step closer to your ultimate goal.

Prepare yourself, for when you turn the page you will enter an exciting, perilous **Fighting Fantasy** adventure where every choice is yours to make, an adventure in which **YOU ARE THE HERO!**

How would you like to begin your adventure?

If you are new to Fighting Fantasy ...

You probably want to start playing straightaway. Just turn over to the next page and start reading. You may not get very far first time but you'll get the hang of how Fighting Fantasy gamebooks work.

If you have played Fighting Fantasy before ...

You'll realise that to have any chance of success, you will need to discover your hero's attributes. You can create your own character by following the instructions on pages 353–354, or, to get going quickly, you may choose one of the existing Fighting Fantasy adventurers described on pages 350–352. Don't forget to enter your character's details on the Adventure Sheet which appears on pages 360–361.

Game Rules

It's a good idea to read through the rules which appear on pages 353–359 before you start. But as long as you have a character on your Adventure Sheet, you can get going without reading the Rules – just refer to them as you need to.

DEAD RECKONING

As the sun sets – a ball of molten iron sinking into the chill waters of the Diamond Sea – you catch sight of Valsinore at long last. With a shout of 'Yaah!' you kick your heels into your horse's heaving flanks and spur it on towards the distant castle. By nightfall you will be home.

You have been away a long time, three years in fact. Three years following the crusading banner of the Knights of Telak. Three years spent in the accursed land of Bathoria, domain of demons and the Lords of Night. Three years fighting the forces of darkness.

In that time you have faced all manner of evils and found yourself in all kinds of life-threatening situations. In fact you almost lost your life on more occasions than you care to remember. But you survived everything that the forces of darkness could throw at you – from an ambush by a pack of werewolves to the seductive enchantments of the Sepulchral Sisterhood – thanks in part to your knightly skills and prowess in battle, but also thanks to your sanctified, charm-wrought sword Nightslayer.

And now, at last, your home is in sight once more. Three years ago you set out from Valsinore Castle on the northern coast of Ruddlestone to join in the crusade to purge Bathoria of the malign influence of the Cult of Death. With the defeat of the Death-Mage Thanatos, your sworn oath fulfilled, you were free to return home. As you recovered from your last battle at a hospice of the White Lady, you sent letters by messenger ahead of you telling of your imminent homecoming, writing one to your sister, Oriana, who was anxiously awaiting news of your safe return, and another to your chamberlain, Unthank, who you had left to look after your estates and safeguard the people of the Sourstone peninsula while you were away. And there is one other who you are eager to see again after so long – your faithful hound who you left to watch over both the castle but more particularly Oriana.

The sky purpling like a bruise as dusk descends, you guide your steed down off the bleak moorland road towards Valsinore Castle, not once taking your eyes off your ancestral home. It is clearly visible now, an imposing silhouette of rising battlements and looming towers. You can also see the village of Sleath that lies close to the castle, in the shadow of the fortress and before that, to the west, the brooding expanse of Wraith Wood. To the east the bleak, windswept moors continue as far as the eastern cliffs of the Sourstone promontory.

But before you reach home, the Moot Road takes you through the desolate wilderness that the ancient tribal people of these lands once called home. Northern Ruddlestone still bears the marks left by these ancient warrior clans; burial mounds dot the landscape along with time-worm druidic stone circles. You gallop past one such circle of standing stones – known locally as the Nine Maidens – as the dusk continues to deepen around you, desperate to be home now after such a long time away. But it is in this treacherous twilight that the trap is sprung.

Three men – dark hoods pulled up over their heads to hide their faces – burst from their hiding places among the standing stones and come at you, armed with swords and axes. Your steed whinnies and rears up on its hind legs in surprise. Exhausted after your long ride, you are thrown from the saddle and land hard on the cold ground. Your horse panics and gallops away as your attackers bear down on you, weapons raised.

You scramble to your feet, Nightslayer already in hand. Ruffians like these shouldn't give you any real trouble, even in your weary state. But as the men close in on you with murder on their minds, you notice the fourth member of their band for the first time as he appears to coalesce from out of the gathering darkness.

He is dressed from head to toe in long black robes, his face hidden behind a grotesque skull-mask. The man does not appear to be armed but in one hand he is holding a glowing sphere of amethyst that seems to swirl with gathering storm clouds. You have encountered his kind before, during your crusade to Bathoria. He is an acolyte of the priesthood of Death himself.

As you keep a watch on him out of the corner of your

eye you prepare to meet the would-be assassins' assault. They are no match for your knightly skills and you have soon dealt all of them flesh wounds. In a few moments the battle will be over. But before you can finish the fight, the death-masked cultist casts his spell.

A ball of crackling black light explodes from the acolyte's crystal, forms into a spear of energy that flashes past the beleaguered murderers and hits you full in the chest. You experience a moment of intense pain like you have never known before as the spell hurls you back onto the road again. And then the pain is gone leaving you feeling numb and cold. Who has done this to you and why, when you were so close to home at last?

You waste no time in getting to your feet and bringing your sword to bear once more. Your assailants suddenly stagger away from you, expressions of abject fear on their faces. Only the Death Acolyte appears unperturbed. You are used to intimidating your enemies but you have never received quite such a reaction before.

One of the men keeps looking down at the ground and then back up at you again, a look of utter, disbelieving horror on his face. In fact, he looks like he's seen a ghost. Curious to know what it is that has the thugs so shaken, you glance down at the ground too.

Bathed in an eerie luminescence is what appears to be a body. Judging by the scorched ragged hole in the middle of its chest you would guess that it is dead, for how could anyone survive such a grievous injury …? It is only then that you realise that the body you are staring at aghast is your own.

Standing over your dead body, you are a glowing ethereal copy of yourself. Your ghostly form is dressed in the same apparel as your corpse and you are even wielding a phantasmal duplicate of your sword Nightslayer, although the real thing is still lying on the ground next to your lifeless body.

The shock you feel at realising that you are dead is nothing compared to the rage and desire for revenge that consumes you now. There will be a reckoning this night, when all those responsible for your untimely death will be made to pay for the evil they have perpetrated against you. Screaming like a banshee, you move to engage your murderers in battle.

Turn to **1**.

1

As you stalk towards the murderous thugs one of the men gives voice to a terrified scream, his face draining of all colour, turns tail and flees. Another drops his weapon in shock, while the third lets out a whimper of fear and collapses to his knees, sobbing like a baby. Only the Death Acolyte appears to be holding things together, his hand moving over his crystal ball, his lips forming the words of some esoteric invocation, no doubt.

These men are responsible for your death and you will have vengeance upon them. But which will you confront first, the three terrified murderers (turn to **25**) or the spell-casting Death Acolyte (turn to **45**)?

2

'That is the correct answer,' the Paladin's ghost intones. He then takes some time to demonstrate how you can make the most of your new, paranormal abilities. (Add 1 to your WILL score and 1 to your LUCK.) Write the number 2 on your *Adventure Sheet* and then roll one die, turning to the paragraph indicated on the table below.

Die roll

1–2	Turn to **120**
3–4	Turn to **230**
5–6	Turn to **293**

The Paladin having offered you what aid he can, bids you farewell before melting back into the moonlight.

Feeling encouraged that you might yet win your own personal battle against the forces of the darkness, you leave the shrine. Turn to 259.

3

Before long you are enveloped within the bounds of Wraith Wood. The trees grow thick and dark around you, although you can still make out the glowing orb of the moon between the leafless branches above you that look like the clawing talons of skeletal hands. Black thunderheads are starting to mass on the horizon, and the wind is picking up. You believe that the wise-woman's hovel lies at its heart, although some say that she is actually a witch. But, all things considered, if anyone can help you, probably a practitioner of the dark arts can.

The blaring note of a hunting horn suddenly breaks the unnatural stillness of the wood and you hear the pounding of hooves on the wind. Following the sound to its source, you look up to see ethereal riders galloping towards you out of the gathering storm clouds, their phantom steeds pounding the air while shimmering spectral hounds sprint ahead of them. This wild hunt appears to be heading directly towards you. Will you:

Stand your ground and unsheathe your phantasmal blade?	Turn to 49
Try to hide from the hunt in the undergrowth?	Turn to 169
Flee from the ethereal huntsmen?	Turn to 190

4

'Curse you witch!' you shout into the cold night air. 'You shall not have your sacrifice!' You are suddenly wracked by the most agonising pain. It feels as if your very soul is being crushed by the taloned hand of Death itself, squeezing the life-force out of you. Roll one die and add 2; you must lose this many STAMINA points, along with 2 SKILL points, 1 LUCK point and 2 WILL points. If you are still alive, if you can really be considered as being alive anymore, turn to **43**. If you do not survive the effects of the Witch's Curse, write the number 43 on your Adventure Sheet and turn to **100**.

5

And so you find yourself within the Inner Ward of Castle Valsinore. To your left, against the western wall, stands the castle cookhouse which abuts onto the grand structure of the Lord's Feast Hall where many a mighty banquet was held in your father's time.

At the far end of the impressive courtyard you can see the gatehouse that stands before the sea-moat, beyond which lies a bridge that leads to the black stone Keep. You fancy you can see something fiery flickering in the darkness there, like sparks rising from a furnace, but before you even get as far as the gate you can see that a wooden scaffold has been constructed at the centre of the courtyard.

The north-eastern quarter of the Inner Ward is taken up by the castle chapel and the private plot of the family graveyard used in more recent times. Beneath the chapel lie the extensive tunnels of the castle catacombs, constructed during the first age of the castle, centuries ago, by your distant ancestors. You yourself have not explored their labyrinthine tunnels. Nurses' tales of giant rats and worse lurking in the dark kept you from ever going down there as a child. Castle legend has it that there is another way into the extensive tomb-tunnels via a passageway at the bottom of the castle well, the stone-clad well-head of which lies to your right, in the south-eastern corner of the courtyard.

The last remaining feature worthy of note is the ruined east wall tower. Known as the Blasted Tower, its upper levels were destroyed long ago by a bolt of lightning that sent the top two storeys tumbling into the Diamond Sea far below. You just need to decide where you want to explore first. Will it be:

The castle kitchens?	Turn to **335**
The feast hall?	Turn to **95**
The chapel?	Turn to **260**
The Blasted Tower?	Turn to **34**
The well?	Turn to **232**

If you would rather not delay here at all, you can approach the last gatehouse that guards the entrance to the sea-moat bridge (turn to **134**) or, if you have the *Spirit* special ability, take to the air and try approaching the Keep directly (turn to **191**).

6

And then you come before the main gate of Valsinore Castle. This was the place where you and your sister played as children and which became your responsibility upon the death of your father at seventy years old, and who had himself been widowed many winters before. But your ancestral home appears anything but welcoming to you now. Its high crenulations loom over you while its torch-lit windows seem to stare down with malignant intent. There is an oppressive atmosphere hanging over the place.

You have seen neither hide nor hair of the Death Acolyte since your encounter with him and his murdering band on the moor turnpike, but you can't shake the feeling that the truth you are searching for will be found within your castle home. But how do you plan on gaining access?

Two guards, armed with halberds, are on sentry duty before the main gate. However, you do know of another way in. Along the eastern wall of the outer ward of the castle is a culvert, a drain that lets filth and waste water out under the wall and down over the cliff edge into the sea. The prospect of crawling up a sewer – even if you are a ghost – does not fill you with glee, and staring up at the looming walls you wonder what it would be like to soar over them in your spectral form.

If you want to try to fly over the battlements, turn to **75**. If you would rather try gaining entry through the

⚃ ⚄

culvert, turn to **36**. Then again, if you simply want to approach the main gate and the guards on duty there, turn to **242**.

7

Re-tracing your steps back through the castle, you come at last to the haunted stable, and there, waiting for you, is the phantom steed. Clambering up onto its back, as if you were still alive and mounting a living, breathing horse, you ride it out of the stables. Once you are out in the open you kick your ghostly heels into the beast's ethereal flanks and spur the horse into a gallop. It races towards the outer wall of the castle and with one great bound leaps over it! It doesn't land on the other side either, but instead, pounding the air with its ethereal hooves, gallops away into the night sky. (If you have the phrase *Best Friend* written on your Adventure Sheet you will no longer benefit from the advantages this brings until you return to Valsinore Castle.)

Rivers and forests, towns and villages, hills and heathland, all rush past below in a high-speed blur. In what seems like no time at all you reach your destination. The phantom steed sets foot on solid ground again and you dismount. Your steed will go no further. But where was it that you were travelling to?

Fetchfen, Village of the Damned? Turn to 441
Frostfinger, the Winter King's tower? Turn to 168

8

'Unthank? He can't be trusted,' Oriana confesses. 'It was him who invited the Knights of the Black Shroud to take up residence here. There's no sign of them during the day but at night they wriggle out of the stonework again like maggots crawling from a rotten apple. And no one other than him and the knights have been allowed into the Keep for months.'

If you want to ask your sister something else, turn to 48. If you would prefer to bid her farewell and be on your way, will you head down into the catacombs (turn to 88), or vacate the chapel and search elsewhere (turn to 445)?

9

You flee from Mother Toadsfoot's cottage as fast as you can, and don't once look back. You are soon deep in the night-shrouded woods again. Eerie cries echo between the night-black trees. An owl hoots and you hear the croaking of toads coming from a reedy pool somewhere nearby.

⚅ ⚅

And then, at last, the forest starts to thin and you emerge on the other side of Wraith Wood. Trees give way to tumbled headstones and you find yourself passing between the overgrown graves of a cemetery. Ahead of you lies the village of Sleath, but before you can reach it, or the castle beyond, you must first cross the neglected graveyard. Turn to **107**.

10

The door is made of some black wood ensorcelled with silver that forms unsettling signs and symbols. As you approach you can feel its power, like a crackling magical shield. The energy field sparks violently and you are suddenly hurled backwards by a powerful burst of magical energy. (Lose 2 STAMINA points and if this has reduced your STAMINA score to zero, or below, write the number 445 on your *Adventure Sheet* and turn to **100**.) The door is resisting your ethereal essence somehow and keeping your ghostly form at bay. You cannot even get close enough to touch it.

The door before you is a Spirit Door, a portal intended to prevent undead spirits like you from passing through it. There is nothing you can do to conquer the spells bound into it – at least, not yet – so you have no choice but to search elsewhere. Add the codeword *Catacombs* to your *Adventure Sheet* and turn to **264**.

11

Now that you have a physical form of sorts again you are able to open the Spirit Door and step through it into the tunnels beyond. These are the true cata-combs. They are a veritable maze of mouldering passageways, forgotten burial chambers and gloomy mausoleums, but you feel another power – unmis-takeably a force for Good – leading you onwards through the labyrinthine passageways.

You come at last to a vast chamber, its roof supported by pillars of black marble. As you enter, iron basket-braziers around the walls burst into flame, revealing the sepulchre in all its terrible splendour. In fact, it looks more like a throne room than a burial chamber. In the distance you can make out tombs and stone sarcophagi but in the middle of the chamber, in front of you is a black marble throne. Seated upon the throne is a beautiful woman wearing luxurious robes, befitting a monarch, and a golden crown. Behind her throne, half-hidden in the shadows cast by the gutter-ing braziers, you can see a host of decomposing figures, watching you with baleful, jaundice-yellow eyes from out of the darkness. The woman is toying with something in her hands. It is your own blessed blade, Nightslayer! You are about to take a step for-ward when common sense halts you.

'Ah, so you've found us,' the woman says, as she examines the sword in her hands. The runes that spell out the name Nightslayer blaze red as they catch the light of a smouldering brazier. She suddenly looks up and you are astonished by just how beautiful she is. Her eyes blaze with a dark intensity as she regards you with an unblinking stare. 'Be welcome here, you belong here after all' – a serpent smile twists her features into those of something not altogether human – 'with your Queen. Now come, bow before me.'

You have a feeling that bowing before her is the last thing you should do, but judging by the zombie host gathered behind her, ready to do whatever she demands of them, it might be your best chance of snatching Nightslayer from her grasp and getting out of here with your soul intact. Will you bow before this Queen of the Damned (turn to **112**), or will you renounce her claim of dominion over you (turn to **246**)?

12

A savage baying suddenly interrupts the old man's musings. 'Moon dogs!' Yorrick gasps, a fearful look entering his eyes as he stares up at the milky orb of the moon high above. Judging by its position in the sky overhead, the hour must be close to midnight. 'Quick! We'd both best be on our way before they find us.' (Add the codeword *Baying* to your *Adventure Sheet*.) Deciding that Yorrick is probably right, thanking him for his help you part company with the old gravedigger and hurry away from your open grave. Will you enter the chapel, if you haven't tried to already (turn to **274**), or choose somewhere else entirely (turn to **445**)?

13

Although you are have the ability to seize control of another's body to use as your own, the idea of even

⚃ ⚁

attempting to possess another living person in order to wear their physical form as you might a suit of armour fills you with unease. If you want to pursue this route to acquire a physical form again, you will need to know where a suitable host can be found, and that means that they have to be somewhere within the castle already. If you know where someone is, and they are alive, then you will also know their name. Convert the first name of the person you want to possess into a number using the code A=1, B=2, C=3 ... Z=26. Add the numbers together, multiply the total by 3 and turn to the paragraph with the same number.

If you do not know of any suitable candidates and simply want to try possessing one of the castle's guards, turn to **301**. However, if you do not wish to continue with this course of action, you will have to try something else. If you have the phrase *Rest in Peace* recorded on your *Adventure Sheet* and you want to pursue this path, turn to **369**. If you have the codeword *Automaton* written down and you want to pursue this path, turn to **427**. If you have no further tricks up your sleeve, turn to **152**.

14

Bertild the blacksmith looks up from her hammering and freezes. 'Then what they've been saying is true,' Bertild gasps and a single tear courses down her soot-smeared cheek. 'Here, come in, come in,' she says, hurrying over to the door and clearing a gap in the salt barrier to let you across before closing the door behind you. 'Tell me, what happened?' the woman mumbles, obviously in some distress.

And so you sit down in the comforting warmth of the forge, in the company of one of your oldest and most trusted friends, and tell Bertild how you were cut down within sight of home for the first time after three years away, and everything that has befallen you since.

'I swear by Verlang and the spirits of the forge,' she says, a grim expression on her face, 'your death shall not go unavenged.'

To hear Bertild say that fills you with hope and you begin to believe that it truly is possible. (Regain 1 LUCK point and add 1 to your WILL score.)

'Valsinore Castle is under a curse,' the blacksmith says. 'These are dark times indeed. But listen to me going on. Tell me, what is it you need to know that you might achieve your vengeance?'

Remembering all the times you spent watching Bertild at her forge, you decide that she might be in possession of unique knowledge that could serve you well in your quest. Will you ask her whether she knows of the existence of any weapons or armour that may aid you in your quest (turn to **51**), ask her if she has any idea as to who would have wanted you killed (turn to **21**), or will you ask her if she knows of anyone else resident within the castle who could help you (turn to **161**)?

⚃ ⚁

15

Over one hundred years ago, the man who now calls himself Chamberlain Unthank, slaughtered the entire population of Fetchfen that his dark gods might grant him the power over death he so desired. And now you have visited this village of the damned and escaped with your soul intact. But you have spent long enough here and it is time to return to Valsinore Castle to bring Unthank's reign of terror to an end. Regain 1 LUCK point and turn to **29**.

16

As you approach the Chamberlain, he snaps his fingers and summons a serving boy to pour him more wine. He appears distracted as he observes the players perform before him and keeps glancing towards a passageway half-hidden by a grand tapestry showing the defeat of the Sourstone Worm by your ancestor, Agravain Wormslayer. Turn to **227**.

17

Tendrils form within the fog, reaching for you, trying to force you to join the macabre dance of the Phantasmagoria. You slice at them with your shimmering blade as you start to fight back against the dream-monster and its hallucinatory nightmares.

PHANTASMAGORIA   SKILL 8   STAMINA 10

If the nightmarish manifestation destroys you, reducing your STAMINA score to zero, write the number 99 on your *Adventure Sheet* and turn to **100**. If you reduce

⬛ ⬛

the Phantasmagoria's STAMINA score to zero, turn to 142.

18

Perhaps it is merely some diabolical illusion, but it feels as though you have been climbing this staircase for hours and you wonder whether you haven't fallen into some hellish trap to which there is no end. And then, after a further half an hour's climb, you enter another ice-rimmed chamber. The chamber is empty, apart from a pedestal formed of black granite and blue ice at its centre, atop which rests a multi-faceted jewel roughly the size and shape of a human skull. As you peer into the shimmering jewel you fancy you can see ghostly faces looking out at you. But you're not imagining things, they really are there, and you can hear them now, speaking to you inside your head – insistent voices demanding to be released from their prison of eons. Something tells you that if the power of the Spirit Stone is connected to those souls bound to it and that if it is to prove of use to you, you should not grant them their request – at least, not yet. But what is more amazing is that you are able to touch and even lift the artefact in your own ethereal hands. Greedily you take hold of the jewel. (Add the Spirit Stone to your *Adventure Sheet* and note down that it has 333 faces.) There is only one way out of this chamber and it is the one you entered by, so turning on your heel, with the Spirit Stone in hand, you set off carefully back down the endlessly winding staircase. Turn to 304.

⚅ ⚅

19

At the crossroads, you peer ahead into the darkness and decide which way to proceed. The moorland road that you have been following continues straight ahead into the village of Sleath. A narrower, but equally well-trodden path leads westwards towards the cemetery that lies outside the village, while a gravelled road bears north-east before turning north again, leading towards the stone bridge over the River Sorrow that must be crossed on the way to Valsinore Castle. So which way will you go now in your quest for revenge? Will you head:

West, towards the graveyard?   Turn to **107**
North, towards Sleath?   Turn to **61**
North-east, towards the bridge and
   Valsinore Castle?   Turn to **121**

20

Outside the Barbican gatehouse once more, choosing something you haven't tried already, will you:

Attempt to pass through into the Inner Ward of the castle?	Turn to **60**
Climb the staircase beyond the left archway?	Turn to **271**
Climb the staircase through the right archway?	Turn to **85**
Find another way into the Inner Ward?	Turn to **393**

21

Bertild looks at you grimly. 'I wouldn't like to say for sure,' she says glancing anxiously into the corners of the smithy. 'Round here, it's like the walls themselves have ears, if you know what I mean.' She leans closer and whispers, 'But I do believe that when you left to go on crusade, evil was already lurking here in Valsinore Castle. But I'll tell you who you do need to look out for, and that's the Knights of the Black Shroud who arrived here a year ago and never left!' Now turn to **140**.

⚄ ⚅

It is then that you hear the splashing sounds of something wading from the breakers behind you accompanied by a croaking cry.

'Oh no, please,' the old man cries, 'not that! Anything but that!'

You turn to see the most appalling abomination emerge from the rising tide and stalk towards you up the beach. It walks on two legs like a man and has the muscular build of an ogre, but its skin is covered with blue-grey scales. It has cruel gutting claws, its fingers are webbed and its bulbous eyes are those of a fish. A crest of spines protrudes from its head and runs all the way down its back to a long, lashing fish tail. The creature opens its mouth, revealing rows of shark's teeth, while the slits of gills in its neck open and close uselessly in the air.

'My tormentor comes to plague me again! Oh, woe. My doom is upon me!' the hermit cries and retreats back into his cave, leaving you to face the monster alone. The fish-beast fixes its eyes upon you and gives another croaking snarl as it continues to stalk towards you.

This is no mere creature of flesh and blood but a demon birthed from the storm-wracked sea; the monster's cruel fish-talons will harm you just as well as if you were still a creature of flesh and blood yourself. Fortunately, your own ethereal copy of

⚁ ⚂

Nightslayer will also be able to injure the demon. Let battle commence!

SEA DEMON   SKILL 9   STAMINA 10

If the Sea Demon 'kills' you, record the number 145 on your *Adventure Sheet* and turn to **100** at once. However, if you manage to slay the demon, turn to **145**.

23

Suddenly the words of the Witch's bargain come unbidden into your mind. *You must slay that which is most dear to you, next time you meet, be it man or lowly beast, or suffer the consequences …*

The witch's bargain hangs like a millstone about your neck, dragging you down into the depths of despair. But the crone was quite clear about the price you would have to pay for her aid. *Another's life-force for yours …*

You have never been faced with such a quandary in all your life. Will you cut Korzen down with your ghostly sword, so that you might continue with your quest unhindered (turn to **138**), or will you leave the dog alive and risk whatever might befall you (turn to **4**)?

24

Whether you are unwilling or unable to subject your physical form to the Demon Gate's demands, you still need to source flesh and blood from somewhere. But where are you going to find an offering of flesh for the gate down here? You could retrace your steps through the dungeon but that would take time, and time is something you do not have. And then the answer strikes you – the putrescent pool! It is *full* of decomposing flesh.

Not relishing the necessity of what you are about to do, you approach the edge of the pit. You scoop a handful of the green-black slime from the pool and are horrified to see it start to eat away at your gauntlet hand. (Lose 2 STAMINA points and 1 SKILL point, for as long as you remain in this metal body.) The surface of the pool suddenly heaves and something truly awful rises from its depths. Turn to **430**.

25

Screaming like a banshee, you launch yourself at the terrified ruffians, who try to run from before your unearthly wrath. In desperation they fight back but even when one of them manages to get a strike in under your guard the assassin's weapon simply passes straight through your ethereal body as if it were nothing but mist – and you do not feel a thing! Their weapons may be useless against you but your phantasmal sword cuts them down just as if you were still wielding the genuine article and not a ghostly replica of Nightslayer.

In no time at all, the three murderers lie dead at your feet on the moorland road. Only the Death Acolyte remains. You can hear him now quite clearly, muttering under his breath in some dark tongue. Do you want to strike the acolyte down immediately, without hesitation (turn to **114**), or will you press him for information as to who it was that wanted you dead (turn to **64**)?

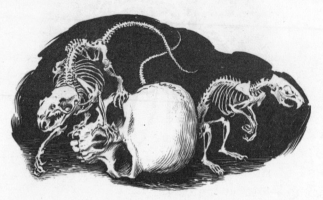

26

You have succeeded in taking over the guard's body. The man's consciousness flees to some dark corner of his mind as you take control. (Add the codeword *Host* to your *Adventure Sheet*.)

Make a note of your spirit-form's current SKILL and STAMINA score, for later use, on your *Adventure Sheet*. While you are clothed in the flesh of the guard you must use the guard's stats which are as follows: SKILL 8, STAMINA 18.

If you are injured in battle you may eat provisions to recover STAMINA points. One meal restores up to 4 STAMINA points and the guard has enough food about his person for 3 meals. He is armed with a non-magical sword, which means that you are now too. If the guard's STAMINA is reduced to 2 STAMINA points of fewer he will be knocked senseless, forcing you to vacate his body. You may then continue fighting in your spirit-form using the stats that you have written down here. Now turn to **429**.

27

'Out of the way now, Rutterkin,' she says as she nearly trips over her pet pig on her way to the table on which lies her Book of Spells. Without looking down at the black-bound tome before her, the crone flicks through it, seemingly at random, until she lets the book fall open at a particular page. She then proceeds to run her fingers over the words scrawled there in a spidery hand.

⚁ ⚁

'Yes, that should just about do it,' she says. 'But it's going to cost yer!'

You explain to the witch that you have no means of paying her. What little Gold you did have is with your body still, back on the Moot Turnpike.

'That's not the sort of payment I had in mind,' she says with a cruel chuckle. If you want to continue with this exercise, turn to 54. If you would rather quit this place and have nothing more to do with the sinister Mother Toadsfoot, turn to 9.

28

'I am sure that Father Umberto could help,' Oriana says. 'He is wise to the ways of the Undead and knows many potent prayer-spells. Wait here awhile, he will not be long.' If you want to wait for the Priest's return, turn to 48. If you would prefer to bid your sister farewell and be on your way, will you head down into the catacombs (turn to 88), or leave the chapel and explore the Inner Ward further (turn to 445)?

29

Back within the walls of Valsinore Castle once again, with the moon commencing its descent towards the horizon, you decide that it is time to find out what secrets lie within the Keep, and so make for the gatehouse and the moat bridge. (If you have the phrase *Best Friend* written on your *Adventure Sheet* you now regain the benefits associated with this.)

⚃ ⚄

Do you have any of the codewords *Baying*, *Banshee* or *Bard* written down on your *Adventure Sheet*? If you have none, turn to **117**. If you have one or two, *Test your Luck*; if you are Lucky, turn to **117**, but if you are Unlucky, turn to **320**. If you have all three, turn to **320** straightaway.

30

The black pit of the freshly-dug hole appears like a whirling void of oblivion, the darkness sucking you in like a whirlpool pulls at a ship tossed in a storm. You cry out, your startled cry of fear becoming a drawn-out howl of horror as you are sucked down, down, down into the blackness of the grave ... and beyond ... Write the number 195 on your *Adventure Sheet* and turn to **100**.

31

The passageway brings you to a flight of stone steps that descend into the lower levels of the dungeons. Considering what you have encountered so far down here, you wonder what horrors await you deeper beneath Valsinore. You follow the steps down into the darkness.

The stairs double back on themselves and lead into another stone-walled passageway. Eventually it bends to the right, but as you turn the corner you cannot help but notice the huge fissure in the floor and one wall of the tunnel. As you watch, through this vast crack a host of undulating, writhing and crawling things emerge and slither, scuttle and wriggle

⚁ ⚁

towards you. All these repulsive vermin have one thing in common – they are all the ghosts of creeping things. If you are in a borrowed body, no matter how repulsive they may look they cannot harm you; you walk right through them and continue on your way (turn to 154). However, if you are in spirit-form then you must battle the ectoplasmic swarm if you are to make it through to the other side. Fight the ghost-vermin as if they were one creature.

ECTOPLASMIC SWARM   SKILL 5   STAMINA 13

If you defeat the swarm, regain up to 7 STAMINA points and turn to 154. If it is the swarm that defeats you, write the number 154 on your *Adventure Sheet* and turn to 100.

32

With a bubbling cry, that makes it sound like she is screaming through a throat full of seawater, the Flibbertigibbet streaks towards you through the tempestuous air. 'You're not laughing at me, are you?' the insane ghost says in challenge, while continuing to cackle away hysterically. 'I laughed at the gibbet and look where it got me!' With that the insane phantom attacks.

FLIBBERTIGIBBET   SKILL 8   STAMINA 8

As the Flibbertigibbet is one of the undead, just like you, she can injure you with her cruelly sharp fingernails. If the insane ghost should defeat you in battle (reducing your STAMINA score to zero), record the number 19 on your *Adventure Sheet* and turn to **100**. If you send the Flibbergibbet on into the next world by reducing her STAMINA score to zero, as the ghost evaporates with a parting cackle of laughter, you suddenly feel revitalised. Restore up to 4 STAMINA points and turn to **19**.

33

In the blink of an eye you are gone. Hidden from sight, you move cautiously towards the gatehouse. But the Hellfire Golem is a magical construct and does not see in the same way that mortal creatures do. Turn to **240**.

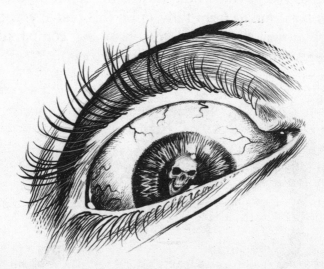

Entering the Blasted Tower through the open arched entrance at its base you start to climb the spiralling stair beyond. Higher and higher you climb until the stairs abruptly run out as you reach what is left of its shattered summit. The cold sea-wind buffets your insubstantial body and whines through fissures in the brickwork. It would seem that there is nothing for you here.

And then another sound can be heard over the keening of the wind and the crash of breakers on the rocks far below. Someone is calling your name and as you watch a sphere of ethereal light forms in the air above you. Something is manifesting at the top of the Blasted Tower. If you want to wait and see what it is, turn to **200**. If you would rather flee before whatever it is has time to form fully upon this plane, you run back down the ruined tower to the comparative safety of the courtyard below (turn to **445**).

35

Before the vampire can transfix you with its hypnotic stare, you turn tail and run. The Nosferatu gives a screeching animal cry and a vast flock of bats pours from between the crypt doors behind it, squeaking shrilly as they set off in pursuit. If you have the *Spirit* special ability, turn to **15**. If not, roll three dice and if the total rolled is less than or equal to your STAMINA score, turn to **15**, as you escape from the vampire's vespertilian servants.

However, if the total is greater, the vampire bats catch up with you and mob you. You soon discover that their vampiric powers are as effective at draining life-force from your ghostly form as they are at drinking the blood of mortals. Roll one die, add 1 and lose this many STAMINA points. If this has taken your STAMINA score to zero, or below, write the number 15 on your *Adventure Sheet* and turn to **100**. If you are still 'alive', you are not out of danger yet as the bat-beast has caught up with you too (turn to **361**).

36

Peering into the culvert you are hit by the appalling stench of the sewer. But, reasoning that nothing unpleasant is likely to stick to your incorporeal form, you press on into the drain regardless. The blue-white glow of your own phosphorescent body lights the way and you soon find yourself climbing what are effectively a set of steps as the channel rises before you into the Outer Ward.

⚅ ⚁

A sudden shrill squeaking drowns out the trickling water of the castle drain and you freeze. Further up the steeply rising tunnel you can see that something has fallen into the sewer and drowned – it looks like a dog. But is that really what happened, you wonder, feeling increasingly ill at ease. For there, blocking the tunnel ahead of you are three rat-like forms that were previously feeding on the carcass. They are huge, with over-large chisel-like incisors, but that's not the worst thing about them. The worst thing is that there is not a scrap of flesh on them. Squeaking hungrily, the undead rats attack. In the confines of the culvert, fight them one at a time.

	SKILL	STAMINA
First SKELETAL RAT	5	4
Second SKELETAL RAT	4	4
Third SKELETAL RAT	5	5

If you manage to do away with all of the undead vermin, turn to **414**. However, if they manage to do away with you, write the number 414 on your *Adventure Sheet* and turn to **100**.

37

As you approach her place at the high table you realise that Oriana is quietly sobbing into her hand-kerchief. She would obviously rather not be here. Turn to 227.

38

Your unearthly interrogator is not done with you yet; it has one more question to ask.

> *'Many have claimed this Keep before,*
> *But who now is lord of Valsinore?'*

If you think you know the answer, again, turn the name of that person into a number using the code A=1, B=2, C=3 … Z=26. Add the numbers together, double the total and turn to the paragraph with the same number. If you do not know the answer, or if the paragraph you turn to makes no sense, turn to 372.

39

'Captain Cador,' you say, your ethereal voice echoing weirdly from the walls of his chamber, 'I am not here to harm you, I want only your help.'

'You wear the face of someone I once knew,' he says, his eyes narrowing in suspicion, 'but I know for a fact that that brave knight is dead.' How does he know that, you wonder?

⚀ ⚅

'It's me,' you say, desperate to convince Cador that it really is you, last of the lords of Valsinore, but he isn't going to be swayed so easily.

'How do I know you're not some hellish doppel-ganger sent here by the forces of darkness to trick me? If you're really who you say you are,' he declares, the light of righteousness blazing in his eyes, 'tell me, what is the name of your own faithful hunting hound?'

If you know the answer to Cador's question, turn it into a number using the code A=1, B=2, C=3 ... Z=26. Add the numbers together and turn to this paragraph. If you do not know the answer, or the paragraph you turn to makes no sense, turn to 380.

40

The stairway leads you at last to a high-ceilinged chamber filled with all manner of detritus, from bro-ken furniture to torn tapestries and the bones of long-dead warriors that have become fused into the icy stalagmites that cover the stone-flagged floor of the chamber, making you wonder who claimed domin-ion here before the arrival of the Winter King in the dim and distant past. But there is no question as to what makes its home here now. Bellowing like a bull, three-metres tall and supported on huge muscular goat-legs, is a savage beast of a demon. The monster's mouth is full to bursting with discoloured, yellow teeth and four cruelly-spiked horns protrude from its bestial skull. Cracking the hellish whip it carries in one hand and shaking the huge demonic axe it holds in the other, the Hellhorn Champion attacks.

HELLHORN CHAMPION   SKILL 10   STAMINA 12

You will soon discover that the Hellhorn's weapons are as potent against undead spirits as they are against mortal flesh. If the Hellhorn slays you, write the number 18 on your *Adventure Sheet* and turn to **100**. However, if you defeat the demonic champion, you leave the ruined feast hall via yet another ascending staircase (turn to **18**).

41

'I don't know about ghosts of your ancestors,' Yorrick starts, 'but I have seen the ghost of your father hereabouts. Up on the battlements it was, at the top of the Blasted Tower. Wouldn't shut up either; something about a dire warning he needed to pass on from beyond the grave.' Now turn to **12**.

'Oh thank you, stranger, thank you,' the ghost of the young woman says in obvious relief.

'But tell me, what manner of creature is it that has you in its thrall?' you ask the restless dead of the graveyard.

The notary looks like he is about to answer when a tremor passes through the graves at your feet. What was that?

'It comes!' the young woman gasps, a terrified look in her eyes.

Abruptly all of the ghosts vanish, as if they have been sucked back into the ground. And then the tremor comes again as the ground in which the dead of Sleath lie rises up before you as a colossal mound of mouldering earth, studded with splintered coffin lids and the remains of those buried within.

This mound of grave dirt shudders once more and takes a lumbering step towards you as arms and legs take shape from within the crumbling conglomeration that now stands before you. The looming humanoid figure exudes a palpable aura of death as it stalks towards you with bone-crunching steps, lumpen arms outstretched, while ghost voices cry from somewhere within it, 'Help us! Free us! Save us!' You have no choice but to draw your ghostly sword once more and engage the Grave Golem in battle.

GRAVE GOLEM   SKILL 8   STAMINA 10

⚃ ⚂

If the Grave Golem wins two consecutive Attack Rounds, turn to **155** at once. If the Grave Golem defeats you, write the number 61 on your *Adventure Sheet* and turn to **100**. If you manage to destroy the grave-dirt monster, turn to **300**.

43

Seeing your old friend again fills you with a renewed sense of hope. And now that the two of you have been reunited, there's no way that Korzen is going to allow himself to be left behind again. Your search of the kennels having turned up nothing else, as you head out into the courtyard of the Outer Ward again, the wolfhound follows you, trotting along at your side.

From now on Korzen will accompany you as you explore Valsinore. This means that whenever you are involved in a battle with a corporeal creature (including demons, undead that have a physical form, such as zombies, and magical constructs, as well as other people and animals) Korzen will harry your opponents, which has the effect of reducing their Attack Strength by 1 point. However, he can do nothing to help you against other incorporeal creatures such as other ghosts; these you will have to face alone. (Regain up to 2 LUCK points, add 1 to your WILL score and record the phrase *Best Friend* on your *Adventure Sheet*.) Now turn to **434**.

44

'Why not?' the monstrous apparition laughs. 'You amuse me, mortal. But remember, I'll be seeing you again.' The Watcher raises its scythe and then brings it down in a reaping motion. Turn to 73.

45

As the three murderers flee in fear, you turn on the individual who actually dealt the killing blow against you. If you want to strike the acolyte down immediately, without showing him any mercy after what he did to you, turn to 114. If you want to demand some answers from him in an attempt to discover who it was that ordered your death turn to 84.

46

You will not go willingly into the dark; you have yet to avenge your untimely death! You feel the pull of the Dead Winds lessen and then a sensation as of rising from the depths of some fathomless ocean overwhelms you and you are floating upwards towards a brightening light high above you. The light is blinding, forcing you to close your eyes.

The sensation of upward motion ceases and you open your eyes to find that you are back in the real world. You have been given another chance and, more than that, you have been revitalised. Restore your SKILL, STAMINA and LUCK scores to their *Initial* levels and add 1 to your WILL score. Now turn to the paragraph with the number you wrote down before you found yourself at the very threshold of the afterlife.

⚁ ⚅

'Time,' you state in as clear a voice as you can manage. There is an audible click, the magically-locked door swings open and you enter the lavish tomb of Aramanthus the White who was court wizard during your father's time. A likeness of the dead wizard lies upon the lid of the black granite sarcophagus that dominates his burial chamber, while various items of magical paraphernalia fill the vault around it. As you are taking in all of the crystal balls, glass alembics and a veritable library's worth of books and scrolls, the ghost of Aramanthus materialises before you.

'Ahh!' the ghost exclaims, a broad smile breaking his wizened features. 'Company at last! Albeit if of the recently deceased variety, but company nonetheless,' the wizard goes on excitedly. 'After all, homunculi are not known for their conversational skills, no offence intended, Fizzgig.'

At this last comment a grotesque, bulbous-bellied, winged imp tumbles out from between a collection of glass instruments sending a number of them crashing to the stone-flagged floor. The creature half-falls and half-flies from its perch, executing an unintentional somersault in mid-air before alighting on top of the wizard's tomb, and then, scowling at the ghost, embarks upon a furious bout of squeaking. The spectral wizard raises a despairing eyebrow, as much as to say, 'See what I mean?'

'But I sincerely doubt you came all this way from the

⚅ ⚄

Other Side to discuss the various merits or otherwise of artificially created life-forms, did you? So, why don't you enlighten me as to the reason for your presence here?'

Sensing that the wizard is a goodly soul who genuinely wants to help, you tell Aramanthus everything that has befallen you since the daylight died, and you with it. But fearing that the longer you linger here, the sooner you might be discovered by those that mean you harm, will you ask the wizard:

About the ghosts of Valsinore Castle?   Turn to **390**
About the evil that has taken root
  within its walls?   Turn to **420**
How to make the most of your ghostly
  abilities?   Turn to **350**

48

The door to the vestry suddenly opens and Father Umberto emerges again. His head is shaved and he is wearing a gleaming golden breastplate, while in his hand he hefts a heavy-headed warhammer.

'My lady!' he shouts aghast and then, before you can move to stop him, he makes a holy sign before pronouncing your fate. 'In the name of Telak the Swordbearer, I return thee to the hellish nether regions that spawned thee!'

There is a sudden blaze of light and you feel as if your ethereal form is being consumed by holy fire that burns with all the fury of a funeral pyre. Write the number 445 on your *Adventure Sheet*, lose 1 LUCK point and turn to **100**.

Remaining exactly where you are, you take your phantasmal blade in hand and wait for the riders to reach you. The ghostly hounds, steeds and their riders descend through the skeletal branches of the trees and alight on the forest floor, barely disturbing the dead leaves that smother the ground at your feet.

'You are bold, spirit, but foolish,' the leader of the hunt tells you, as he reins his horse in before you. 'Do you not know who I am?' He is dressed in the garb of a nobleman and a ghostly, but nonetheless lethal-looking crossbow hangs from his saddle.

Another legend of these parts speaks of a ghostly hunt led by the spectre of one Baron Blood who, when the moon shines bright, seeks out lost souls trapped on the Earthly Plane, to carry them back to the Realm of the Damned. You have heard superstitious peasant folk speak of Baron Blood many times, but you had never thought to meet him face to face.

'You are Baron Blood,' you tell him, 'Lord of the Wild Hunt.'

'Then you know why I am here.'

'I do indeed, but this is one lost soul you won't be carrying away to the Realm of the Damned.'

⚅ ⚄

'A challenge!' the huntsman says, delighted.

'A challenge,' you reply, never once taking your eyes from the ghost.

'Very well, what's it to be?' Baron Blood asks. 'Will you face me in single combat or would you prefer to try your luck against my hounds?'

If you choose to face the Baron in single combat, turn to **79**. If you would rather pit yourself against the spectral hounds of his Wild Hunt, turn to **220**.

50

If you successfully recovered the Spirit Stone from its resting place you will know how many faces it has. Add 100 to the number of faces and turn to this paragraph. If you do not know how many faces it has, lose 1 LUCK point. There is no time to try anything else now; there is only just time to defend yourself from the scything blade of the Shadow King. Choose the weapon that you want to use to battle this Death Lord carefully and then turn to **249**.

51

'Weapons a ghost could wield,' Bertild ponders and then a twinkle enters her one good eye. 'Legend has it that hidden somewhere within Valsinore Castle is the Amethyst Blade, a magical blade with sinister life-draining powers, but from its description it could be a weapon of Evil as much as one employed by the forces of Good. And I don't know if you could wield it in your present state.' The blacksmith suddenly looks glum again. 'There was one thing that might have helped but it was taken.'

'What was it?' you ask.

'I fashioned the most wonderful suit of automaton armour, a device of great artifice that would not only protect its wearer to the utmost degree but could actually fight for them. It took me the best part of a year to construct. I had almost perfected it when those dread knights of Unthank's broke in and stole it away from me.'

'Do you know where it is now?'

'I believe it was taken to the lock-up in the Barbican. The knights guard it night and day and no one's allowed in or out of there now.' Now turn to **140**.

52

As you pass by the gibbet tree, you suddenly hear a hysterical cackle of laughter and turn to see the woman gliding towards you over the moors, hands outstretched. Her skin is coloured the horrible grey-green of decomposition and half her face is missing, as if something has eaten it away. There are tresses of bladderwrack and kelp knotted in her wet hair and her talon-like fingernails are thick with dark sand. As there is no escaping the ghost of the drowned woman, you prepare to defend yourself.

Test your Luck. If you are Lucky, you unsheathe your sword in time (turn to **32**). If you are Unlucky, you are still pulling your weapon free of its spectral scabbard as the ghost attacks. Turn to **32** to fight her anyway, but you must automatically lose the first Attack Round.

53

Stepping past the massive beast, you stand at last before the mirrored shield. If you still have a physical form you can take it with you. (Add the Soul Shield to you *Adventure Sheet* and add 1 to your SKILL score, even if this takes it above its *Initial* level.) If you are in your ethereal form, there's nothing you can do other than exit the chamber again. Whether you take the shield or not, you ultimately leave the Moon Dog's cell (turn to **182**).

54

Speaking in a dark tongue that you do not understand, Mother Toadsfoot crafts her spell. You immediately feel power flowing through your body, even though you have no body to speak of. Restore your SKILL and STAMINA scores to their *Initial* levels and add 1 to your WILL score. Make a note of the number of this paragraph on your *Adventure Sheet* and then roll one die. On a roll of 1–3, turn to **230**; on a roll of 4–6, turn to **263**.

'Now we come to the question of payment,' the crone says, smiling horribly, her crooked teeth looking like a row of broken tombstones. 'You must slay that which is most dear to you, next time you meet, be it man or lowly beast, or suffer the consequences.'

'Curse you, witch!' you gasp in appalled shock. 'What have you done?'

'Another's life-force for yours. Fair's fair! It has to come from somewhere. Nature will see that the debt is paid, one way or another.'

You get the feeling that the witch has cursed you rather than helped you. (Add the phrase *Fool's Bargain* to your *Adventure Sheet* and lose 2 LUCK points.) If you want to attack the old crone in your fury, turn to **356**. If you would rather get away from this place as quickly as you can, before any greater ill can befall you, turn to **9**.

55

Darting from left to right, backwards and forwards to confuse the magical construct, you gradually lure the gatehouse's guardian away from the archway. It is then that you make your move. *Test your Skill*. If you succeed, turn to **337**. If you fail, turn to **240**.

56*

A little further along the passageway you come to another door, this time on your left. However, this one is made from the same black wood as the Spirit Door that first prevented you from entering the Keep and has the same arcane symbols etched into it in silver. Unless you still have a physical form, and know what to do, you will not be able to pass beyond this door. When you are ready to proceed along the passageway, turn to **436**.

57

'I believe so,' Cador replies, 'although it has been some weeks since I saw her last myself. She never leaves her apartments in the Inner Ward, or so I hear. Spends all her time in her solar or at the castle chapel. If your plan is to free her from her captivity there is something I must tell you.' Turn to **269**.

58

You re-appear on the Earthly Plane in the middle of the Inner Ward, bathed in cold, silver moonlight, looking up at the dominating shadowy presence of the Keep. Never before has it appeared so unwelcoming, so unlike home. You understand now that this is where the source of the evil power within Valsinore Castle lies. And if you are to vanquish it, that is where you need to go now.

But you also heard Chamberlain Unthank mention two other places that, from the way he was talking about them, may well hold the key to defeating that same power. If you want to try travelling to one of these places, turn to **188**. If you would rather not waste the hours left between now and dawn and want to approach the Keep, turn to **117**.

59

As the last of the knights falls to the floor, a noxious black gas rising from the pile of armour and black cloth that is all that is left of its physical form, you cross the chamber to another archway that leads to another spiral staircase. However this one both ascends and descends through the tower. If you want to go up it, turn to **166**. If you want to go down it, turn to **115**. If you would rather return to the ground floor and the portcullis gate, turn to **20**.

60

You approach the portcullis with trepidation. If you have the codeword *Gateway* written on your *Adventure Sheet*, turn to **5**. If not, how do you plan on getting past the portcullis? Choosing something you haven't tried already, will you:

Use the *Poltergeist* special ability (if you have it)?	Turn to **291**
Use the *Apparition* special ability (if you have it)?	Turn to **5**
Climb the staircase beyond the left archway?	Turn to **271**
Climb the staircase through the right archway?	Turn to **85**
Find another way into the Inner Ward?	Turn to **393**

61

Night lies over the sleeping village like a bejewelled cape, the wind chasing black clouds across the sky, like a wolf after a shepherd's flock. Ahead of you lie the stone-built buildings and thatched cottages of Sleath. There are few lights visible in the windows of the village although you see plenty within the windows of Castle Valsinore. Most of the villagers, who predominantly work on the land, have already retired for the night.

The tolling of the temple bell rings through the cold night air, the sound deadened by the capricious whipping wind. And then the soughing of the wind becomes what can only be a moaning voice. The voice is joined by others, all wailing in torment, and they are getting closer. You can see a phosphorescent mist moving towards you like a sentient cloud over the fields that lie between you and the village. This is no natural mist. As you watch, anguished faces, their eyes closed, surface from within it.

The troubled dreams of the villagers have manifested as this nightmarish monster of the Spirit World. There is nothing you can do as the unearthly fog slithers towards you over the wind-ruffled grass. And then it is all around you, enveloping you, smothering you, threatening to overwhelm you with its insanity as the nightmares of the populace of Sleath become manifest reality to your own tortured mind.

Roll two dice. If the total rolled is less than or equal to your WILL score, turn to **17**; if it is greater, turn to **105**.

62

You come at last to yet another chamber, high up within Frostfinger. Two more spiral staircases lead onwards but the archway leading to the one to the left is blocked by a solid sheet of ice. The only way that you are going to be able to get beyond this icy gate is if you have the *Apparition* special ability. If you do, and you want to follow the staircase to the left, turn to **18**. If not, or you want to take the right-hand staircase anyway, turn to **40**.

63

'There are plenty, let me tell you,' Yorrick says, a look of resignation on his face. 'I've seen ghosts flying around the battlements the last three nights in a row, and some of the serving maids claim to have heard a spider the size of a horse scuttling about on the roof of their sleeping quarters. But that's nothing compared to what's happening down in the catacombs. Other spirits have told me that the Wraith Queen is holding court down there, protected by her zombie generals. Of course, I wouldn't want to go down there and check myself – know what I mean?' Now turn to **12**.

64

'Who did this?' you shout. Your voice does not sound quite like your own; it has gained an echoing, ethereal quality. 'Who commanded that I be struck down on the highway, when I was so close to the end of my epic journey?'

⚀ ⚁

The skull-masked acolyte does not answer you but continues to wave his hand over his crystal ball and then utters the words, 'Begone, spirit! In the name of the Finisher, I banish you from this place to dwell in the Realm of the Damned forevermore!'

It suddenly feels as if a powerful gale is blowing over the moors although you can see no sign of it rippling the grass or tugging at the robes of the Death Acolyte. And then it feels as though you are in danger of being carried away, sucked up by this whirling ethereal maelstrom, and you can hear screaming ghostly voices on the wind.

Roll two dice. If the total is less than or equal to your WILL score, turn to **114**. If the total is greater than your WILL score, turn to **136**.

65

And in the blink of an eye, you become invisible to human sight. As you slip between the jugglers and fire-eaters, Chamberlain Unthank suddenly gets to his feet and, having banged on the floor with the metal-sheathed tip of his staff and achieved silence, he raises his goblet and announces, 'To absent friends!' No one responds to his hail.

Unseen as you are you could approach anyone you wanted to and eavesdrop on their conversations or observe them to work out what is going on here. Will you:

⚁ ⚅

Approach your sister?	Turn to **37**
Approach Chamberlain Unthank?	Turn to **16**
Approach Blondel the Bard?	Turn to **130**
Move among the acrobats and mummers?	Turn to **227**

66

As you enter the kennels you hear the dogs chained up within whining in fear. Wolfhounds and lean hunting dogs cower before your ghostly presence or start barking ferociously, but you know that none of them can hurt you. However, their barking may well alert others within the castle to your presence. (Add the codeword *Barking* to your *Adventure Sheet*.)

But one of those animals present does not tremble and whine in your presence but instead runs up to you, barking in delight and wagging its tail. It is your own hunting hound, Korzen, your faithful companion who you have not seen for three years, since you left him behind to keep your sister Oriana and the castle safe from harm.

If you have the phrase *Fool's Bargain* recorded on your *Adventure Sheet*, turn to **23**; if not, turn to **43**.

67

The cottage door is suddenly flung open by a scrawny old woman wearing a plain black robe and with a shock of wild white hair streaming out from around her head.

'Who's that? Who's there?' she demands, peering into the night through eyes clouded with cataracts. 'Come on, speak up, I knows yer there. I can smell yer!' She is totally blind.

The expression on her face suddenly becomes one of startled fear and she raises her bony hands ready to defend herself. 'You're one of them, aintcha!' she snaps. 'So your master's sent you to do away with me at last, has he? Well, we'll see about that!'

The old crone weaves her hands through the air in front of her as if preparing to cast a spell. If you want to draw your phantasmal sword ready to defend yourself, turn to **356**. If you would rather speak up and tell the wise-woman you mean her no harm, turn to **399**.

68

As soon as the metal-eating fungal spores touch the rusted, bloodstained ironwork of the Demon Gate they set to work. The Demon Gate crumbles into nothing but a rust-red powder with a fading cry of, 'Flessshhh!' leaving you free to continue on your way. Cross the Ironbane off your *Adventure Sheet*, regain 1 LUCK point and turn to **243**.

69

A bony tail suddenly comes out you out of nowhere and whips you off your feet. (If you still have a physical body lose 2 STAMINA points.) You now have no choice but to fight whatever it is that is coming into being here. Turn to **110**.

70

Then the voice comes again.

> *'No breastplate, shield, or armoured helm,*
> *Can 'gainst my blade defend.*
> *Prince and pauper, knight and maid,*
> *All face me in the end.*
> *No weapon forged, can strike me down,*
> *No arrow, sword or lance.*
> *King and servant, rich and poor,*
> *Shall join me in my dance.*
> *Who am I?'*

If you think you know the answer to this riddle, turn it into a number using the code A=1, B=2, C=3 ... Z=26. Add the numbers together and turn to this paragraph. If you do not know the answer, or if the paragraph you turn to makes no sense, then turn to **372**.

71

Bravely you throw yourself at the Golem and land a resounding blow against it. But to your horror your ethereal blade does not even leave a mark on its iron carapace. The magic powering the arcane automaton is resistant to your own paranormal powers. The Hellfire Golem retaliates with all its might. Unfortunately the magical construct is perfectly capable of harming you. Roll one die, divide the number by 2 and (rounding fractions up) deduct this number many STAMINA points. If this has taken your STAMINA score to zero, or below, write the number 278 on your *Adventure Sheet* and turn to **100**. If not, turn to **278**.

72

The small room you enter appears to have once been a prison cell, and you wonder why it wasn't locked. But then its occupant isn't going to be going anywhere in a hurry; hanging from the wall opposite by lengths of rusted chains is the skeleton of a man. You quickly examine the skeleton but it shows no signs of springing to life and certainly has nothing of value to you. It is as you are turning to leave that you become aware of the hollow knocking of bone on wood and stone. And then you see them. They look like spiders, large spiders, but rather than having soft hairy bodies they are clad in bony armour, like crabs. Three of these bizarre undead arachnids have squeezed through a hole in the roof of the cell and are now scuttling over the door, preventing you from getting out again. If you want to leave this cell you are going to have to fight them altogether.

	SKILL	STAMINA
First BONE SPIDER	7	6
Second BONE SPIDER	6	6
Third BONE SPIDER	6	5

If you manage to defeat all of your adversaries you will be able to leave the cell and continue on your way (turn to **255**). If your spirit-form should 'die' during your struggle against the Bone Spiders, write the number 255 on your *Adventure Sheet* and turn to **100**.

73

There is a flash of blinding black light and then the rushing roar of the wind in your ears again. You feel as if you are being sucked violently backwards, away from the purgatory in which you have been languishing, back to the mortal realm.

Suddenly all is still and quiet once more. You look around you in stunned disbelief. You are indeed back in the land of the living, even though you are still in spectral form – but at least you're back. You have been given another chance and, more than that, you feel re-energised. Return your SKILL, STAMINA and LUCK scores to their *Initial* levels, and add 1 to your WILL score. Also add the codeword *Judgement* to your *Adventure Sheet*.

Now turn to the paragraph with the number you wrote down before being banished to the borders of the Lands of the Dead.

74

If you are going to catch up with Chamberlain Unthank and your sister, you are going to have to get through his dread knight bodyguards first. Fight them together.

⚁ ⚀

	SKILL	STAMINA
First DREAD KNIGHT	9	8
Second DREAD KNIGHT	8	8

The knights are armed with swords imbued with necromantic power. If one of the knights wounds you, roll one die; on a roll of 5–6 the cursed blade will cause you 3 STAMINA points damage, instead of the usual 2. If the Dread Knights put an end to you, write the number 394 on your *Adventure Sheet* and turn to **100**. If you manage to defeat them both, turn to **394**.

75

Gazing up at the peg-toothed silhouette of the battlements high above you, you picture yourself breaking free of the pull of gravity and letting the rising wind carry you over them. If you have the *Spirit* special ability, turn to **94**. If not, roll two dice. If the total rolled is less than or equal to your WILL, *Test your Luck*; if you are Lucky, write the number 94 on your *Adventure Sheet* and turn to **293**. If you fail either roll, you are unable to defy gravity, even in your wraith-like form, and so must resort to finding another way into the castle. Will you try gaining entry through the sewer outlet (turn to 36) or would you rather approach the guards at the gate (turn to 242)?

76

The witch sits down on one side of the table and invites you to take a seat opposite her. She then begins her conjuration, her eyes rolling up into her head as she calls her familiar spirit by name. 'Come, Pyewackit, come to mother.'

The temperature in the hovel suddenly drops, frost forming on the inside of the windows. As you watch aghast, something manifests in the air between you and the witch. It has a body like that of a monkey, only it is covered in the iridescent blue and green plumage of a parrot, it has the backward-jointed legs of a cockerel and the face of a demon. It hovers before you, a cruel sneer splitting its ugly visage.

'Pyewackit, answer me this, who is responsible for this one's murder?'

Her familiar spirit writhes as if in pain, mewling like a child.

'Why do you not answer me?' Mother Toadsfoot pushes.

'Another would command me,' Pyewackit snarls from between gritted teeth.

'Tell me!' the witch shrieks. 'Answer your mother!'

⚅ ⚀

The demon utters something intelligible in some netherworld tongue, unable to resist its mistress any longer.

'Do not try to trick me, demon,' the witch roars at her familiar.

'Ask me no more!' the imp squeals, its unnatural form contorted in pain, its face a picture of agony. 'The Lord of Shadows comes.'

Before your very eyes, the demon's feathers darken to the colour of blood and its skin blackens.

'Command me no more!' it growls in a much deeper voice, suddenly lashing out at the witch with claws as sharp as blades.

Giving a weak cry of pain herself, the old woman slumps face first onto the table, blood pouring from a savage wound in her neck. Her familiar spirit then turns to you and snarls, 'Now you shall die a second death!'

Hastily unsheathing your phantasmal blade you prepare to defend yourself against the familiar's demonic talons.

PYEWACKIT   SKILL 7   STAMINA 6

If Mother Toadsfoot's familiar does indeed grant you a second death, write the number 9 on your *Adventure Sheet* and turn to **100**. If you defeat the unbound demon, turn to **9**.

⚁ ⚁

77

Shutting the door again, you continue on your way. You might have been able to help the wretched Iago; leaving him to his fate was a callous act. Lose 1 LUCK point and turn to **416**.

78

The Dead Winds pull you over the bleak and rugged terrain towards the edge of a mighty gulf that bisects the scarred landscape. In the distance, in the shadow of the rumbling storm clouds you can see an arched gate, made from monolithic blocks of obsidian. An avenue of standing stones forms a processional path that ultimately leads to the gate. You can feel yourself being inexorably drawn towards it, but you cannot shake the feeling that if you pass beyond that stone arch then there will be no going back. You begin to rail against your fate; you have unfinished business in the mortal realm. You will not go willingly into the Lands of the Dead knowing that your murderer has yet to be brought to justice in the world above. Roll two dice. If the total rolled is less than or equal to your WILL score, add the codeword *Devourer* to your *Adventure Sheet* and turn to **46**. If it is greater, turn to **327**.

79

Baron Blood jumps down from the back of his horse, leaving his steed pawing at the ground impatiently. 'To the death!' he cries as he draws his own spectral blade and the two of you join in combat.

⚃ ⚁

BARON BLOOD   SKILL 10   STAMINA 10

You will soon discover that the Baron's own ethereal blade can harm you just as readily as your ghostly blade cuts down your enemies. If the Lord of the Wild Hunt kills you, write the number 290 on your *Adventure Sheet* and turn to **100**. If it is you who wins the duel, turn to **129**.

80

Against all the odds, you have managed to break through the holy wards Father Umberto had blessed himself with as protection from the machinations of undead spirits, and taken control of his body. (Add the codeword *Host* to your *Adventure Sheet*.)

Make a note of your spirit-form's current SKILL and STAMINA score, for use later, on your *Adventure Sheet*. While you are wearing Father Umberto's physical form, you must use his stats which are as follows: SKILL 10, STAMINA 19.

If you are injured in battle you may eat provisions to recover STAMINA points. One meal restores up to 4 STAMINA points. Incredibly you manage to find food enough for 2 meals. Father Umberto looks very different to how he did when you first encountered him. He is now wearing a gleaming golden breast-plate, while in his hand he hefts a heavy-headed war-hammer. If you make a successful strike against an opponent with the warhammer roll one die; on a roll of 3–6 you cause 3 STAMINA points of damage, rather

than the usual 2. (Make a note of this on your *Adventure Sheet*.)

You also now know what Father Umberto knows, and that includes a potent prayer-spell to banish undead spirits. (Also add the *Banish Spirit* special ability to your *Adventure Sheet*.)

If the warrior priest's STAMINA score is ever reduced to 2 STAMINA points or fewer, he will be knocked senseless and you will be forced to leave his inert body. Fortunately, you can keep on fighting in your ghost-form, using the stats that you have written down here. Now turn to **429**.

81

Catching sight of you, a serving wench lets out an ear-splitting scream, and then everybody is looking your way. As terrified people flee before you, two men at a corner booth leap to their feet, grim expressions of pleasure on their faces. The first is dressed completely in black, with a broad-brimmed hat on his head, and a velvet cape around his shoulders. He is also festooned with all manner of charms and is holding a finely-wrought, basket-hilted silvered rapier in one black-gloved hand. His companion looks like nothing less than a thug. The rogue's nose has obviously been broken on more than one occasion, the tattoo of a spider's web covers one side of his shaven head – although he still sports a bushy beard – and a contraption that looks like a silver bear trap hangs from his waist by a chain.

⚅ ⚀

'Do not fear, good people of Sleath,' the black-clad man addresses the tavern's clientele. 'I'll rid you of your plague of ghosts starting with this one, or my name's not Josef Van Richten, ghost hunter extraordinaire!' He advances towards you, adopting a fencer's stance, and shouts, 'Streng, with me. Now have at you, foul fiend!' You have no choice but to draw your own phantasmal blade to defend yourself.

	SKILL	STAMINA
JOSEF VAN RICHTEN	10	9
STRENG	8	8

The Ghost Hunter and his henchman attack you both together, using silver weapons designed to harm undead creatures, such as you. If both Van Richten and Streng wound you in two consecutive Attack Rounds, turn to **208**. If you should die for a second time in this battle, write the number 259 on your *Adventure Sheet* and turn to **100**. However, if you manage to defeat both your opponents, turn to **248**.

82

You climb higher and higher. You have no idea how much time has passed, but it must be half an hour at least. Just when you are wondering if this staircase will ever end, you emerge into another frozen chamber to be greeted by a long, low hiss. It is bitterly cold. Standing before you, at the heart of its lair, surrounded by the frozen bones of its previous victims, is a grotesque creature. It has a bloated green stomach, like that of some monstrous toad, and a hideously

⚃ ⚅

misshapen head supported atop a blubbery neck. Its circular, extended mouth is full of needle-sharp teeth and surrounded by fat purple lips. But it is its extended, sickle-like claws that give this monster its name. There is something otherworldly about this particular Coldclaw that gives you the impression that you are as much in danger as any living creature would be. In fact the chill malice being exuded by this creature starts to affect you, even though you are a ghost. Roll two dice and if the total is greater than your WILL score you must reduce your Attack Strength in the battle to come by 1. Now fight!

COLDCLAW   SKILL 10   STAMINA 11

If the Coldclaw is the end of you, write the number 40 on your *Adventure Sheet* and turn to **100**. If you win, you cross the hellishly cold chamber and stop before a pair of icy stone staircases that both lead further up into the tower. Will you take the stairway to the left (turn to **40**) or the one to the right (turn to **62**)?

83

'First it was the Keep,' Cador explains. 'No one was allowed in there, apart from him. Word was that he was spending all his time in the castle archives, looking for something, but I don't know what. We wouldn't see him for days at a time but other than that life at the castle continued pretty much as it always had. But then the rumours started circulating that he was making something in there – a machine of some sort – but again nobody knew quite what exactly.

'Then, like I said, just over a year ago, one night, in the middle of a terrible storm, thirteen knights turned up at the gates, seeking shelter. Unthank invited them in and they never left. We were banished from the Inner Ward and the knights were set to guard the Barbican. And they've got something in there under lock and key, something that Unthank doesn't want anybody else getting their hands on.

'What I do know is that events have been building up to something, something big, and whatever it is, it's going to happen this very night. I'm sure of it. As a result, there is something else I must pass on.' Turn to 269.

'Who commanded that I be struck down on the highway, so close to home?' you demand, your voice sounding not quite like your own, having gained an echoing, ethereal quality. 'Who was it that ordered my murder?'

The skull-masked acolyte does not answer you but continues to wave his hand over his crystal ball and then utters the words, 'Begone, spirit! In the name of the Finisher, I banish you from this place to dwell in the Realm of the Damned forevermore!'

It suddenly feels as if a powerful gale is blowing over the moors although you can see no sign of it rippling the grass or tugging at the robes of the Death Acolyte.

⚃ ⚁

And then it feels as though you are in danger of being carried away, sucked up by this whirling ethereal maelstrom, and you can hear screaming ghostly voices on the wind.

Roll two dice and then subtract 3 from the total. If the total is now less than or equal to your WILL score, turn to **114**; if it is greater than your WILL score, turn to **136**.

85

Ascending the spiral staircase you enter the Barbican's guardroom located on the first floor. And there are three guards waiting for you within – three more of the dread knights you met guarding the portcullis. Silently, the undead warriors unsheathe their accursed weapons and surround you, blocking off an easy means of escape. In the confines of the guardroom fight these Dread Knights two at a time.

	SKILL	STAMINA
First DREAD KNIGHT	8	8
Second DREAD KNIGHT	8	9
Third DREAD KNIGHT	9	8

If a knight wounds you, roll one die; on a roll of 5–6 the knight's cursed blade will cause you 3 STAMINA points of damage. If your battle with the knights ends badly for you, write the number 20 on your *Adventure Sheet* and then turn to **100**. If you manage to defeat them all, turn to **59**.

⚃ ⚃

86

You enter what would appear to be an alchemist's chamber. Benches and tables are covered with all manner of glass alembics, crucibles, jars of powdered compounds and flasks of curiously-coloured liquids. There is even a stuffed crocodile suspended from the ceiling. However, one thing draws your attention more than any other. It is a lavish flask that appears to be made from black glass, either that or its contents are black. It is sealed with a clasp-bound stopper and etched into the glass are the words 'Oil of Midnight'. Nothing else interests you as much as this so if you want to take the flask with you as you leave, record the Oil of Midnight on your *Adventure Sheet*, and then turn to 436.

87

'Well there's Aramanthus, former court wizard, although you'll need to go down into the catacombs to find him. There's a set of steps in the chapel that leads down into the tomb tunnels but rumour has it you can enter them through the castle well too, although I wouldn't know about that myself.' Now turn to 12.

88

And so you find yourself in the dripping castle catacombs. It was within these dank tunnels that Castle Valsinore's first founders were laid to rest when it was their time to go into the ground. The otherworldly glow emanating from your own ethereal presence illuminating the way onward, you come at last to a crossroads. You can see that the passageway in front of you, and the one to your left, both end at solid looking doors. The tunnel to your right leads further into the dark with no sign of stopping. Which way do you want to go? Will you:

Continue straight on?	Turn to **10**
Head left?	Turn to **235**
Follow the passageway to your right?	Turn to **109**
Leave the catacombs and return to the Inner Ward courtyard?	Turn to **445**

89

'It is you!' Captain Cador exclaims in relief, his tensed body suddenly sagging with relief. 'You came back!'

'Yes,' you reply, 'to avenge my murder.' You fill him in on all that has happened to you since you were cut down on the moors beside the Nine Maidens, concluding by saying, 'And I believe that I shall find the answers I am looking for here within Valsinore.'

Cador in his turn tells you that his guards are no longer permitted to patrol past the Outer Ward, Chamberlain Unthank having apparently invited a mysterious order of knights to take over those duties roughly a year ago. 'So,' he finishes, 'how can I help? What do you want from me?'

'Information,' is your simple reply.

'What do you want to know?'

⚃ ⚀

Will you ask Cador whether your sister, the Lady Oriana, is safe (turn to **57**), about the changes Chamberlain Unthank has made in your absence (turn to **83**), or about where you might find other allies within the castle (turn to **189**)?

90

You are able to pass through solid objects, such as walls and doors, as if they weren't there at all. Record the *Apparition* special ability on your *Adventure Sheet* and turn to the paragraph with the same number as the one you were just instructed to write down.

91

Since you have bested his zombie executioner, Unthank has had a change of plan. 'After me!' you hear him shout as he descends from the platform, dragging Oriana after him. 'I've something else in mind for this one,' he tells his knights.

The zombie dead at your feet, you set off after Chamberlain Unthank as he drags Oriana through the archway and onto the bridge heading for the Keep. *Test your Luck*. If you are Lucky, turn to **394**. If you are Unlucky, turn to **74**.

92

You slip past the woman and gaze up at the skeleton hanging from the gibbet. Thanks to the attentions of wind and rain, carrion birds and rot, the hanged villain's face is now nothing more than the mould-blackened face of a skull, although it has noticeably elongated canines. A medallion bearing the image of a wolf's head hangs about the corpse's neck on a rusted iron chain, and you notice that the corpse's fingernails have the appearance of animalistic claws. You find yourself wondering what crimes the villain committed to earn a hanging in the first place.

The woman's sudden scream of laughter catches you completely by surprise. You spin round to see her sweeping towards you over the moor, and stare into a partially decomposed horror of a face. A crab crawls through a hole in the woman's drowning-bloated cheek while tangles of seaweed stream out from around her head. When she is within reach she lashes out at you with broken fingernails caked with gritty sand. Turn to **32** as you are forced to fight her, but as you are surprised by the ghost, you must automatically lose the first Attack Round.

93

You can feel the relentless volcano-fury of the Golem coming off it in waves. How are you going to get past such an awesome obstacle as this? Will you:

Attack the Hellfire Golem?	Turn to **71**
Try to dodge past it?	Turn to **55**
Use the *Shade* special ability (if you have it)?	Turn to **33**
Use the *Spirit* special ability (if you have it)?	Turn to **312**

94

And then you are rising high into the sky, soaring over the battlements and enjoying a spectacular bird's-eye view of the castle below. You have never seen Valsinore in this way before. Directly below you lies the Outer Ward, containing stables, kennels, the blacksmith's forge and the guards' barracks. Beyond a second gatehouse lies the more densely defended Inner Ward, containing the kitchens, feast hall, chapel and graveyard, beneath which lie the castle's ancient and extensive catacombs. And then, over the sea-moat, rising from a spur of black rock, is the castle's indomitable Keep. You notice that although you can see lights flickering elsewhere in the castle, the Keep is in total darkness – not something you would have expected to see at all and a sight that fills you with dread.

Now that you are airborne, do you want to continue flying over the castle towards the Keep to investigate further (turn to **125**), or would you prefer to come back down to earth and alight in the Outer Ward below (turn to **414**)?

95

As you enter the castle feast hall you are surprised to be met by the sounds of carousing. A travelling troop of tumblers, acrobats, jugglers, fire-eaters and mummers are doing their best to get those present into the spirit of celebration but it doesn't appear to be working.

⚀ ⚂

The top table groans under the weight of the food arrayed upon it. There is everything from suckling pig, to peacock, to quails and honeyed hams, and all manner of drink to wash everything down with. It is a veritable feast, but despite the great quantities of food on display, nobody seems particularly interested in consuming any of it.

Seated at the table is Chamberlain Unthank, who is watching the players and tumblers with a disdainful look on his face while beside him sits your sister, the Lady Oriana, who is staring unhappily at a plate of untouched sweetmeats. In a nearer corner of the hall Blondel the Bard is coaxing a reluctant melody from the lyre he holds in his lap.

If you want to reveal yourself, in all your ghostly glory, to those present, turn to **348**. If you would rather remain unobserved and already have the *Shade* special ability, turn to **65**. If you do not have this ability, roll two dice. If the total rolled is less than or equal to your WILL, *Test your Skill*; if you are pass this test, write the number 65 on your *Adventure Sheet* and turn to **230**. If you fail either roll, turn to **348**.

96

The horse whinnies and brings its hooves crashing down on the ground just in front of you, the straw of the stall catching fire, burning with ethereal green flame. Once again, you are fighting for the fate of your immortal soul.

⚃ ⚀

PHANTOM STEED   SKILL 7   STAMINA 8

If the insane animal spirit destroys you, write the
number 434 on your *Adventure Sheet* and turn to **100**.
If you destroy the Phantom Steed, a quick search
reveals that there is nothing else of use to you here
and so you leave the haunted stables. (Recover up to
4 STAMINA points and turn to **434**.)

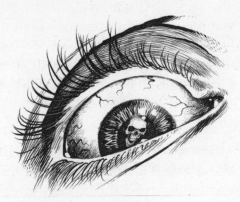

97

You pass straight through the wooden planks forming the door and into the noise and light of the
Cockcrow Inn. You suddenly realise that you have
entered a tavern full of people by walking right
through the door. If you are happy to let the people
see you, turn to **81**. If not, and you have the *Shade* special ability, turn to **299**; otherwise, in that instant, you
wish that you weren't there. Roll two dice. If the total
rolled is less than or equal to your WILL, *Test your
Skill*; if you are successful, write the number 299 on
your *Adventure Sheet* and turn to **230**. If you fail either
roll, turn to **81**.

'That villain?' the Watcher roars, its scream of rage echoing across the bleak wilderness with all the force of a landslide, causing the distant crags to split asunder and boulders to topple from their jagged peaks. 'He is known to us,' the spectre goes on. 'He has cheated death for too long. His journey to this place is long overdue; his life should have run its course long ago.'

The Watcher reaches inside its cloak once again and this time takes out another life-timer. You see the trickle of sand falling from the top bulb to the bottom is unmoving, as if frozen in time.

'He has signed pacts with darker powers, in his own blood, that he might live beyond a man's natural span of three score years and ten. But the time is coming when he will have to make good on those promises he made so long ago. Take this,' the Watcher says, handing you the black hourglass.

You automatically reach out a hand and take it – and to your amazement find that you can handle the object. (Add the Black Hourglass to your *Adventure Sheet*.)

'You will know when the time is right to use it,' the Watcher tells you. 'And remember, a fool is just a fool but a man's best friend can be his greatest ally.'

Now turn to **73**.

Now turn to **73**.

99

Sleath is quiet, but there is one place that shows little sign of anyone going to bed just yet, and that's the Cockcrow Inn that stands on the northern edge of the village square. A warm orange glow exudes from its windows while sounds of carousing can be heard coming from within.

On the southern edge of the square stands the neglected shrine that was built up around the tomb of an ancient champion of Good, sadly now long forgotten. On the eastern side, where the dwellings are few and far between, a gaudy tent has been pitched on a patch of scrubby grass. The midnight-blue canvas has been embroidered with silver sequin stars, crescent moons and other more exotic astrological sigils. A banner hung outside reads, 'Madame Zelda – Mistress of Mystery'.

There is one other place in particular that draws your attention and that is the Burgomaster's grand house on the western side of the square. You cannot see any lights in any of its windows but you can feel the lure of the place deep down in your bones – at least you would if you had any! Perhaps Burgomaster Jurgen could help you make some progress in your search for answers.

What do you want to do now? Will you:

Visit the Cockcrow Inn?	Turn to **118**
Explore the shrine?	Turn to **229**
Investigate the tent of Madame Zelda, Mistress of Mystery?	Turn to **368**
Approach the Burgomaster's house?	Turn to **437**
Leave the village?	Turn to **6**

100

And then you are no longer upon the Earthly Plane and the Dead Winds are carrying you over to the Other Side of the veil that exists between the world of the dead and the world of the living …

Before you lies a barren expanse of grey rock and sand. Above, the sky is as grey as the ground, and full of dark storm clouds in turmoil. Thunder rumbles over distant mountains that rise to jagged black peaks that seem to claw at the storm-wracked sky.

If you have the codeword *Endgame* written on your *Adventure Sheet*, turn to **400**. If you have the codeword *Judgement* on your *Adventure Sheet*, turn to **279**. If you have the codeword *Watcher*, turn to **286**. If you have the codeword *Devourer*, turn to **327**. If you none of these codewords recorded on your *Adventure Sheet*, turn to **78**.

· ·

The front door is in sight when suddenly three apparitions manifest in front of you. The first is a woman dressed entirely in grey, the second a nobleman wearing clothes that are no longer in fashion and carrying his head under one arm, the ghostly impression of a finely-balanced rapier in his hand, and the third a bodiless, floating skull.

'What do you think you're doing here?' the grey lady shrieks.

'This house is already haunted!' the decapitated noble informs you.

And then the building's resident spooks are hurtling towards you. The skull's jaw drops open and a bloodcurdling scream rends the air around you. You have no choice but to fight the three, furious ghosts.

	SKILL	STAMINA
GREY LADY	6	6
HEADLESS NOBLE	8	8
SCREAMING SKULL	7	4

Fight the ghosts all at the same time. For as long as the Screaming Skull is still bound to the mortal realm, you must reduce your Attack Strength by 1 point as it keeps up its spine-chilling wail. If any of the ghosts should kill you, write the number 259 on your *Adventure Sheet* and turn to **100**. As soon as you manage to banish two of the spirits back to the Netherworld, regain STAMINA points up to half the STAMINA total of the ghosts you defeated and turn to **406**.

102

'Fool!' the apparition roars in a voice like the banging of coffin lids. 'You cannot cheat death!' And then it flies at you, scythe raised, ready to cut you down where you stand.

Roll dice to calculate Attack Strengths for yourself and the Watcher as you would in a normal battle: the Watcher's SKILL score is 12. If your Attack Strength is higher, you block the sweeping scythe (turn to 73). If the Watcher's Attack Strength is higher, turn to 279. If both Attack Strengths are the same, roll again.

103

You can only use your ability to fly if you do not have a physical form, or you are prepared to quit it and leave all equipment, provisions and the like behind and cross off any relevant codewords. If you are not in a position to do this or are not willing to do this, turn back to 154 and try a different option. If you are, you easily soar over the putrid pool and land on the stone-flagged floor on the other side without anything untoward happening. Turn to 421.

104

If you successfully recovered the Spirit Stone from its resting place you will know how many faces it has. Turn now to the paragraph with the same number. If you do not know how many faces it has, lose 1 LUCK point and turn to 132.

⚁ ⚄

105

You are beset by the most horrific visions – all the products of the fevered minds of the sleeping villagers. There must be something truly evil haunting these lands to produce such vivid and hideous nightmares among the local populace. You thought you had seen all the horrors the world had to offer within that benighted realm of Bathoria, but you were wrong; the horrors you witnessed there were as nothing compared to the nightmares now conjured in your mind by the predatory Phantasmagoria. You are left a gibbering wreck, your undying mind driven to the brink of insanity by what you have seen. Lose 2 WILL points, 1 SKILL point and 2 LUCK points. Now turn to 17.

106

Having climbed the stair quite some way you enter a frozen chamber but as you do so you notice the temperature start to rise. A dull glow fills the chamber and the ice covering the stone walls begins to melt. It is then that you notice the creature hunched on the far side of the chamber, blocking your way to another staircase. It is over two metres tall, its upper body and arms knotted with muscle, while its lower body is that of a goat. It opens a mouth brimful of tusk-like teeth and issues a bellowing challenge. Lowering its horned head it charges, demon-axe in hand. Demons are as lethal to spirits as other undead so you have no choice but to fight the Hellhorn.

⚁ ⚄

HELLHORN SKILL 9 STAMINA 10

If the Hellhorn's demon-axe does for you, write the number 82 on your *Adventure Sheet* and turn to **100**. If you defeat the chamber's guardian, you are able to leave by following the staircase that leads upwards from this floor (turn to **82**).

107

The graveyard looks like it has been neglected for some time. Headstones lie tumbled amidst briars and thick tussocks of grass while a number of free-standing tombs look like they have been broken into – or perhaps the bodies interred within have broken out.

You are halfway across the cemetery when the first of the ghosts appears. It is that of a young woman, her face emaciated. The ghost rises from the turfed mound of a grave. 'Help us, stranger,' the young woman pleads.

Another figure steps out of a crumbling mausoleum. This time it is the spectre of a severe-looking old man dressed in the clothes of a notary. 'Yes, help us,' he begs, 'for we are slaves to a foul fiend that will not let us depart this world.'

'Free us,' says the ghost of a bearded woodsman who sits up through the turf of an unmarked grave, 'that we might go to our eternal rest.'

What is it that has bound these ghosts to this place and that fills them now with such dread, having

⚃ ⚃

made their afterlives a misery? Will you help them? Can you help them? If you want to try, turn to **42**. If not, turn to **150**.

108

You re-appear on the Earthly Plane in the middle of the Inner Ward, bathed in cold, silver moonlight, looking up at the dominating shadowy presence of the Keep. Never before has it appeared so unwelcoming, so unlike home. You understand now that this is where the source of the evil power within Valsinore Castle lies. And if you are to vanquish it, that is where you need to go now. Turn to **117**.

109

You wander aimlessly along the mouldering tunnels, further and further under the foundations of Valsinore Castle with really no idea of where you are going. Roll one die. One a roll of 1–3, turn to **139**; on a roll of 4–6, turn to **158**.

110

The last few bones slot into place and then the Bonebeast is complete. But what is it that stands before you now? From the bones of which monster was it formed? Roll one die. On a roll of 1–2, turn to **153**; on a roll of 3–4, turn to **183**; on a roll of 5–6, turn to **212**.

111*

The passageway comes to an end a little further on, at a black wood door riven with silver sigils and esoteric runic patterns. It is another Spirit Door and unless you have a physical form of some kind you will not be able to pass beyond it. When you are ready, you will have to retrace your steps and take the alternative route through the dungeons (turn to **154**).

112

You kneel before the Queen at the foot of her throne and look up into her midnight-black eyes. And then her mask slips and you see her for what she really is – no beauty of flesh and blood but a hellish, undead wraith – but by then it is too late, you are already under the dominion of the Wraith Queen. You will remain here as a member of her undead court until the end of time. Your adventure is over.

113

'Prepare to learn what an eternity in torment is really like!' the Shadow King roars. Whatever the outcome, this will be one battle you will remember for the rest of your life, no matter how long – or short – that amount of time may be!

SHADOW KING   SKILL 13   STAMINA 18

If you are wielding the Amethyst Blade, you may increase your Attack Strength by 1 point for the duration of this battle and any successful hit you make against the Shadow King will cause him 4 STAMINA points of damage rather than the usual 2. If you are using your blessed blade Nightslayer, you may also increase your Attack Strength by 1 point but each successful hit you make will cause 3 STAMINA points of damage. If, against all the odds, you manage to defeat the Shadow King in single combat, turn to **450**. However, if he should be victorious, there will be no coming back from the dead this time and your adventure, like your life, will be over ...

114

Resisting the pull of the Death Acolyte's spell you rush at the black-robed spell-caster, shrieking in fury. A shocked expression enters the man's eyes and he starts to back away from you. But he is not done with his magic yet. Still holding the crystal ball in one hand he begins another conjuration. Not waiting to see what it is he is attempting to cast now you join in battle with the Death Acolyte.

DEATH ACOLYTE   SKILL 7   STAMINA 7

If the acolyte wins an Attack Round, turn to **186** at once. If you reduce the Death Acolyte's STAMINA score to 3 points of fewer, without him wounding you once, turn to **156**.

115

Descending the staircase you enter a stinking prison cell. At your sudden arrival, its single prisoner turns mad-staring eyes upon you and starts to laugh hysterically. You are shocked to see that it is Toadstone the Fool that is imprisoned here. He was court jester in your father's time and he's still wearing his same motley costume even now, although it is stained with filth and hangs off his skinny frame. Eventually the insane cackling subsides. 'Fancy seeing you here,' he says, and once he's started talking it seems he just can't stop.

'How long you been away now? Three years is it? Who'd've thought it? They're holding a slap-up feast tonight but I don't suppose you'll be going will you, seeing as how you've got *no body* to go with? I guess you heart's not in it. I hope there aren't any vampires going. They like everything served in bite-sized pieces!'

The poor fool is obviously completely mad, but he wasn't always like this. You wonder what can have happened – what he must have seen – for him to lose his mind like this.

'So what's it like being a ghost?' he asks. 'My mum wanted to marry a ghost. I don't know what possessed her! But you'll have to forgive me, I've not been myself lately. When I die I want my epitaph to be, 'I told you I was ill'! But anyway, enough about me, have you seen the changes they've made while you've been away? I know something they don't know. I know about their little strongroom at the top of this tower. Thing is it's got this amazing lock but to unlock it you need to reverse the combination. Hey, here's a good one. What's got six legs and flies? A witch giving her cat a ride on her broomstick!' This terrible joke sets him off again, giggling uncontrollably to himself.

You're not going to get any sense out of this poor wretch and so prepare to be on your way again. As you leave the cell and its insane occupant, Toadstone tries one last joke on you. 'Here, I used to be a werewolf but I'm all right nowww!'

If you want to climb back up the spiral staircase right to the top of the tower, turn to **166**. If you would rather return the Barbican and return to the portcullis gate, turn to **20**.

Staring into the phantom steed's baleful eyes, exerting your will against it, you manage to calm it down and bring it under your control. The horse ceases its unearthly whinnying and stands patiently within its stall instead. It does not look like it is going anywhere and knowing where there is a horse that is a ghost like yourself, could prove useful – you never know! (Add the codeword *Steed* to your *Adventure Sheet*.) Searching the stables further doesn't uncover anything else that might be of use to you so you leave to look elsewhere. Turn to **434**.

117

Do you have the codeword *Oriana* written down on your *Adventure Sheet*? If so, turn to **376** at once. If not, turn to **134**.

118

As you approach the raucous tavern, you see that the door is closed against the encroaching night. If you have the *Poltergeist* special ability, turn to **148**. If you have the *Apparition* special ability, turn to **97**. If you have neither you cautiously approach the door, recalling that the one thing everyone knows about ghosts is that they can pass through solid objects. Roll two dice. If the total is less than or equal to your WILL score, make a note of the number 97 and turn to **90**. If the total rolled is greater than your current WILL score you are unable to enter the inn, turn to **259**.

119

Your old friend Bertild gladly allows you to take control of her body, so that you might gain access to the Keep and complete your quest. (Add the codeword *Host* to your *Adventure Sheet*.)

⚁ ⚅

Make a note of your spirit-form's current SKILL and STAMINA score, for later use, on your *Adventure Sheet*. While you are wearing Bertild's muscular form you must use her stats, which are as follows: SKILL 11, STAMINA 21.

If you are injured in any way, for as long as you are wearing Bertild's body, you may eat provisions to recover STAMINA points. One meal restores up to 4 STAMINA points and Bertild has enough food for 3 meals. Looking around for a (suitable) weapon you decide to take Bertild's blacksmith's hammer. If you make a successful strike against an opponent while using the hammer roll one die; on a roll of 4–6 you cause 3 STAMINA points of damage, rather than the usual 2. (Make a note of this on your *Adventure Sheet*.)

If Bertild's STAMINA is reduced to 2 STAMINA points or fewer she will be knocked senseless, forcing you to leave her body. However, you may continue fighting but now in your spirit-form, using the stats that you have made a note of here. Turn to **429**.

120

Through sheer strength of will, you can, on occasions, move objects in the real world. Record the *Poltergeist* special ability on your *Adventure Sheet* and turn to the paragraph with the same number as the one you were just instructed to write down.

121

As you approach the sturdy stone bridge you hear the clip-clopping of hooves and then another spectre materialises in front of you. It is that of an old knight from ages past and his noble steed, faithful even unto death and beyond. The ancient knight is unhelmeted, a flowing white beard hanging down over his torn tabard and battered breastplate. He has a lance couched at his side. 'Halt!' he calls out in a reedy voice, challenging you. 'No spirit may pass!' If you are determined to cross the knight's bridge, turn to **175**. If you would rather submit to the knight, turn to **391**. Alternatively you could try wading across the river and not worry about the bridge at all (turn to **313**).

122

Climbing over the motionless body of the Golem, its metal body *plinking* as it cools, you set foot on the bridge at last. The bridge spans the natural sea-channel that lies between the headland on which the Outer and Inner Wards of Valsinore Castle were constructed, and the separate spur of rock on which the imposing Keep stands. Below you the waves crash and white water spumes where the sea is funnelled into the narrow channel, forcing the surging waves into the cliffs, sometimes even sending sprays of water cascading over the bridge itself. You are halfway across when something rises from the tumultuous surge beneath. It is little more than a gaping maw of shark-like teeth surmounting a sinuous serpentine body. With a primeval roar, the moat monster attacks. (If you have fought the bridge's serpentine guardian already, but it remains undefeated, amend its stats accordingly before attempting to best it again.)

MOAT MONSTER   SKILL 9   STAMINA 11

If you win two consecutive Attack Rounds you can escape from the sea serpent by running for the Keep at the far end of the bridge (turn to 449). If the serpent destroys your physical form it submerges beneath the waves again (cross off the relevant codeword and turn to 173). If you manage to defeat it, turn to 449.

And so you return to the guard barracks and find Captain Cador keeping watch there, despite the very late hour. Entering his room you attempt to take over his body. If you have the codeword *Braveheart* written on you *Adventure Sheet*, turn to 172. If not, roll two dice and add two to the number rolled. If the new total is less than or equal to your WILL score, turn to 172. If it is greater, Captain Cador resists your attempt to seize control of his mortal body and sends you packing with a slash of his blessed blade. Lose 2 STAMINA and if this has reduce your STAMINA score to zero or below, write the number 13 on your *Adventure Sheet* and turn to 100; if not, turn back to 13 to try another subject.

124

You must fight the faceless Tenebrae together.

	SKILL	STAMINA
First TENEBRAE	7	7
Second TENEBRAE	8	7

If you manage to defeat these creatures of darkness, regain up to 7 STAMINA points and turn to **132**. However, if they are, quite literally, the death of you, write the number 132 on your *Adventure Sheet* and turn to **100**.

125

As you soar over the castle, you become aware of dreadful keening cry. Through the wind-whipped night straight ahead you can see a host of phantasmal forms. Some are little more than skull-like faces trailing misty tails behind them, like ethereal comets, while others are fully-formed apparitions. You had never realised Valsinore had so many ghosts. Then the wraith-like creatures sense your presence and their seagull cries intensify as they surge towards you on the wind. Fight the Ethereals as if they were one creature.

ETHEREALS   SKILL 8   STAMINA 13

The Ethereals tear at you with their phantasmal claws and weaken your resolve with their terrible keening cries. If they should reduce your STAMINA score to zero or below, write the number 414 on your *Adventure Sheet* and turn to **100**. If you reduce their combined STAMINA to zero it means that you have repelled their attack and they break away from you to circle the Keep, their eerie howls echoing from the sea-lashed cliffs below. If you still want to approach the Keep, turn to **191**. If you would rather alight within the courtyard of the Outer Ward, turn to **414**.

126

Standing at the foot of the tower, gazing up at it, you can see no sign of any windows or other entrances higher up. The only way in is under an icicle-encrusted archway, the frozen spikes of water making it look like you are about to enter the gaping jaws of some colossal Ice Demon. But step between them you do.

Inside the tower, every surface is covered in a thick layer of ice and a chill wind wails eerily as it is channelled down two ascending icy spiral staircases from somewhere high above, and into the entrance hall where you now stand. Both staircases lead upwards, but which will take you to the treasure you seek? Choose a staircase. Will it be the one:

To the left?	Turn to **82**
To the right?	Turn to **106**

127

A sound like thunder rumbles across the rift and you realise that the Watcher is laughing at you. 'A second chance?' the otherworldly guardian shrieks. *Test your*

Luck. If you are Lucky, turn to **44**. If you are Unlucky, turn to **279**.

128

You hastily hurl the pouch containing the Ironbane spores at the Iron Maiden and then stand well back. The pouch bursts open on contact with the magical metal construct, surrounding it in a cloud of corrosive spores. You watch, transfixed, as the solid iron body of the torture device is eaten away until all that is left is a pile of rust-red powder on the floor. Not wanting to spend another moment in this gruesome place, you leave the torture chamber as quickly as possible. Turn to **56**.

129

With your 'killing' blow, you pierce the huntsman's ghostly heart with the tip of your ethereal blade. With a shrill, blood-curdling scream, the Baron's spectral form appears to evaporate before your very eyes. But even as his body dissolves like mist on the wind you feel yourself become imbued with phantasmal strength. Regain up to 5 STAMINA points and add 1 to your WILL score.

You suddenly find yourself at the heart of a whirling maelstrom as with whinnying cries, unearthly howls and desperate cries, the rest of the Wild Hunt is forcibly returned to the Realm of the Damned once more. (Regain 1 LUCK point.) Alone again, you set off once more for the wisewoman's hovel. Turn to **290**.

130

Blondel the Bard is strumming away at his lyre without much gusto, a disinterested expression on his face as he half-sings and half-hums along. You can tell that his heart's not in it. You know Blondel of old; he was minstrel to your father just as he was to you, when you were still the guardian of Castle Valsinore. If you want to announce your presence to him, turn to 147; if not, turn to 227.

131

'I know you,' Myrddin the hermit gasps. 'You're from the castle. But I've not seen you these three years past. And now here you are, at my door, as it were, and a ghost to boot. What happened to you?'

Your voice echoing strangely on the sea-breeze, you tell the hermit all that has passed since you were struck down on the road.

'But who would employ a servant of darkness like a Death Acolyte to do away with you?' Myrddin asks, appalled. 'Although, that said, there has been a disturbance hereabouts for some time now. Talk of strangers at the castle, people beset by restless dreams, and the Black Dog has been heard to howl again. I've heard it said that Burgomaster Jurgen of Sleath has even gone so far as to call on the services of a ghost hunter.'

Myrddin certainly seems to know a lot, especially for a hermit who's supposed to have cut himself off from the rest of society. Talk of strangers at Valsinore concerns you and makes you wonder as to your sister's safety. You've seen evidence yourself of other hauntings but the mere mention of a ghost hunter has you intrigued.

As he's in such a talkative mood, and apparently not fazed by your spectral nature, you decide to press the hermit for more information. But will you ask him about:

Recent goings on at the castle?	Turn to 314
Your sister?	Turn to 344
The ghost hunter?	Turn to 374

132

A sound like a thunderclap bursts across the circle of standing stones and you know that Unthank the Necromancer has achieved what he set out to do this night through his dark ritual. Gasps of 'The Shadow King comes!' rise from the remaining cultists, who all fall to their knees in obeisance. All except for Unthank.

'Behold the Lord of Shadows!' he declares staring up at the moonless sky above the Nine Maidens, 'The ruler of the night! Your lord and master!'

Something is condensing out of the moonless night at the very centre of the stone circle. As you watch, dumfounded, a looming figure, twice as tall as a man takes shape, clothing itself in the very fabric of the night. It looks like a giant wearing ancient armour

⚅ ⚀

forged from the metal of the night beneath a shroud of darkness, an ornate crowned helm on its head. But it is its face that stops you in your tracks – for it doesn't have one. All that lies beneath its armoured helm are two malevolently glowing coals that burn red like a pair of dying stars. And then the lunar eclipse passes and the apparition is revealed in all its malignant glory.

Peering down at the ground, it fixes the necromancer with its malevolent gaze. Then it reaches forth its hand and a blade of pure darkness forms within it. It raises the two-metre long blade above its head, pauses for a moment, and then brings it down in a sweeping arc – and Unthank is cut down with a single stroke.

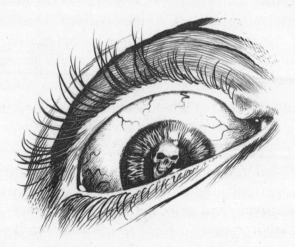

'Arrogant fool,' the dread apparition snarls in a voice like the slamming of crypt doors. (Add the codeword *Retribution* to your *Adventure Sheet*.)

The cultists start to whimper in fear. You suddenly feel colder than you have ever felt in your life and the hairs on the back of your neck start to rise. But that shouldn't be possible …

If you have the codeword *Revenant*, or *Host*, or *Armoured* still written on your *Adventure Sheet*, turn to **275**. If not, turn to **448**.

133

Before you even reach the woman, without turning round she suddenly addresses you. 'I used to laugh at the gibbet. So did, Wolfric. 'E said the roadwardens would never catch 'im, but they did. Hanged him too, for what 'e did, but 'e's not laughing now is 'e?'

She suddenly bursts into hysterical, cackling laughter and then spins round to face you. Her skin is the disgusting grey-green colour of decomposition and half her face is missing, as if something has eaten it. You then see that lengths of seaweed have become knotted in her hair.

'But I couldn't go on without 'im, could I?' the hideous apparition goes on, drifting towards you over the heather, wet sand dripping from her clothes, crabs crawling from the fleshless spaces between her ribs, and saltwater dribbling from between her fish-eaten lips with every sentence she speaks. 'Drowned myself, so that we'd both go over into the next world together, so that we need never be apart,' she giggles. 'Well I got my wish, didn't I? We've never been apart since!' she howls turning back to look up at the blackened skeleton swinging from the gibbet. Giving voice to a blood-curdling hysterical scream she suddenly launches herself at you, broken fingernails outstretched. Turn to 32.

134

As you approach the gatehouse that guards the entrance to the bridge spanning the castle's sea-moat, by the wan light of the moon you see that there are no guards present, the portcullis is raised and the way onward appears clear. If you want to approach the moat-bridge on foot, turn to 276. Alternatively, if you have the *Spirit* special ability and want to use that as a way to approach the Keep and avoid having to cross the bridge altogether, turn to 214.

135

Letting the black-bound spell book fall open in your hands you are immediately confronted by three spells which may be suitable given the circumstances. The only problem is that although you can pronounce the words written in human blood, you do not actually understand the meaning of the dark tongue of necromancy.

And then two of the shadowy Tenebrae are gliding towards you over the damp grass and frosted heather, reaching for you with their claws of darkness. You are going to have to make a decision and fast. Which spell will you read?

Dae deht fos tirip seh thsin abot?   Turn to **162**
Senok radeh truoc cusot?   Turn to **244**
Li vef oeca feht nignor tsebot?   Turn to **151**

If you don't want to risk invoking the powers of necromancy, turn to **124**.

136

The roaring of the unearthly wind surrounds and consumes you. The moorland road begins to fade from before your eyes and you feel as if you are being sucked up by a whirling maelstrom of otherworldly energies. And then you are gone from this world. Write the number 288 on your *Adventure Sheet* and turn to **100**.

137

Test your Luck. If you are Lucky, turn to **205**. If you are Unlucky, turn to **69**.

138

It only takes a moment and then the vile deed is done. You are almost overwhelmed by guilt. Korzen waited faithfully for three years for your return and then, when you did, his loyalty bought him nothing but death. (Lose 2 LUCK points and 2 WILL points.) But the witch has had her due and, as she said would be the case, you are saved from suffering any physical side-effects yourself. Cursing the witch's black soul to Hell for what she has made you do, barely able to continue with your quest now that it has cost you so much, you leave the kennels. Turn to **434**.

139

The catacombs echo to the constant *drip-drip-drip* of water. You are just thinking that you must be alone down here when a figure appears to congeal from the shadows ahead of you. The figure is wearing a hooded cloak. Without any warning, it suddenly spins round, knotted talon-like hands raised ready to strike, and you see that beneath its hood there is nothing but darkness, a darkness that not even your ghostly luminescence can penetrate – the dark oblivion of the Void. You are shocked to the core (lose 1 WILL point) and then find yourself fighting for your continued survival upon the Earthly Plane as the mind-numbing horror that is the Nightshade attacks.

NIGHTSHADE   SKILL 10   STAMINA 8

The touch of the Nightshade is deathly cold, as cold as the grave, but worse than that, every time it makes a successful strike against you, it drains off a portion of what little life-force you have left. This causes you 2 STAMINA points damage as normal but also increases the Nightshade's STAMINA score by 1 point! If the Nightshade proves too powerful an opponent and drains all of your life-force, write the number 445 on your *Adventure Sheet* and turn to **100**. However, if you manage to best this undead horror, recover up to 4 STAMINA points and turn to **207**.

140

Hearing the rattle of shifting coals coming from the forge, Bertild breaks off abruptly and you both turn to see what's making the noise. Unbelievably something is climbing out of the forge fire, two small figures formed from the coals and clinker itself, stirring the flames into crackling life as they do so. They drop from the fire onto the floor and stalk towards you, spitting and hissing like popping embers.

'We are discovered!' Bertild exclaims. 'Someone has been eavesdropping on our conversation,' she says as she stumbles to her feet, taking up her hammer and grabbing a red-hot poker from the fire. Bertild takes on the first of the clinker creatures while you deal with the second.

CLINKER   SKILL 6   STAMINA 6

If the magical creature defeats you, write the number 434 on your *Adventure* Sheet and turn to **100**. If you destroy the spark-spitting Clinker, Bertild, having beaten her opponent into a pile of cold ash, turns to you and says, 'You had best be away from here before anything else finds you, and so I bid you farewell and good luck!' You cannot fault Bertild's assessment of the situation and so leave the smithy, as the blacksmith restores the salt barrier behind you. Add the codeword *Ironheart* to your *Adventure Sheet* and turn to **434**.

141

The room you enter is like some nightmarish art gallery, containing, as it does, all sorts of grim statues depicting monstrous creatures, hellish demons and grim memento moris of skulls and human skeletons. But by far the largest and most impressive is the looming statue of a cloaked and hooded skeleton with the wings of some black-winged carrion bird spread wide behind it. Gripped in the statue's claw-like hands is an even more macabre scythe. It looks like it has been fashioned from the spine of some great beast while its blade glints blackly in the dim torchlight cast by wall-mounted braziers. It appears to be made from one huge piece of amethyst. Do you want to lift the weapon from the statue's clutches (turn to 412), or would you prefer to leave the room and proceed deeper into the dungeons (turn to 154)?

142

You have broken the dark enchantment holding the dream-monster together and freed the people of Sleath from their tortured dreams. With a lingering scream, like that of a child waking from a horrid dream, the Phantasmagoria breaks apart and dissolves like mist on the wind. At the same time, you feel your ghostly form absorb part of its unreal essence. (Regain up to 5 STAMINA points.)

Alone again on the road, you decide where to go next in your search for answers. If you want to enter

⚀ ⚁

Sleath, turn to **99**. If you want to skirt past the village and make for Valsinore Castle instead, turn to **6**.

143

Surely a will as strong as yours can bring a horse under control. Roll two dice and subtract 1 from the total rolled. If the new total is less than or equal to your WILL score, turn to **116**; if it is greater, turn to **96**.

144

A chill wind blows flurries of snow and ice flakes across the surface of the lake like winter waves. The ice gleams an eerie white in the moonlight. As the ever-present wind blows a dusting of snow from the surface of the lake you see something trapped in the ice below your feet. You almost lose your footing in shock as you see the frozen features of a terrified warrior looking back at you, locked in the ice for all eternity. Looking to your right you see another, and another. It's the same to your left. In fact, they're everywhere, corpses frozen within the surface of the lake. What manner of place have you come to? (Lose 1 WILL point.)

The sound of the ice cracking echoes across the surface of the lake and you freeze in your tracks. There comes another loud crack and this time you locate the source of the sound; what you see fills you with horror. Breaking free of the ice, ancient battle-axe still in hand, an ice-rimmed bearskin cloak about its shoulders, is one of the frozen warriors. You can see the blue veins of the corpse beneath its pallid grey skin, the moisture in its body frozen solid. As it pulls itself free of the ice, what looks like breath frosts on the air before it. The warrior's eyes are vacant and its face expressionless, but it stumbles towards you, bringing its weapon to bear, determined to stop you reaching the tower. Hearing the sounds of more corpses breaking free of their icy graves you realise that you are in trouble now. As you engage the Ice Ghost in battle, more of the frozen undead warriors slowly drag themselves towards you.

ICE GHOST   SKILL 7   STAMINA 6

Roll one die and add 7 to the number, giving you a result between 8 and 13. Now deduct your current SKILL score from that number; this is the number of Ice Ghosts you must battle to get to the other side of the lake, but you must fight at least one. If after fighting at least one ghost you think that the challenge is too great, you may return to the lake shore and from there return to Castle Valsinore (lose 1 LUCK point and turn to **29**). If any of the ghosts finish you off, write the number 126 on your *Adventure Sheet* and turn to **100**. However, if you defeat all of your opponents, you make it to the island at last (turn to **126**).

145

Leaving the beach you return to the cliff-tops and from there set out across the moors in the direction of Valsinore Castle. But then a crossroads comes into view. Turn to **19**.

🎲 🎲

146

Another ten metres on and you come to another door on your left. This one is covered in curtains of spider-webs and looks like it hasn't been opened in a very long time. If you are capable of opening the door and want to enter the room beyond, turn to 72. If not, you continue on along the passageway (turn to 255).

147

'Blondel,' you hiss, without revealing yourself just yet.

The bard breaks off his playing and looks about him. 'Who goes there?' he challenges, taken completely by surprise.

'It is I,' you say as you materialise again before his very eyes.

'By Saint Zillah's bones!' he splutters. 'Begone, demon. Do not try to tempt me with your evil wiles, doppelganger. Leave my soul in peace, vile fetch!'

This was not quite the welcome you were hoping for. And then, equally unexpectedly, Blondel takes up his lyre again and begins to play. But there's something unsettling about the melody he is playing now and the words of the song sound more like the words of a spell of exorcism!

Roll two dice and add 2 to the number rolled. If this new total is equal to or less than your WILL score, turn to 187. If it is greater, write the number 227 on your *Adventure Sheet* and turn to 100.

⚃ ⚁

148

Through sheer strength of will you use your supernatural powers to turn the handle and open the latch. The door blows open with a bang in the wind and suddenly the eyes of all those inside turn to see who it is entering the inn. If you are happy to let the people see you, turn to **81**. If not, and you have the *Shade* special ability, turn to **299**; otherwise, in that instant, you wish that you were invisible as well as a ghost. Roll two dice. If the total rolled is less than or equal to your WILL, *Test your Skill*; if you are successful, write the number 299 on your *Adventure Sheet* and then turn to **230**. If you fail either roll, turn to **81**.

149

And then you are through. (Add 1 to your WILL score.) Stumbling over the threshold and down the steps on the other side, you find yourself within a chapel of rest. Standing in the centre of the sanctuary is a marble sarcophagus bearing the carved relief image of a noble paladin reclined in prayer, his stone sword clasped in his hands upon its lid. Moonlight shines through a stained glass window at the far end of the shrine that appears to depict the same Templar Knight of Telak, wearing the garb of that holy order, but with his helmet under one arm.

As you watch, the moonlight within the chamber seems to solidify and then runs together like quicksilver, forming the ghostly impression of the knight there in front of you. You can sense a palpable aura of Goodness around him.

'Who summons me from the Battle at the End of Time against the forces of darkness?' the Paladin demands, his silvery eyes fixing on you.

You mumble a hasty apology, saying that you did not mean to. The knight suddenly looks beyond you, as if sensing something you cannot.

'Ah, I understand,' he says, 'the Shadow King would manifest within this reality at this place and time as well. Then he must be stopped! But my powers are limited here, I am bound to this place, but if I were able to pass on my knowledge to another ...'

He looks at you again, a severe expression upon his perfect, chiselled features. 'But are you worthy?' he says, somewhat arrogantly. 'A challenge!' he declares, before you have time to answer him.

> 'As I was travelling to Analand,
> I came across three hunting bands.
> Each band had seven knights,
> Each knight had seven squires,
> Each squire had seven hounds.
> Hounds, squires, knights and bands,
> How many were travelling to Analand?'

If you know the answer to the Paladin's riddle, add one to the number and turn to the paragraph that has the same number as this total. If you do not know the answer (or if you get it wrong) there is nothing more the Paladin will do for you and he simply dissolves into moonlight once more; you have no choice but to leave the shrine (turn to 259).

150

Making your embarrassed excuses you hasten on your way through the graveyard, the mournful wailing of the ghosts trapped here chasing you between the tumbled tombstones. 'You have doomed us all,' the notary calls, 'so cursed shall your afterlife be too!'

It suddenly feels as if a sinister shadow has fallen across your soul. (Lose 1 LUCK point and 1 WILL point.) Leaving the ghosts to their fate, whatever it may be, you make your way beyond the boundary wall of the cemetery at last and find yourself on the road that leads into Sleath. Turn to **61**.

151

A curious radiating glow floods your being and you feel reinvigorated, in mind as well as body. Regain up to 5 STAMINA points, 1 SKILL point and 1 LUCK point, and add 1 to your WILL score. Now turn to **124**.

152

Unable to enter the Keep and confront the dark power that now holds dominion of Valsinore Castle, you are robbed of your ultimate revenge. You are doomed to haunt the stronghold that was once your home forevermore. Your adventure is over.

⚅ ⚁

The bones that make up the body of the Bonebeast are mainly those of dragons, wyverns and the various other worms slain by your ancestors around the time of the Rise of Kakhabad. So prepare yourself for a titanic struggle indeed.

DRAGONKIND BONEBEAST SKILL 11 STAMINA 12

If the Bonebeast wins an Attack Round, roll one die and consult the table below to discover what damage it inflicts upon you.

Die Roll	Attack and Damage
1–3	Terrible Claws – the Bonebeast savages you with its cruelly sharp claws. Lose 2 STAMINA points.
4–5	Tail Lash – the dragon-thing's tail hits you, knocking you off your feet. Lose 2 STAMINA points and reduce your Attack Strength by 1 point for the duration of the next Attack Round as you get up again.
6	Savage Bite – the monster catches you in its mouth and sinks its fangs into you. Lose 4 STAMINA points.

If you manage to defeat the Bonebeast, turn to **236**. Alternatively, after three Attack Rounds have elapsed you can attempt to flee by running for the descending staircase. If you want to do this you must forfeit one Attack Round and suffer the consequences, but if your gamble pays off, turn to **205**. However, if your battle with the Bonebeast results in your ethereal form being destroyed, write the number 110 on your *Adventure Sheet* and turn to **100**.

154

The passageway ends at a sturdy oak door but some-one has been careless, and left it open. Passing through into the chamber beyond you are hit first by the size of the space and secondly by the absolutely appalling smell. The room, if it can be called that, is at least thirty metres long, its high ceiling supported by crumbling pillars ten metres tall. Burning braziers illuminate the vast vaulted space also allowing you to see the pool that lies at its centre. In fact this pool looks more like a vast sewer.

The pool crosses the chamber from one side to the other without leaving so much as a ledge for you to skirt round it. And it is no wonder that such a dis-gusting stench fills the chamber. The pool is filled with a stomach-turning soup of putrefying flesh and worse. Amidst puddles of foaming bile you see leg bones, skulls, ribcages and calcified hands poking above the surface. Looking at the pool you have no idea how deep it could be, but there is a way across it. One of the pillars that once helped support the roof now lies across its width, forming huge stepping stones across the middle of the pool.

On the other side of the vile pool of putrescence another tunnel leads away from this chamber, deeper underground, but this exit is blocked by a spiked iron gate cast with a grinning demonic face. You will obviously need to cross the pool to proceed any further and find your nemesis, but by what means? Will you:

Use the *Spirit* special ability (if you
    have it)?   Turn to **103**
Cross by means of the broken pillar?   Turn to **179**
Step into the pool in the hope that you
    can wade across it?   Turn to **222**
Attempt to leap across to the
    other side?   Turn to **261**

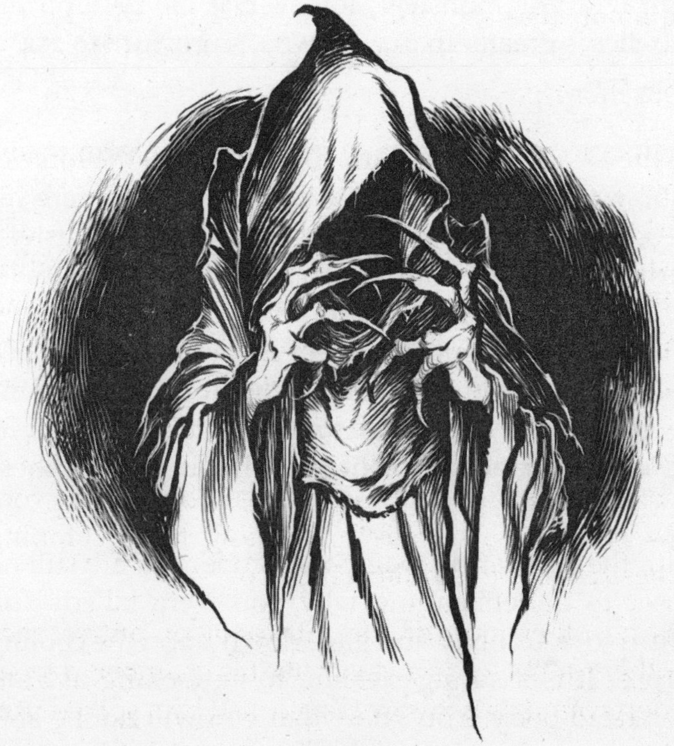

155

The Golem sweeps you up in its huge arms and crushes you against its chest. Human faces, screaming in torment, ooze from between the broken graves that make up the undead monster's body and you realise that the Grave Golem is trying to trap you inside itself as it has those wretches buried within Sleath's cemetery.

Roll two dice. If the total rolled is less than or equal to your WILL score, you resist the Golem's power and slip free of its clutches; return to 42 and finish your fight with the monster. However, if the total on the two dice is greater than your WILL score, turn to 254.

156

As the Death Acolyte starts to succumb to the force of your wrathful vengeance a look of panic enters his eyes. He abruptly quits his spell-casting and instead hurls the crystal ball at your feet. The amethyst sphere explodes with the force of the black energies bound within it. For a moment everything goes black and then the light of the rising moon returns and the world appears once more around you, limned in its monochrome radiance. But of the Death Acolyte there is no sign.

With the murdering magic-user gone, you are still no closer to understanding why you were killed. You return to your body and gaze down upon the cooling corpse. It is a strange feeling to be looking at your own dead body. You know that you will not be able to rest now until you have solved the mystery of your own murder and exacted your revenge against the one who wanted you out of the way. But where will you go first in your search for answers?

You gaze out across the wind-swept promontory towards the distant Valsinore Castle. Ahead of you, directly to the north, lies the village of Sleath, the castle a black shadow now against the horizon behind it. To the north-west lies the tangled expanse of Wraith Wood where, rumour has it, a Wisewoman dwells. Perhaps she could help you in your search for answers. To the north-east, the moors peter out at the edge of the sea, where – when you were here last at least – a hermit monk dwelt, down on the seashore. Perhaps he might be able to help you. However, to the east you can see the dark hill of a burial mound and you feel a strange pull to this place that you cannot explain, just as you do in fact to the stone circle of the Nine Maidens where you were attacked. Will you:

Approach the burial mound?	Turn to **409**
Succumb to the lure of the Nine Maidens?	Turn to **257**
Explore one of the other options open to you?	Turn to **217**

157

Snatching a torch from a wall-bracket, you prepare to fight this undead monstrosity. You know you have chosen the correct weapon when you hear the thing shriek in fear and recoil from the searing flames.

⚃ ⚀

NECROS   SKILL 10   STAMINA 12

If the Necros hits you, the acidic slime coating it will burn you whether you have a physical body or not, due to the fact that it is also one of the Undead, although like no other you have ever seen. In return, your burning brand will burn it for 2 STAMINA points of damage with every successful strike. If you manage to overcome this appalling undead horror, turn to **401**. If the Necros puts an end to your spirit-form, write the number 243 on your *Adventure Sheet* and turn to **100**.

158

This part of the catacombs is thick with spider webs. However, spiders shouldn't trouble you in your ethereal form and so you press on. But the further you go the thicker they become. Where the moisture-clad webs are at their thickest you are not entirely surprised when a monstrous arachnid descends from the ceiling above. Shock quickly turns to horror when you see the monster's face for the first time; where you would have expected to see the blunt head of a spider, with its myriad black pearl eyes and venom-dripping fangs, there in its place is a malevolent travesty of a human face. Hissing horribly, the demonic Death Spider stalks towards you, determined to snare your soul within its unearthly web and drag you to its own hellish dimension.

DEATH SPIDER   SKILL 12   STAMINA 9

⚀ ⚀

If the Death Spider wins two consecutive Attack Rounds, turn to **177**. If not, keep fighting until either you or the monster is destroyed. If it is you who 'dies', write the number 445 on you *Adventure* Sheet and turn to **100**. If it is the demon's spirit that is returned to the Realm of the Damned, turn to **207**.

159

The will of the Shadow King, one of the Lords of Death, is a powerful force indeed, a tangible force like some crushing tentacle of evil. But you have not fought your way through hosts of Undead, facing untold dangers to be resurrected from the dead only to fail now. Chamberlain Unthank may be dead, and your need for vengeance satisfied, but now an even greater evil threatens the future of these lands, as great an evil, in fact, as that defeated by the massed forces of the Crusade against Evil that cleansed Bathoria.

'I shall not bow before you!' you scream in defiance at the undead entity. 'Your servant Unthank the Necromancer failed to destroy me, even though he tried, and so shall you fail too!'

Thunder rumbles over and around the stone circle again and it takes a moment for you to realise that the Shadow King is mocking you with laughter. If you have the codeword *Retribution* written on your *Adventure Sheet*, turn to **419**. If not, turn to **375**.

🎲 🎲

You clamber up into a filthy, draughty chamber that reeks of the smell of the crusted droppings that cover every perch and every alcove. You are in what used to be the loft where the falconer kept his trained birds of prey. But there is no sign of the falconer now, other than for a human skeleton, picked clean of flesh and half-buried in bird droppings. Nor is there any sign of his birds, only you wouldn't be surprised if they all ended up inside the blasphemy now picking at the lamb's carcass trapped in its talons. In life it must have been something the size of a Roc or a Giant Vulture, and has characteristics of both, but it is hard to be certain now the thing is somewhat decomposed – its flesh hanging in tatters from its bones, its jaundice-yellow eyes rolling in the orbits of its fleshless skull. Whatever it was in life, now that it is dead its hunger is insatiable. Giving a savage squawk the undead bird launches itself at you on featherless wings of torn dead skin.

CARRION BIRD   SKILL 7   STAMINA 7

If the undead avian 'kills' you, write the number 20 on your *Adventure Sheet* and turn to **100**. If you slay the Carrion, you find nothing for you here in the stinking aviary and so make your way back down through the tower to the Barbican gate (turn to **20**).

161

'Would that Aramanthus was still alive,' Bertild says glumly, 'he could have helped you, I'm sure of it. I don't know who to trust round here, these days. The Captain of the Guard's a good man but distrustful of others too. Likewise, I hear the Priest still does what he can to halt the spread of evil, but he hardly ever leaves his chapel now for fear of what lies beyond the limits of that sanctuary. The Bard's hardly ever out of Chamberlain Unthank's presence and appears to be one of the favoured few of the court. The Porter's a dead loss, these days; let's just say he has trouble with spirits of his own. But my information's a little out of date; movement between the wards is restricted. And no one's permitted to enter the Keep anymore.' Turn to **140**.

162

As you speak the words of the invocation, the shadow-born Tenebrae scream in pain and dissolve back into the darkness they were originally summoned from. Regain 1 LUCK point, add 1 to your WILL score and turn to **132**.

163

As you make for the village of Sleath and your ancestral home, a crossroads comes into view, as does the gibbet that stands before it at the top of a steep escarpment on the moors. The wind is picking up now as it blows in across the black gulf of the Diamond Sea to the east. It bats at the mouldering body hanging from the end of the hangman's noose, lank hair billowing out around its head. Standing close by, her shawl pulled tight around her shoulders against the wind, her ragged dress billowing in the sea-breeze, is a red-haired woman. You can't help but wonder who the gibbet-body was in life. Perhaps this woman knows. As you look at her more closely, you see that a flickering green aura surrounds her body. Do you want to:

Approach the woman?	Turn to **133**
Study the body hanging from the gibbet?	Turn to **92**
Proceed along the road towards the crossroads?	Turn to **52**

164

Upon entering the stables you are met by the earthy smell of the horses tethered inside. The animals whinny and stamp their hooves in agitation as you pass by them. You notice that one animal is saddled and then, as you look closer, you are amazed to see that it is the horse you were riding back to the castle. You had forgotten about it until now but it makes you wonder … If your horse has made it back here, then what has happened to your corpse?

As you ponder the fate of your own dead body, the stables become bathed in an eerie green light as something manifests within an empty stall opposite you. As you watch, a phantom horse materialises there. Its eyes are blazing witch-lights while ectoplasm drips from its foaming lips. The horse appears to be wild and it has you completely trapped. If you want to get out of the stables you are going to have to get past this phantom creature first.

As the horse rears up on its hind-legs, ready to bring its hooves crashing down on your head you hastily decide how to react. If you want to draw your sword to defend yourself, turn to **96**. If you would rather try to calm the horse-ghost, turn to **143**.

165

At the last possible moment the bolt of black lightning is drawn towards the mirrored shield on your arm, hitting it and dissipating harmlessly. Now nothing stands between you and your longed-for revenge, other than Unthank the Necromancer himself. If you still have a Black Hourglass and want to use it now, turn to **410**. If not, turn to **428**.

166

The stairs end before a heavy-looking oak door, painted black and inlaid with ornately-tooled silver filigree that marks out esoteric symbols within the wood. The door has a handle but lacks a keyhole. Instead, in the middle of the door is a set of three tumblers, each one bearing the digits 0 to 9 upon their knurled surfaces. Obviously, to be able to open the door you need to know the code to the combination lock. But even if you do possess such knowledge, it's useless to you if you cannot move the tumblers.

⚂ ⚄

If you think you know the combination and you have the *Poltergeist* special ability, turn to **411**. If you have the combination but not the ability, but you still want to try to force the tumblers to move, roll two dice. If the total rolled is less than or equal to your WILL, roll three more dice; if this second total is less than or equal to your STAMINA score, write the number 411 on your *Adventure Sheet* and turn to **120**. If you fail either roll, you are unable to operate the combination lock; you will either have to leave this wing of the gatehouse (turn to **20**), or use the *Apparition* special ability to try to get round the problem, if you both have that special ability and you want to use it here (turn to **181**).

167

'But what is justice?' the Watcher intones. 'Answer me that.' If you reply by saying that justice means revenge, turn to **226**. If you want to say that you want a second chance so that you might achieve justice for yourself, turn to **127**.

168

You are standing at the shore of a frozen lake, on the distant, ice-locked arctic Diamond Islands. At the centre of the lake's ice sheet stands a rocky island, and from it rises a colossal tower of blue ice and black stone. The icicle-pointed spurs of its battlements seem to reach all the way to the realm of the gods, it's so high. This is Frostfinger, the tower of the Winter

King, a place of legend, cursed by demons, but if the information you're acting on is correct, it is also the resting place of the mysterious Spirit Stone. Before you can start looking for this arcane artefact you are going to need to cross the lake to reach the island. If you have the *Spirit* special ability and want to use it, turn to 126. If not, you set out across the frozen lake (turn to 144).

169

With the Wild Hunt bearing down on you out of the sky you turn and flee deeper into the wood. You throw yourself into cover beneath the growth of bracken obscuring the root bole of an old oak, just as the hunt's hounds and horses alight in a clearing between the trees. The unearthly barking of the dogs echoes between the black trunks of ash and elder and you hear someone command the pack to, 'Seek them out, wherever they might be!'

As you wait, lurking in the dense undergrowth, you hear the padding footsteps of the hounds getting closer accompanied by an urgent snuffling sound. And then they find you. (Lose 1 LUCK point.) Snarling rabidly, the ethereal hunting dogs go for you. Fight the Phantom Hounds altogether.

	SKILL	STAMINA
First PHANTOM HOUND	7	5
Second PHANTOM HOUND	6	5
Third PHANTOM HOUND	6	6

⚅ ⚀

If you die a second death at the jaws of the hounds within 4 Attack Rounds, record the number 290 on your *Adventure Sheet* and turn to **100**. If you are still 'alive' after 4 Attack Rounds, the leader of the Wild Hunt calls off the dogs. Turn to **220**.

170

As you proceed through the hall you are suddenly bathed in brilliant, arctic light, and find yourself unable to move. You can see nothing all around you but for the blinding whiteness. And then out of the light a rasping, inhuman voice speaks.

> *'Each thing has its allotted span,*
> *But how many years is the life of man?'*

If you think you know the answer to this riddle, turn to the paragraph with the same number. If not, or if the paragraph you turn to makes no sense, then turn to **372**.

171

Having rid yourself of the Black Dog of Barrowmoor, you set off again for the sea-cliffs. Before long you are negotiating the goat track that leads from the windswept moors to the pebbled beach and dark sea below.

Your feet make no sound as you walk over the pebbles, the only sounds are the wash of the tide and the rattle of stones tumbled by the breakers. Ahead of you, further along the headland, you can see a cave mouth that stands above the band of seaweed left by the tide, illuminated by a crackling driftwood fire. This must be the hermit's home. You only hope that he can help you.

And then he's there, standing at the entrance to his cave, staring out into the night at the moonlit breakers. 'Hello? Is there anybody there?'

He is dressed in a plain grey habit, tied at the waist with rope, a long, straggly grey beard clinging to the hollows of his hunger-lean face, although the top of his head is completely bald. Then he sees you, and his ruddy complexion pales in the moonlight. *Test your Luck*. If you are Lucky, turn to **131**. If you are Unlucky, turn to **447**.

172

Your mind, with all the knowledge you have gained, inside Captain Cador's highly-trained body will make a ruthlessly effective combination. (Add the codeword *Host* to your *Adventure Sheet*.)

Make a note of your spirit-form's current SKILL and STAMINA score, for later use, on your *Adventure Sheet*. While you are controlling Cador's body you must use his stats, which are as follows: SKILL 12, STAMINA 20.

If you are injured in any way, for as long as you are wearing Cador's body, you may eat provisions to recover STAMINA points. One meal restores up to

4 STAMINA points and Cador has enough food for 2 meals. The captain of the guard is armed with a blessed blade (not unlike your own Nightslayer, only not as powerful) which is capable of harming undead, demons and magical creatures.

If Captain Cador's STAMINA is reduced to 2 STAMINA points or fewer while you are in possession of him, he will be knocked unconscious, forcing you to release his body from your influence. However, you may continue fighting in your spirit-form, using the stats that you have made a note of here. Turn to **429**.

173

You already know that to proceed any further you will need a physical body, and yet you have just lost yours. But do you know of another means of acquiring one? If you have the phrase *Rest in Peace* written on your *Adventure Sheet*, turn to **369**. If you have the codeword *Automaton* written down, turn to **427**. If you have the *Spook* special ability and wish to choose this path, turn to **13**. If you have none of these things, turn to **152**.

174

You could not possibly use your sister to exact your revenge! She is the last surviving member of your family line. If she should die, then so will your family's bloodline and that is something you are trying to prevent. As a result, the Lady Oriana is not a suitable candidate for possession. Lose 1 LUCK point and 1 WILL point. Turn back to **13** and try someone, or something, else instead.

175

'You do not get past Sir Calormayne of Ravenscar that easily,' the knight roars, spurring his horse forwards at a gallop. 'Prepare to meet your doom!' His charger pounding towards you, the old knight suddenly doesn't appear quite so weak and feeble after all. You are forced to draw your sword and defend yourself once again.

GHOSTLY KNIGHT   SKILL 10   STAMINA 10

If you defeat the knight in single combat, you are able to cross the bridge unhindered and you also feel yourself filled with renewed energy. (Regain up to 5 STAMINA points and turn to **6**.) If the knight bests you in mortal combat, write the number 6 on your *Adventure Sheet* and turn to **100**.

176

With a strange, almost musical cry the bard's conscious flees to some distant corner of his mind as you take control of his body. (Add the codeword *Host* to you *Adventure Sheet*.)

Make a note of your spirit-form's current SKILL and STAMINA score, for later use, on your *Adventure Sheet*.

While you are wearing the body of Blondel the Bard you must use his stats which are as follows: SKILL 8, STAMINA 15.

If you are injured in battle you may eat provisions to recover STAMINA points. One meal restores up to 4 STAMINA points. You hastily gather scraps left over after Unthank's bizarre midnight feast and collect enough for 4 meals. Blondel carries a short sword in a scabbard at his waist, which is not enchanted, and his lyre, which is. (Make a note of this on your *Adventure Sheet*.)

If Blondel's STAMINA score is ever reduced to 2 STAMINA points or fewer, the Bard will be knocked out, and you will be forced to leave his unconscious body. You can keep on fighting in your spirit-form, however, using the stats that you have written down here. Turn to **429**.

177

The Death Spider seizes your ethereal form in its hellish fangs and, making the most of your vulnerable state, tries to drag you into the middle of its web, which is its extra-dimensional link to the Realm of the Damned. *Test your Luck*. If you are Lucky return to **158** and keep fighting until either you or the monster is destroyed. If you are Unlucky, the Death Spider succeeds in dragging you into the centre of its web. Write the number 445 on you *Adventure* Sheet and turn to **100**.

178

As abruptly as it appeared, the light is gone, plunging the entrance hall into darkness once more. But, undaunted, you continue on your way until it opens out into a vast chamber and you begin to realise how much the Keep has been altered in the time you've been away.

The interior of the vast structure is now nothing more than a shell. The upper floors and internal walls have been pulled down, the rubble from this mass destruction piled in great drifts of brick and stone at the sides of the vast chamber so created. Where once the skeletons of those beasts slain by the lords of Valsinore Castle were displayed in all their ossic glory, now there is only a pile of broken bones. On the other side of the chamber, at the north-west and north-east corners of the Keep, you can see two still-intact spiral staircases, leading up, towards the battlements, and down, into the dungeons, respectively.

But it would seem that there is life in these calcified remains yet. As you enter the chamber, some of the bones start to move, rattling across the stone floor towards each other, joining together as if they remember how they once connected in life. And yet bones from all manner of shattered skeletons are joining together in this way as something monstrous manifests within the shell of the Keep. How will you deal with this latest threat? Will you:

Race across the chamber towards the
north-west staircase?   Turn to **69**

⚃ ⚃

Try to make it to the north-east
staircase?   Turn to **137**
Prepare to fight whatever it is that is
manifesting here?   Turn to **110**

179

Cautiously, you step out onto the broken column spanning the putrid pool. If you are in your ethereal form you easily make it across to the other side without anything untoward occurring (turn to **421**). If you are inhabiting a physical body you must *Test your Luck*. If you are Lucky you also make it safely to the other side (turn to **421**), but if you are Unlucky, one of the broken pieces of column tips under your weight, sending you stumbling into the foul pool (turn to **222**).

180

The welcoming ruddy glow of the working forge draws you through the darkness towards the blacksmith's workshop. The blacksmith has left the door open, as always, to stop the heat inside becoming unbearable. The heat even warms your chill phantom form. You cautiously peer inside.

It is just as you remember it. You have fond memories of this place. As a child you would while away hours within the sphere of its warmth, watching Bertild the smith working at her forge, shaping pieces of armour on the anvil or perfecting sharp-edged weapons.

⚁ ⚀

And Bertild's there now, working at her forge. Bertild is a tall, thick-set woman, with heavily-muscled arms and shoulders and is unmistakeable thanks to the eye-patch she wears over her left eye where a sliver of red-hot iron once caught her in the eye. She wears a heavy-duty leather apron and has a heavy-headed hammer in one thick-gloved hand and the piece of metal she is working held in a pair of tongs in the other.

You are about to enter the smithy when you notice that salt has been poured in a line across the threshold. If you want to cross this salt barrier, turn to **231**. If you would rather call out to the blacksmith first, turn to **14**.

181

Instinctively closing your eyes, you take a confident step forwards. Immediate and inexplicable pain courses through your body like an electric shock and you are thrown back from the door, unable to pass through it. Roll one die and add 1; this is the amount of STAMINA damage you suffer. If this has finished you off, write the number 20 on your *Adventure Sheet* and turn to **100**. If you are still alive, as it were, unless you think you know the combination and want to try to open the door (turn back to **166**), there is nothing you can do but leave the tower (turn to **20**), or descend the staircase to the bottom, if you haven't already done so, by turning to **115**.

⚀ ⚁

182

The passageway brings you to a flight of stone steps that descend into the darkness below. Considering what you have encountered so far in the dungeons, as you follow the steps down into the gloom, you wonder what horrors await you deeper beneath Valsinore.

The stairs double back on themselves and then you find yourself in another stone-walled passageway. A sound like a rattlesnake's tail vibrating causes you to freeze and you peer into the murk ahead of you. A little further on a new passageway branches off to the left. The tunnel also continues ahead of you, but clinging half to the wall and half to the ceiling by its large ivory dew-claws is a hideous creature that appears to be an amalgam of a large lizard of some kind with a rattlesnake's tail, its scaly skin mottled green and brown. However its head looks horribly like a fleshless human skull, although the nictitating golden eyes in that skull are undoubtedly reptilian and a forked tongue darts from its open mouth tasting the stale, musty air of the dungeons. If you want to continue along the corridor, you are going to have to fight the Catacomb Crawler. If you are prepared to do this, turn to **219**. If not, you could try taking the turning to the left before the creature becomes aware of your presence (turn to **203**).

183

The Bonebeast has been created from the bones of fantastical beasts such as a manticore, a chimera and a basilisk, so you know the battle you are about to fight is going to be legendary!

CHIMERICAL BONEBEAST   SKILL 9   STAMINA 11

If the Bonebeast wins an Attack Round, roll one die and consult the table below to discover what damage it inflicts upon you.

Die Roll	Attack and Damage
1–2	Terrible Claws – the Bonebeast savages you with its cruelly sharp claws. Lose 2 STAMINA points.
3–4	Tail Lash – the Bonebeast's tail hits you, knocking you off your feet. Lose 2 STAMINA points and reduce your Attack Strength by 1 point for the duration of the next Attack Round as you get up again.
5–6	Savage Bite – the undead monster sinks its fangs into you. Lose 3 STAMINA points.

If you manage to defeat the Bonebeast, turn to **236**. Alternatively, after three Attack Rounds have elapsed you can attempt to flee by running for the descending staircase. If you want to do this you must forfeit one Attack Round and suffer the consequences, but if your gamble pays off, turn to **205**. However, if your battle with the Bonebeast results in your ethereal form being destroyed, write the number 110 on your *Adventure Sheet* and turn to **100**.

184

A cold sweat breaks out on your forehead and you find yourself gritting your teeth as you struggle to force the very powers you seek to destroy to aid you in their own destruction. But somehow, against all the odds, you manage it.

As you continue to read the spell of banishment the codex found for you, the veil between worlds is torn asunder and the ghosts of a thousand damned souls rush through the tear in the fabric of reality, and surround the Shadow King with a whirling vortex of spectral light. You watch in awe as the spirits tear the Shadow King's insubstantial form apart with their spectral talons. The Death Lord does his best to defend himself from their relentless assault but in the end he is simply overwhelmed. Soon there is nothing left of the Shadow King but a few traces of inky darkness at the heart of the whirling spirit vortex and then, with one last howl of fury and frustration, even that is gone as the evil entity is dragged back to the Realm of the Damned. With an explosive thunderclap boom, as of slamming tombs, the rent in reality closes again. Turn to **450**.

185

You find yourself inside an utterly appalling room. It is a torture chamber – there can be absolutely no doubt about that. The implements of the torturer's trade are everywhere – braziers, chairs covered in iron spikes and all manner of confining irons litter the dungeon cell or hang by chains from the ceiling. But none are as deserving of awe as the two-metre tall iron maiden that stands in the centre of the chamber. It has been made to mimic the shape of the human body, having two arms and two legs, as well as a trunk and head. But you could never have guessed how closely it resembles a human being until, with a squealing of rusted iron joints, the horrific torture implement comes to life. Stomping across the floor on its iron-shod feet it blocks your way out of the torture chamber. If you have some Ironbane and wish to use it, turn to **128**, otherwise you have no choice but to fight the magically-animated Iron Maiden, which is as capable of injuring you as you are of damaging it.

IRON MAIDEN   SKILL 8   STAMINA 10

If you are fighting the magical metal construct with a crushing weapon – such as a hammer of some kind or your own iron fists – or a magical weapon, each successful strike your make against it will inflict 2 STAMINA points of damage. Ordinary bladed weapons (such as a battleaxe or a dagger) will only cause 1 STAMINA point of damage with each successful hit. If you destroy the torture chamber's guardian, you leave its cell as quickly as possible (turn to **56**). If, during the battle, your spirit-form perishes, write the number 56 on your *Adventure Sheet* and turn to **100**.

186

Rather than fighting back with an ordinary weapon, the acolyte defends himself by blasting you with more of his dark magic. One of these bolts of black energy hits you and you are consumed by pain. It is as if the acolyte's spell has burned your ethereal form and causes you 2 STAMINA points of damage.

Continue your battle with the Death Acolyte. As soon as you reduce the evil magic-user's STAMINA score to 3 points of fewer, turn to **156** at once. However, if your STAMINA score is reduced to zero, write the number 288 on your *Adventure Sheet* and turn to **100** immediately.

187

Resisting the arcane power of the Bard's magical lyre you quickly make yourself invisible again and flee from his presence. Add the codeword *Bard* to your *Adventure Sheet* and turn to **227**.

188

Both the village of Fetchfen and Frostfinger, the Tower of the Winter King, lie many leagues from Valsinore Castle. To travel there on foot would take days, time which you just don't have. But then perhaps you know of a less conventional way to travel. If you have *Spirit* special ability, turn to **218**. If not,

⚁ ⚅

but you have the codeword *Steed* written on your *Adventure Sheet*, turn to 7. If you have neither of these things, there is no way that you would be able to travel to either place and return again before daybreak, and you have a feeling that whatever is going to happen will happen before Valsinore Castle sees the dawn of another day. Lose 1 LUCK point and turn to 117.

189

'The cook's busy in the kitchen's preparing Unthank's midnight celebratory feast, the priest barely ever leaves the sanctuary of the chapel, and of course the blacksmith's still here, plying her trade over on the other side of the courtyard. The bard's about the only one who has anything to do with Unthank. For some reason he's still welcome at court.

'The fool went mad long ago. Unthank has him locked up in a cell in the Barbican. I can hear him laughing hysterically on nights when the moon is full. The old gravedigger's still here too. Certainly seems to have plenty to keep him occupied these days.

'But if you're planning to exact your revenge on whoever it might be that's got it coming to them, there's something else you should know.' Turn to 269.

190

Without looking back again, you turn tail and run. Your ghostly feet still seem to beat the ground beneath you as you tear away between the crowding black tree trunks. You can hear the pounding hooves of the horses and the panting of the unearthly hounds quite clearly now behind you. And then they are upon you. A spectral boot is planted firmly in the middle of your back and you are sent tumbling to the ground, under the phantom steeds' hooves.

Roll one die and add 2 to the number rolled. This is the number of STAMINA points you lose. If you are still 'alive', turn to **220**. If the trampling you have just received has granted you a painful second death, write the number 290 on your *Adventure Sheet* and turn to **100**.

191

As you approach the solid black blockhouse shape of the Keep, grotesquely leering Gargoyles, that you don't remember being there before, tear themselves free of their stone-carved plinths and launch themselves from their lookout posts at the four corners of the Keep's battlements. They swoop towards you on leathery wings, reaching for you with their stony claws. As a pack of the monsters mobs you, you do your best to defend yourself, but you soon discover that their stony hides are impervious to your ethereal blade. Unfortunately, the same cannot be said of your ghostly form and their diamond-hard talons. Roll one die and add 1; this is how many STAMINA points damage you suffer as the Gargoyles attack you in mid-air. If you survive the attack, realising that you are not going to be able to reach the Keep this way, you quickly descend to the Inner Ward beneath and are relieved to see the Gargoyles return to their perches atop the keep (turn to **445**). If you do not survive the Gargoyles' assault, write the number 445 on your *Adventure Sheet* and turn to **100**.

192

Returning to the feast hall, you find Blondel the Bard cowering in a corner, both Chamberlain Unthank and the Dread Knights of the Black Shroud having departed. Before he has time to try any tricks to escape you, you bring the full power of your will to bear against him. Roll two dice. If the total rolled is less than or equal to your WILL score, turn to **176**. If it is greater, the minstrel resists your attempts to seize control of his body, plucking the strings of his lyre to create unsettling discords that upset your etheric field, forcing you to flee. Turn back to **13** to try another approach.

193

To reach the steep cliffs that border the Grimcrag Coast you must first cross the undulating terrain of Barrowmoor, named so after all the ancient tumuli that dot the landscape in this far-flung corner of the kingdom. The moon is climbing steadily into the sky as night lays claim to the land.

A dreadful howl suddenly shatters the eerie silence of the moors, carrying to you over the chill wind that is

194

blowing in from the sea. You are reminded at once of the story your father told you and your sister when were both still children – the legend of the Black Dog of Barrowmoor. The Black Dog – or Barghest as legend also knows it – is a phantom dog, the howling of which precedes a death in the family. But on this particular night it would appear to be a little late. After all, you're already dead!

With a savage snarl, ghostly jaws slavering at the prospect of feasting on your soul, its eyes burning coals, the Barghest materialises out of the night in front of you. You had thought this hellhound to be nothing but a ghost story used to bring disobedient children into line. And it *is* a ghost story, only now you're in it!

BARGHEST   SKILL 7   STAMINA 6

The black dog's phantasmal claws can harm you just as if you and the dog were both living creatures. If the Barghest's savage attack should kill you, write the number 171 on your *Adventure Sheet* and turn to **100**. If you manage to defeat the dog, as its spirit dissipates on the wind, you feel your own ghostly body absorbing some of the Barghest's power, and you luxuriate in the new strength flowing through your ethereal form. Regain up to 3 STAMINA points and turn to **171**.

194

With pistoning steps the Hellfire Golem pounds towards you, gauntlet-fists the size of anvils ready to pound you to a pulp. The magical machine opens its mouth in another inferno roar and you see the white-hot fury that rages at its molten core. The only way to get past the Golem is to defeat it in battle! (If you have fought the Golem already but it remains undefeated, amend its stats accordingly before fighting it again.)

HELLFIRE GOLEM   SKILL 9   STAMINA 12

Unless you are using a magical weapon of some kind, if you make a successful strike against this magical automaton roll one die; on a roll of 4–6 you will only cause the Golem 1 STAMINA point of damage. If you lose an Attack Round roll one die and then consult the table below to see what damage you suffer. (You may use Luck to reduce any damage caused in the usual way.)

Die Roll	Attack and Damage
1–3	Fists of Fury – the Golem pounds you with its sledgehammer fists. Lose 2 STAMINA points.
4–5	Engine of Destruction – the Golem goes berserk, fists whirling like windmills, its blows delivering double damage. Lose 4 STAMINA points.
6	Inferno Blast – a gout of searing hellfire, hot enough to melt iron, blasts from its gaping maw. You are caught by this blast; roll one die and lose that many STAMINA points.

⚁ ⚃

If the Golem destroys your physical form, cross off the relevant codeword and turn to **173**. If you manage to overcome the rampaging Golem, regain 1 LUCK point, add the codeword *Hellfire* to your *Adventure Sheet* and turn to **122**.

Resisting the pull of the grave by force of will alone, you turn your attention to the man working away at the headstone. Suddenly aware of your presence he lowers his tools and turns to face you. But rather than react with fear he smiles at you benevolently.

'I wondered whether you might make an appearance,' he says, a twinkle in his eye. 'It's alright,' he adds, 'I'm used to seeing dead people.'

You know this toothless wretch of old. Yorrick is chief ratcatcher, drain un-clogger and gravedigger.

'I've been getting this ready for you,' Yorrick says, pointing at the headstone with his chisel.

He picks up a skull from the disturbed earth he has dug to form the new grave. Holding it in one hand, he gazes intently into the skull's empty eye-sockets, then takes hold of the loosened jawbone with his other hand and wobbles it, opening and closing the skull's mouth as he says, 'Gottle-a-gear! Gottle-a-gear!'

'I know,' you say, your eyes on the open grave, chilled to the very core of your being – what there is left of it.

⚁ ⚁

'Terrible shame, it is. Terrible shame. So, what are you doing here anyway?' the gravedigger asks. 'Revenge is it? A black and deep desire to avenge the wrong done you and see justice served?'

Glad to have someone who understands your predicament, you and Yorrick quickly fall into a conversation about the various merits of revenge over justice and vice versa.

'So I guess you'll be needing some help,' he says at last, a solemn expression on his age-lined face. 'I can't offer you much, but they do say that a little knowledge is worth more than gold. And although they also say dead men tell no tales, I wouldn't be so sure about that, if I were you. I spend most of my time in the company of the dead and they tell me plenty. So, what do you want to know?'

Will you ask Yorrick about:

Ghosts within the castle who might
  help you?   Turn to **87**
Which ghosts might seek to harm you? Turn to **63**
The spirits of your ancestors?   Turn to **41**

196

And so you clash swords with the Dread Knights of the Order of the Black Shroud, a company that calls its number from amongst the ranks of the Undead. They will not be easy to defeat and you will have to fight the broadsword-wielding warriors at the same time.

	SKILL	STAMINA
First DREAD KNIGHT	9	9
Second DREAD KNIGHT	8	9

The undead knights' blades smoulder with dark energy, runes cast into them glowing like red-hot coals. If a knight wounds you, roll one die; on a roll of 5–6 the knight's cursed blade will cause you 3 STAMINA points damage, rather than the usual 2. If the Dread Knights dispatch you, sending you over to the Other Side, write the number 20 on your *Adventure Sheet* and turn to **100**. However, if you manage to defeat them, turn to **323**.

197

In your spirit-form how are you ever going to give the Demon Gate the offering of flesh it demands? The putrid pool is full of decomposing flesh but in your ethereal state you cannot even make use of that. You have no choice but to retrace your path through the dungeon to find another way of acquiring the gruesome offering needed to open the gate. But it is as you are preparing to cross the pool again that its surface heaves and something truly awful rises from its depths. Turn to **430**.

Your attention is diverted from the cleaver-wielding Cook by the arrival of two black-robed knights. Through their visors you catch glimpses of faces spoiled by rot. They are of the Order of the Black Shroud, who many believe to be only a legend, for they draw their number from the ranks of the already dead! But they are here, now, in front of you and you must fight them together.

	SKILL	STAMINA
First DREAD KNIGHT	8	9
Second DREAD KNIGHT	8	9

The undead warriors' blades smoke with dark energy and if one of them wounds you it will go badly for you; roll one die and on a roll of 5–6 the cursed blade inflicts 3 STAMINA points damage, rather than the usual 2. If the Dread Knights dispatch you, sending you on your way over to the Other Side, write the number 445 on your *Adventure Sheet* and turn to **100**. If you manage to defeat them, you decide that you need to get out of here as quickly as possible, before more of the silent knights turn up, but which way will you go; out through the cookhouse door (turn to **445**), or along the passageway that the knights entered by (turn to **95**)?

199

Courageously you step up to the doors again. Pain flares through your body a second time. Lose a further 2 STAMINA points and if this reduces your STAMINA score to zero or below record the number 259 on your *Adventure Sheet* and turn to **100**. However, if you are still in this world, roll two dice and add 2. If the total rolled is less than or equal to your WILL score, turn to **149**. If it is greater, try as you might you cannot penetrate the Circle of Protection that surrounds the sanctuary. You will simply have to turn to **259** and explore elsewhere.

200

Unable to take your eyes off the manifesting form, you watch as the ghostly luminescence assumes the shape of an older man, wearing the armour of a warrior-knight. You recognise it as your late father's armour, but then the ghost *is* that of your father.

'My child,' the ghost booms portentously, 'it grieves me to see you in the same state as I, but although my time is run, things are not too late for you. I come to warn you. Trust not the trusted, heed not the helpful and gird yourself against the night for the Lord of Shadows waits at the gate and death comes in his wake.'

Bewildered by your father's ghostly warning, you do not know what to make of his words as his ethereal form begins to break up on the wind and is carried away on the gusting wind. The last thing you hear before he is gone again for good are the words: 'Seek the sword under hallowed ground and the shield beyond the door.' And then there is nothing more.

Seeing your father again spurs you on to see your betrayers brought to justice and your own death avenged. Add 1 to your WILL score, 1 to your LUCK and then turn to **445**.

201

You make your way up onto the battlements and are afforded the most marvellous view of the cold, black expanse of the Diamond Sea beyond. The walls of Valsinore Castle seem to rise up out of the very bed-rock of the Sourstone promontory. A drop from the gargoyle-encrusted battlements of the Keep would see a man plummet straight down into the sea.

'There's one!' a startled voice suddenly cries out and you turn from enjoying the moonlit view and come face to face with the two guardsmen patrolling the battlements, on the lookout for danger. The two men are armed with pole-axes which they grip tightly in shaking hands. If you have one or more of the code-words *Bell*, *Barking*, *Barracks* or *Blacksmith* recorded on your *Adventure Sheet*, turn to **223** immediately. If not, how will you react to the two guards? Will you:

Try to talk to them?	Turn to **253**
Try to scare them away?	Turn to **239**
Engage them in combat?	Turn to **223**

202

The skeletal worm strikes, seizing hold of your ethereal form between its jaws and sinking fangs half a metre long into your incorporeal form. The fangs cause you as much harm as they would if you had still been a thing of flesh and blood, as the monster's poisonous bite taints your very soul. Lose 4 STAMINA points and 1 WILL point. If you are still in the land of the living, turn back to **232** and finish your battle with the legendary worm. If the worm's corrupting bite has finished you off, however, write the number 88 on your *Adventure Sheet* and turn to **100**.

203

Trying to move as quickly and yet as stealthily as possible, you lunge for the turning to the left. You may choose whether to *Test your Skill* or *Test your Luck* here. If you succeed or are Lucky, turn to **154**. If you fail or are Unlucky, turn to **219**.

⚁ ⚀

204

You wake the Burgomaster the only way you can think of, by moaning and wailing like a banshee. The tubby Burgomaster snorts and blearily opens his eyes. A split second later he is sitting bolt upright in bed screaming in abject terror.

'Murder!' he screams. 'Murder! Send for the Ghost Hunter! Send for Van Richten, there's another one here now! Help! Oh, horror! Help me, someone, please!'

Nothing you can do now will calm the distressed Jurgen and you can hear muffled voices and the sound of running feet coming from downstairs. As the Burgomaster has raised the alarm, you feel that you have little choice but to leave the house as quickly as you can. *Test your Luck*. If you are Lucky, turn to **406**. If you are Unlucky, turn to **101**.

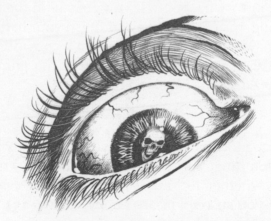

205

Descending the staircase you enter the dungeons that lie beneath the great Keep. This is an area you had little to do with when you were alive but now that you're dead you have little choice but to explore the dungeons; your nemesis awaits you somewhere within the dark passageways and half-forgotten cells.

It is not long before you come to a plain wooden door in the right-hand wall of the passage. The only thing of interest about it is the sign that has been written on a torn scrap of parchment in what appears to be red ink – although it could well be blood – and nailed to the door. It reads, 'KEEP OUT!' but you can't help noticing that the door is slightly ajar. If you want to enter the chamber beyond, turn to **185**. If you would rather continue on your way, turn to **56**.

206

As you exert your will against the old man, a curious thing happens. You steadily find yourself probing further and further into the porter's mind until suddenly you are looking out at the world through his eyes. You have actually managed to possess the body of the porter. He's still inside there with you too, scared and confused, but his body is yours to command – at least for the time being. Add 1 to your WILL and, having made a note of this paragraph first, turn to **343**.

Looking down at the porter's callused hands and lice-ridden rags you are possessed of an unbelievable thirst and almost overwhelmed by the need to empty your bladder. It is a weird sensation, controlling another's body. While you are still in control of the porter's body, you stumble over to the capstan and, putting all of Falstaff's strength into it, set to turning it.

Slowly, via a series of trundling gears, the portcullis rises through a slot and into the roof. Once you think it is high enough you lock off the capstan so that it can't be lowered again. You are only just in time. You feel your mental grip slipping and with a shudder your spirit-form is expelled from the porter's body. You can't say you're sorry to say goodbye to his body; and to think that you thought being dead was bad! (Add the codeword *Gateway* to your *Adventure Sheet* and regain 1 LUCK point.)

As the porter stumbles down the stairs yelling in nerve-shredding terror, you decide what you want to do next. Will you continue up into the gatehouse through the archway opposite (turn to **160**), or will you return to the ground floor gate and re-assess your options there (turn to **20**)?

207

Having wandered these tunnels of the dead for what feels like far too long, you eventually find yourself back where you started. So where will you go now?

Along the tunnel ahead of you? Turn to **10**
Along the tunnel to the left? Turn to **235**

⚃ ⚅

Out of the catacombs and back to the
Inner Ward courtyard? Turn to 445

208

'Quick, Streng,' Van Richten calls to his companion, 'deploy the spirit snare!' His henchman responds at once, hurling the modified trap towards you.

Your first reaction is that the trap will pass straight through you but then it snaps shut, its silvered teeth snagging your ethereal form. You let out a blood-curdling scream of agony as pain like you have known only once before – when you died – shoots through you.

'I have a suitable receptacle ready,' the Ghost Hunter says.

As you struggle to free yourself from the spirit snare, Van Richten unstoppers a silver flask and mutters something incomprehensible under his breath. You suddenly feel as though the world around you is swelling in size beyond all reason and then there is a pop and you hear the squeak of the bung being pushed back into the neck of the bottle.

Van Richten holds the flask up to his face and peers at you with undisguised disgust. 'That's another one dealt with,' you hear him say before he stows the flask in his strongbox. There is no way out of the ghost trap for you and so your adventure must end here.

⚀ ⚂

209

You make it safely to the shore and from there depart the frozen domain of the Winter King once and for all. Turn to **29**.

210

And so you come once more to the forge. Despite the lateness of the hour, Bertild the blacksmith is still working away at her anvil and forge, hammering a finely-wrought blade into shape as you enter her sanctuary to take possession of her body. If you have the codeword *Ironheart* written on your *Adventure Sheet*, turn to **119**. If not, roll two dice and deduct one from the total. If the final total is less than or equal to your WILL score, turn to **119**. If it is greater, the blacksmith's mind resists your attempt to seize hold of her physical form; turn back to **13** and try someone, or something, else.

211

You creep towards the stone circle, through the heather, under the cover of the darkness brought about by the eclipse, but there are creatures present that do not need light to detect the life-forces given off by either the living or the ethereal dead. Two of the shadowy creatures observing the ceremony leave the circle and drift towards you, ready to take what little life you have left. If you have the *Banish Spirit* special ability and want to use it now, turn to **162**. If not, turn to **124**.

212

The form the Bonebeast has taken on is like that of some eons-dead reptile species. Although its fore-bears may be long dead, the Bonebeast is nonetheless a formidable opponent.

LIVING FOSSIL BONEBEAST   SKILL 10   STAMINA 10

If the Bonebeast wins an Attack Round, roll one die and consult the table below to discover what damage it inflicts upon you.

Die Roll	Attack and Damage
1–3	Terrible Claws – the living fossil tears at your body with its savagely sharp claws. Lose 2 STAMINA points.

4–5   Tail Lash – the Bonebeast's tail hits you, knocking you off your feet. Lose 2 STAMINA points and reduce your Attack Strength by 1 point for the duration of the next Attack Round as you get up again.

6   Savage Bite – the fossil-thing takes you in its mouth, its huge jaws closing around your body. Lose 6 STAMINA points.

If you manage to defeat the Bonebeast, turn to **236**. Alternatively, after three Attack Rounds have elapsed you can attempt to flee by running for the descending staircase. If you want to do this you must forfeit one Attack Round and suffer the consequences, but if your gamble pays off, turn to **205**. However, if your battle with the Bonebeast results in your ethereal form being destroyed, write the number 110 on your *Adventure Sheet* and turn to **100**.

213

And so you return to the Barbican and the portcullis windlass room, wherein you find Falstaff the porter, fast asleep and snoring loudly, his precious cider bottle clenched tight to his chest. You meet little resistance as you force your mind inside the body of the porter, the drunkard's own consciousness running to hide in some corner of his being in a confused, alcoholic haze. (Add the codeword *Host* to you *Adventure Sheet*.)

Make a note of your spirit-form's current SKILL and STAMINA score, for later use, on your *Adventure Sheet*. While you are possessing the porter's body you must use the drunkard's drink-dulled stats, which are as follows: SKILL 7, STAMINA 16.

If you are injured in any way, for as long as you are wearing Falstaff's filthy body you may eat provisions to recover STAMINA points. One meal restores up to 4 STAMINA points. Falstaff's cider jug contains three tots, the equivalent of three meals. However, every time you drink a measure of cider, for the duration of the next battle you are involved in you must reduce your Attack Strength by 1 point. The porter's only weapon is a cudgel, but it will have to do for now, until you can find something better.

If Falstaff's STAMINA is reduced to 2 STAMINA points or fewer while you are in possession of his body, he will be knocked unconscious, forcing you to relinquish control of him. However, you can fight on in spirit-form, using the stats that you have made a note of here. Turn to **429**.

214

You soar over the gatehouse, over the sea-moat and approach the south face of the forbidding black Keep. You hear the crack of shattering stone followed by the beating of leathery wings. The gargoyles set to guard the Keep from aerial assault launch themselves from their battlement roosts and dive towards you, cruel talons outstretched.

Unbelievably, your ethereal sword cannot penetrate the stony hides of these enchanted monsters. However, their diamond-hard talons will ravage your ghostly body as well as they would flesh and blood. All you can do is try to fend off their savage attacks as you try to land again, and negate the enchantment that has set them on you in the first place. You must fight the Gargoyles as if they were one creature.

GARGOYLE PACK   SKILL 9

Roll one die and add 1; this is the number of Attack Rounds you must fight against the monsters before you are able to make it to the ground again, on the far side of the moat-bridge. If the gargoyles 'kill' you before that number of Attack Rounds have passed, write the number 337 on your *Adventure Sheet* and turn to **100**. If you survive long enough to make it to ground again, regain 1 LUCK point and turn to **337**.

215

The faint phosphorescence of your own ghostly form illuminates the interior of the barrow. It is cold and damp and you can see worms, centipedes and beetle larvae writhing about in the rich loam of the earth-cut passageway. The malign presence you felt outside the barrow permeates the atmosphere like a fog of evil intent. But despite its nature, it still draws you onwards, deeper into the mound.

You emerge from the tunnel into the burial chamber itself. A vile stench hangs in the stagnant air of the chamber and seems to be coming from the thing slumped in a stone throne on the far side of the chamber. It is the grey-green rotting corpse of the ancient king that was buried here hundreds of years ago with all his worldly possessions.

You cannot help noticing that most of the dead king's possessions have rotted away over time and that what treasures do remain are tarnished with the patina of eons. You also can't help noticing the piles of mouldering bones surrounding the king's throne. The bones appear to be human, and some of them appear to have been gnawed down to the marrow.

Suddenly the dead king's eyes flick open. 'An intruder!' the corpse hisses, a forked tongue darting out from between fleshless lips. 'Is this another villain come to steal my crown?'

The corpse springs to its feet; it is surprisingly agile for a mouldering corpse. The dead king fixes you with its putrid green stare.

'No, not a common thief,' it hisses, 'but a noble knight, a knight of the living dead.' Warily you

⚄ ⚃

unsheathe your spectral sword. 'A vengeful spectre, one who would rid the world of its own kind,' the ghoulish creature goes on. 'But you are too late, noble knight. The Lord of Shadows comes and none shall stand in his way. He shall reap such a harvest of souls that soon the whole world shall know his name.'

What is the dead king talking about? Whatever it is, his doom-laden prophecy fills you with a sense of doubt and foreboding. (Lose 1 LUCK point and reduce your WILL score by 1.)

'Silence, grave-worm!' you cry, raising your phantom sword high above your head 'Take your vile prophecies with you into the next world.' With that, the ghoul king leaps at you with filth-encrusted talons raised.

GHOUL KING   SKILL 9   STAMINA 8

If the Ghoul King manages to strike you, he causes 2 STAMINA points of damage. He also drains a measure of the very essence of your soul to grant him greater power. For every three wounds the Ghoul King delivers you must lose 1 SKILL point as well and increase his SKILL score by 1 point in return. If the Ghoul King kills you outright, reducing your STAMINA score to zero and granting you a second death, write the number 295 on your *Adventure Sheet* and turn to **100**. If you slay the Ghoul King, knowing that nothing you could possibly want could be found within the dead king's foetid tomb, you escape from the barrow as quickly as you can. Turn to **295**.

⚁ ⚁

216

A host of maggots suddenly erupts from the worm-eaten flesh of the undead Gatekeeper and tries to burrow its way into your body. If you have the codeword *Host* or *Revenant* written on your *Adventure Sheet*, roll one die and lose that many STAMINA points as the hungry maggots chew their way through your flesh. Now return to **243** and see the battle through to its end.

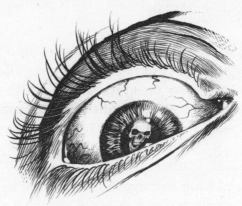

217

Roll two dice. If the total rolled is less than or equal to your WILL score, turn to **237**. If it is greater than your WILL score, turn to **257**.

218

No longer bound by gravity, you launch yourself into the chill, wind-whipped air. (If you have the phrase *Best Friend* written on your Adventure Sheet you will no longer benefit from the advantages this brings until you return to Valsinore Castle.) The Sourstone promontory rushes past below you and then you are passing beyond the bounds of the kingdom of Ruddlestone, towns, villages, rivers, forests, hills and heathland all rushing past below in a blur. You will be at your destination in no time, but where is it that you are travelling to?

Fetchfen, Village of the Damned?   Turn to **441**
Frostfinger, the Winter King's tower?   Turn to **168**

219

The Catacomb Crawler moves with lightning speed and you are forced to put your hand to your weapon before the creature can bite or claw you with its equally vicious teeth or talons.

CATACOMB CRAWLER   SKILL 9   STAMINA 7

Despite its appearance, the reptilian Catacomb Crawler is not one of the Undead but a living thing. This means that if you are in your spirit-form, it cannot actually hurt you and you will be able to slay it with ease. However, it could still destroy your physical form, if you have one, although your ghost will then be able to destroy it with ease. With the Catacomb Crawler dead, one way or another, do you now want to continue along the tunnel ahead of you (turn to **111**) or would you rather take the new turning to the left (turn to **154**)?

220

You suddenly find yourself surrounded by the ghostly members of the Wild Hunt. You're not going anywhere. Their noble leader points at you with his loaded phantasmal crossbow and declares, 'I am Baron Blood, Lord of the Wild Hunt, and I demand some sport!'

He takes aim and fires, the quarrel of the crossbow zipping through the air and striking a lighting-sundered oak a hundred metres away.

'You see that tree?' he cries. You nod. 'Make it to that tree before my hounds can catch you and you go free. Fail to make it to that tree in time and your soul is mine! Do you understand?' You nod again. 'Then go!'

There's no time to think or plan; all you can do is start running. You set off at a sprint, ghostly lungs still gasping for breath even though you no longer breathe. You run as if your very soul depended on it, which it does. But how can you possibly outrun Baron Blood's phantom hounds?

If you want to rely on cunning and good fortune to get the better of the hounds, turn to **270**. If you would rather rely on brute strength and your own relentless determination, turn to **310**.

221

Unbelievably, with the hellish hounds snapping at your heels, you make it to the tree and fling your arms around the Sundered Oak. You stare in wonder

⚃ ⚃

as the crossbow bolt embedded in the bark crumbles into silver dust. With a shrill, spine-chilling scream, the Baron's spectral form dissolves like mist on the wind. (Add 1 to your WILL.)

You suddenly find yourself at the centre of a whirling maelstrom as, with whinnying cries, unearthly howls and blood-curdling screams, the rest of the Wild Hunt is forcibly returned to the Realm of the Damned once more. (Regain 1 LUCK point.)

Just as the huntsman promised, having bested his Wild Hunt, you are free to continue your search for answers upon this Earthly Plane. Turn to **290**.

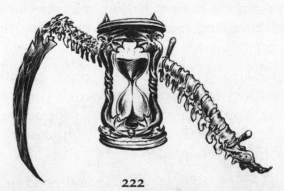

222

You are soon up to your knees in rotting human remains. Despite everything that you have witnessed this night, this situation appals and repulses you, and it unsettles you deeply. (Lose 1 WILL point.) Just when you think things couldn't get any worse, the surface of the pool heaves and something truly awful rises from amidst the stinking, decomposing remains. Turn to **430**.

223

The guardsmen level their weapons at you and charge. Seeing as how they are not armed with enchanted or holy weapons, the guardsmen are defenceless against you and in a moment you have silenced them – forever! But they were good men, only doing their job, and they did not deserve such an ignominious end. Lose 1 LUCK point and turn to **434**.

224

You are not quick enough. The squid-like beast smashes the frozen surface of the lake to smithereens, forcing you to retreat to the island again. With no way of crossing the watery barrier, you are doomed to haunt this island for evermore, or at least until the lake surface freezes again, but by then you will be too late to stop your nemesis' evil plan. Your adventure is over.

225

As you draw closer to the man he burps loudly in surprise and the stench of stale cider wafts over you, making even your ethereal form recoil. But press on you must, if you are to ever manage to open the portcullis. ''Ere, wot are yoo doin'?' he challenges as you loom over him, your spectral brow knotted in concentration as you pit your will against his. Roll two dice. If the total rolled is less than or equal to your WILL score, turn to **206**; if it is greater, turn to **247**.

226

'I was cruelly murdered, cut down in my prime before my life could run its course,' you say.

The Watcher looks at the hourglass again. 'It would appear that you are right, that destiny is not done with you yet. But who was it that desired you death? What is the name of this villain?'

If you know the name of the villain you are seeking, turn it into a number using the code A=1, B=2, C=3 ... Z=26. Add the numbers together, reverse the digits and then turn to this paragraph. If you do not know the name of the one who had you killed, you are forced to beg the Watcher to give you a second chance (turn to **127**).

227

The door to the feast hall bangs open and the entertainment abruptly stops. A tall, imposing figure, wearing the tabard and armour of a crusader knight enters the chamber, his anxious squire trotting to keep up. Chamberlain Unthank is on his feet immediately and at his sycophantic best.

'My lord,' he simpers, bowing obsequiously, 'what a pleasant surprise. We were not expecting guests at our lowly feast.'

'Then whose benefit is this for?' the crusader snaps, indicating the table groaning with food.

'Ah, this was to honour the return of one of our own from the Dark Crusade,' Unthank invents quickly.

You know this man!

'That is who I have come here to pay my respects to,' the crusader announces. 'We fought together at the Siege of Sanctiphrax. I have undertaken a pilgrimage to cleanse my soul after witnessing the horrors I did in Bathoria. I was in the region and remembered my old friend and thought I'd pay a visit.'

You were right! It is Marrok of the Eldermark. Yours was a friendship forged in battle. You saved his life when an undead wyvern attempted to carry him from the field of battle, and he saved you from a pack of rabid Werewargs.

'Then I am very sorry to inform you that your journey has been a wasted one,' Unthanks says with false gravitas. He then goes on to tell the crusader of how you were struck down within sight of the castle by a band of bloodthirsty cut-throats.

⚃ ⚁

'A pox on this place!' Marrok exclaims in grief and anger. 'What has befallen this accursed castle? On the way here my squire and I were also beset by a pair of undead Golems until they were repelled by the strength of our holy purpose.'

You are overjoyed to see your brother-in-arms again but are also fully aware of your precarious position here within the castle. Do you want to reveal yourself to him and recruit him to your cause that he might help you discover what is going on here yourself (turn to **267**), or would you prefer to keep watching and see what befalls (turn to **298**)?

<hr />

228

You find Marrok where you left him, in the castle feast hall. He has fallen asleep, his squire beside him, in a corner of the now otherwise empty chamber. Seizing this opportunity, you exert your will against his in an effort to take over his body. Roll two dice and add 2. If the total rolled is less than or equal to your WILL score, turn to **444**. If it is greater, Marrok wakes and, on seeing your ghostly form hovering before him, leaps to his feet.

'Mighty Telak!' he shouts. 'That you would take on the guise of a great and noble warrior to do your evil shall be your undoing, I curse you to Hell for all eternity! For Telak and for Valsinore!' Marrok doesn't believe it is really you and comes at you, his blade bared.

⊡ ⊞

If you would allow yourself to be cut down by the noble knight, write the number 13 on your *Adventure Sheet* and turn to **100**. If not, you are going to have to fight him, no matter how much you might loathe the idea.

CRUSADER   SKILL 11   STAMINA 11

Marrok's sword Deathsbane, is a holy weapon and so will harm you in your undead state. In fact, for every successful strike that the crusader makes against you, roll one die and on a roll of 5–6 you lose 3 STAMINA points instead of the usual 2. If Marrok slays you, write the number 13 on your *Adventure Sheet* and turn to **100**. If you cut him down first you must lose 1 LUCK point and 1 WILL point for having to kill your battle-brother. Then turn to **13**.

The stone-built shrine was obviously once an impressive building bearing all manner of stone-carved ornament – everything from noble knights battling dragons to scythe-wielding angels of death – but it is now choked with briars and does not look like anyone has been inside for a long time, even though one of the rotted wooden doors is hanging half off its hinges. Approaching the open door, you step over the threshold.

Pain courses through your spectral body and you are thrown violently back from the entrance. It feels as if a lightning bolt has just passed right through you.

(Lose 2 STAMINA points and if this reduces your STAMINA score to zero or below record the number 259 on your *Adventure Sheet* and turn to **100**.)

Knowing what awaits you now if you try to enter the shrine, do you want to try again (turn to **199**), or would you rather leave and try somewhere else (turn to **259**)?

230

You are able to make your incorporeal form invisible to the human eye, dissolving into the shadows with a single thought. Record the *Shade* special ability on your *Adventure Sheet* and turn to the paragraph with the same number as the one that you were just instructed to write down.

231

Salt has long been held to be an effective deterrent against witches and the Undead and, no matter how much you might not like it, you are now one of the Undead. As you come close to the barrier it feels as if you have hit an invisible wall of potent energy that burns your ethereal form. Lose 4 STAMINA points, 1 SKILL point, 1 LUCK point and 1 WILL point. If you are still 'alive', turn to **14**. If not, write the number 434 on your *Adventure Sheet* and turn to **100**.

Peering down into the well you can just about make out the reflection of moonlight on the black mirror of the water far below. It is supposedly possible to get into the castle catacombs from the chamber that lies at the bottom of the well. However, legend also has it that after your ancestor Agravain fatally wounded the Sourstone Worm, which had been terrorizing the area for some months, it slithered into the castle well to die, polluting the water until a priestess made it whole again with a spell of cleansing. (If you have the phrase *Best Friend* written on your *Adventure Sheet* for as long as you are underground you must lose the benefits usually gained from this.)

Cautiously you clamber into the well, your faintly glowing form illuminating hand-holds between the moss and fern-covered stones that line the inside of the shaft. Eventually the well opens out into a large natural chamber within the bedrock of the Sourstone headland on which Valsinore stands. Making use of clefts in the rock now you manage to make it down to the edge of the pool from which the well's water is drawn and are stunned by what you see there.

The northern edge of the pool is littered with millions of bleached white bones. There are so many, piled in great mounds at the water's edge, that some have tumbled into the pool itself, creating calcified islands formed from the skeletons of everything from men to dogs to cattle and even horses. Beyond this bone-yard

⚁ ⚅

a circular passageway does indeed lead away into the darkness, under the foundations of the castle chapel.

Fizzing and spitting like Dwarfish black-powder igniting, sparking green witch-lights rise like will-o'-the-wisps from the still black waters and then vanish, at speed, into the piles of bones surrounding the pool. With a clatter of bones loud enough to wake the dead, a massive skeletal form rises from out of the piles of broken skeletons in front of you. It has the appearance of a monstrous serpent, formed from the strange conglomeration of bones that litter the cave, and its head is the skull of some huge snake, or possibly even a basilisk. Green witch-fires blazing in its eye-sockets, the spirit of the Sourstone Worm strikes.

SKELETAL SERPENT   SKILL 9   STAMINA 12

If the serpent wins an Attack Round, roll two dice and if you roll a double, turn to **202** immediately. If the ghost of the Sourstone Worm should 'kill' you, write the number 88 on your *Adventure Sheet* and turn to **100**. If you manage to defeat this monstrous Undead creature, turn to **292**.

233

Unstoppering the flask you hurl it at the advancing Shadow King. The effect is instantaneous. Where the oil splashes over the night-born body of the Undead Lord it burns like acid, eating away at the Shadow King's form. The Shadow King roars in pain and fury and you barely have time to draw your own weapon before he is on you. When you come to fight the Shadow King, reduce his STAMINA score by 6 points and his SKILL score by 2, but for now, turn to **249**.

234

Making your way upstairs you come at last to the Burgomaster's bedchamber and, as luck would have it, his chamber door is ajar. You slip inside and by the phosphorescent glow given off by your own spectral form you see the Burgomaster fast asleep in bed. You can hear him too; he is snoring loudly. An empty carafe of wine sits on his bedside table. So far, he has no idea that you are there. If you want to risk waking the Burgomaster, turn to **204**. If you would rather let sleeping dogs lie, and prefer to explore downstairs, turn to **325**.

235

The door at the end of the passageway is an ornate affair, decorated with a complex pattern marked out in bands of gold. On it is inscribed the following verse:

> *A wizard of great power and might,*
> *Lies sleeping through eternal night.*
> *If you would with him consult,*
> *And seek to enter this stone vault,*
> *If you wouldst the wizard see,*
> *Answer then this riddle-me-ree.*
>
> *You can waste it, make it, kill it, take it,*
> *But like the tide, no king can break it.*

If you know the answer to the riddle, turn the word into numbers using the code A=1, B=2, C=3 … Z=26. Add the numbers together and turn to this paragraph. If you do not know the answer, or if the paragraph you turn to makes no sense, you cannot gain access this way. If you have the *Apparition* special ability and want to use it now, turn to **284**. If not, you will have to search elsewhere within the catacombs (turn to **264**).

236

At your killing blow, the necromantic magic holding the Bonebeast together is dispelled in a burst of noxious energy, and it crumbles into a pile of skeletal remains once more. Amidst all the bones and rubble that fills the interior of the Keep, you find scraps of treasure and a few other items of interest, which are only going to be of any use to you if you still have a physical body with which to carry them. If you do, and you want to pause for a bit of treasure-hunting, turn to **273**. If not, which way do you want to go from here; up the north-west spiral staircase (turn to **294**), or down the north-east stair (turn to **205**)?

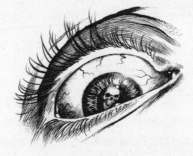

237

Resisting the weird otherworldly lure of the stone circle, you set out across the night-dark landscape, heading north. Your feet carry you forwards just as they did in life and you can even feel the stony surface of the road beneath them. But which way are you headed?

North, towards the village and
   Valsinore Castle?   Turn to **163**
North-west, towards Wraith Wood?   Turn to **3**
North-east, towards the sea-cliffs?   Turn to **193**

238

The bolt of black lightning hits you square in the chest. Instantly, a howling wind, with the voice of a million screaming souls, picks you up and carries your spirit-form away to the netherworld. (If you have the codeword *Revenant*, or *Host*, or *Armoured* written on your *Adventure Sheet* cross it off now.) Write down the number 132, and turn to **100**.

239

Screaming in terror the two guards flee. 'Attack!' they shout, 'We're under attack from the Undead!' A warning bell starts to toll in the guardhouse and you know that in moments every guard in the Outer Ward will have been alerted to your presence. (Add the codeword *Battlements* to your *Adventure Sheet*.)

⚀ ⚁

You feel that the only thing you can do to avoid detection is to leave the Outer Ward and head further into the castle. Turn to **317**.

240

Just when you are thinking that you have avoided the infernal machine, the Golem turns towards you and, opening its furnace-mouth, vomits a great gout of flame over you. Its hellish breath washes over you, burning you just as badly as if you were still a creature of flesh and blood. Roll one die, add 1, and lose that many STAMINA points. If this flame-attack has taken your STAMINA score to zero or below, write the number 134 on your *Adventure Sheet* and turn to **100**. If not, turn to **278**.

241

Certain that the ritual is at its height, if you don't act quickly you will forfeit your sister's life. But what can you do to disrupt the blasphemous rite? Will you:

Try to penetrate the stone circle by stealth?	Turn to **211**
Use a Jet Amulet (if you have one)?	Turn to **258**
Use a Black Hourglass (if you have one)?	Turn to **296**
Use a Spirit Stone (if you have one)?	Turn to **104**
Use the *Codex Mortis* (if you have it)?	Turn to **135**

242

The main entrance to Valsinore Castle stands within the imposing edifice of the Outer Gatehouse. Two guards stand on duty here but there are other defences besides them, including the sturdy gates themselves, a heavy iron portcullis, murder holes, a siege ballista and a second portcullis. Nobody gets in or out unless the castellan wills it. But that person should be you, and right now you are on the wrong side of the gate.

As you move in sight of the gate you consider what would be the best way to gain entrance. If you have the *Spectre* special ability and wish to use it, turn to

272. If you have the *Shade* special ability and wish to use it, turn to **334**. If you possess neither of these abilities, or do not want to use them, you will just have to approach the gatehouse as you are (turn to **395**).

243

Beyond the Demon Gate you descend another flight of steps and enter a rock-cut tunnel that is shored up with the rib bones of some great creature – a Bullwhale perhaps – so that it feels as if you are walking down the gullet of some rapacious behemoth. But eventually this ends too and you find yourself entering a near-spherical underground cavern. Ahead of you, across a narrow stone causeway, stands a column of rock upon which rests a circular gateway of black stone. Surrounding the column is a fiery pit, the hungry flames filling the cavern with an infernal glow. You are certain that you have reached the deepest part of the dungeon now but there is no sign of the villain you have been pursuing. The only figure present is a large, rotting corpse, standing beside the black gate, wearing ancient rusted armour and carrying a skull-headed mace – a potent weapon against both the living and the dead. Somehow you know that to find your nemesis you must pass through the gate – wherever it may take you – but to earn that right, you are going to have to battle the gruesome Gatekeeper first. Stepping onto the bridge you prepare to meet your destiny.

GATEKEEPER   SKILL 10   STAMINA 10

If the Gatekeeper wounds you, roll one die. If you roll a 6, turn to **216** immediately. If you roll any other number, fight on. If you manage to best the Gatekeeper, turn to **309**. If the Gatekeeper vanquishes you in battle and your spirit-form is destroyed, write the number 309 on your *Adventure Sheet* and turn to **100**.

244

As you shape the words, the air around you thickens perceptibly. Surely it cannot be possible for the eclipse to get any darker, but that is how it feels to you now. Unknown to you, your spell has enhanced the powers of the shadow-born horrors that are about to attack you. (Lose 1 LUCK point.) Now turn to **124**, but before you fight the Tenebrae, increase their STAMINA scores by 2 and their SKILL scores by 1.

245

Suddenly, unbelievably, the stone shifts. Through willpower alone you have managed to influence an inanimate object in the physical world despite being a ghost yourself. Write the number 215 on your *Adventure Sheet* and then turn to **120**.

246

'Very well,' the Queen says, her sinister smile remaining in place, her eyes blazing with emerald witchlights. 'Then by hellfire, brimstone and pestilence, I decree that you shall die a second death, here and now. But which shall it be? Choose the manner of your undoing!' How will you answer?

'By hellfire!'	Turn to **340**
'By brimstone!'	Turn to **262**
'By pestilence!'	Turn to **283**
'Do your worst! I do not intend to die again!'	Turn to **305**

247

You bear down on the old man, your features twisting into those of some hellish apparition. 'Listen to me, old man, and listen well,' you growl in a bestial voice that surely cannot be your own. But before you can say any more the porter gives a strangled gasp, his eyes roll up into his head and he pole-axes onto the floor face-first, not dead drunk this time, just dead. What good is another dead man to you? (Lose 1 LUCK point.)

Unable to do anything about the portcullis now, will you continue up into the gatehouse through the archway opposite you (turn to **160**), or will you return to the ground floor and re-assess your options (turn to **20**)?

248

As the Ghost Hunter and his henchman drop dead, the life gone from them, the screaming begins again. But the people's fear triggers a hideous transformation within you. Your ethereal form warps and swells and you take on a terrifying aspect more demon than human. This only feeds the villager's fear still further, and they run screaming from the building, into the night.

But this wasn't what you wanted! (If you don't already have it, write down the *Spectre* special ability on your Adventure Sheet and lose 1 LUCK point.) Managing to regain control of yourself at last, you hurtle out of the open door and away from the village of Sleath altogether. Turn to **6**.

249

Are you fighting the Shadow King with a magical or holy weapon? If so, turn to **113**. If not, turn to **346**.

⚃ ⚄

'So, is the deed done?' Chamberlain Unthank asks the Death Acolyte.

'The deed is done,' the other replies darkly.

'And there weren't any … complications?'

The Acolyte does not answer immediately. 'The spirit was willing even though the flesh was weak, but I dealt with it.'

'Good,' the Chamberlain says, steepling his fingers in front of his face. 'Nothing can be allowed to upset my plans. They have been years in the making, ever since I swore my soul to the Darkness all those decades ago back in Fetchfen, the place of my birth. Tonight our lord shall rise and then all shall know the name of Unthank and bow before me or else suffer my wrath. When the eclipse comes ultimate power shall be granted to me and then the dead of an entire kingdom shall answer my call to war.'

'Everything is ready, my lord?' the cultist asks.

'Almost everything. I still need a suitable sacrifice, but I have someone in mind. And we shall succeed, have no fear of that. The only thing that would make me absolutely certain of our success would be if I had the Spirit Stone in my hands right now. The Order of the Black Shroud have searched long and hard but the wards of the Winter King have thwarted them in their efforts to locate his tower, Frostfinger. But no matter, the eclipse fast approaches and with it my ultimate victory over the grave!'

You cannot quite believe what you are hearing! It was Chamberlain Unthank, the one you set to guard your ancestral home and ensure your sister's safety who was behind your murder all along. And it sounds like your death was only the beginning of his nefarious schemes. He must be stopped or else it won't be only Valsinore Castle that is under his control, and it won't be only your blood on his hands.

'We are discovered!' Unthank suddenly hisses, shooting anxious glances all about him. 'We have a spy in our midst. Someone has been eavesdropping on our conversation. But no matter, with a word it is done.'

The Chamberlain mutters something barely audible and wholly inhuman under his breath and an unearthly gale rises from nowhere to wail and whirl about the secret meeting chamber. It is at that moment that the traitor screams over the roar of the gale, 'Spirit, begone!'

The howling wind rises, forming a spiralling whirlwind with you at its heart. The veil between worlds is suddenly torn asunder and you are sucked through as the Dead Winds carry you over into the next world. Write the number 58 on your *Adventure Sheet* and turn to **100**.

251

Captured by Baron Blood's Wild Hunt, there is nothing you can do as the huntsman pulls you up onto the back of his horse. Howling and whooping, Blood's hunters gallop away into the night and beyond the veil to the Realm of the Damned as you despair for the fate of your soul. Record the number 290 on your *Adventure Sheet* and turn to **100**.

252

You are halfway across when the frozen surface of the lake fractures and a thick, rubbery tentacle smashes through. The tentacle waves about in the wind-whipped air, as if looking for something and then is withdrawn again. You can see something moving there beneath the ice – something massive. You start to run. There is another crash as a second tentacle smashes through the ice and then a third, sending great fissures skittering out across the lake, plunging back into the ice sheet, opening up great areas of rippling water. Moving water is inimical to undead spirits like you and if you don't pick up the pace, the lake monster's actions could leave you trapped between the island and the shore, unable to go anywhere because of the natural magical barrier formed by the water. With your very destiny depending on it you start to run. Roll three dice. If the total rolled is less than or equal to your STAMINA score, turn to **209**. If the total rolled is greater than your STAMINA score, turn to **224**.

253

You try to tell the guardsmen that you mean them no harm but actually want their help, but the two men are practically out of their wits with fear and don't listen to a word you say. It's anybody's guess how they're going to react. Roll one die. If you roll 1–3, turn to **223**; if you roll 4–6, turn to **239**.

254

You struggle to resist the lure of the Grave Golem but the monster is too powerful for you, engorged as it is with the essence of those souls already bound to it. You become bound to the Golem – neither able to continue with your quest, nor able to pass over into the Lands of the Dead – doomed for all eternity. And so your adventure ends here, in eternal torment.

255*

The passageway turns left and a little further on another door appears out of the gloom to your right. This too is a Spirit Door, constructed from black wood and enchanted silver, and unless you still have a physical body you will not be able to pass beyond it. When you are ready to proceed along the passageway, turn to **31**.

256

'Revenge is a black and deep desire,' the Watcher intones. 'Revenge is a dish best served cold, as cold as the grave. Is revenge really what you wish for? And remember, you should be careful what you wish for,

for you might just get it.' If you want to change your mind, turn to **102**. If you want to stick with your original answer, turn to **226**.

257

Unable to resist the curious attraction of the Nine Maidens, you approach the standing stones, feeling the ground beneath your feet with every ethereal step you take, although the heather passes through you as if your body was nothing but smoke. Where to your mortal eyes the Nine Maidens looked like nothing more than a circle of weathered stones, flecked with moss and lichen, you can now see tendrils of eldritch power rising into the night's sky like coruscating trails of multi-coloured flames. And you can hear the plaintive singing of women, although you can see none.

⚁ ⚃

You come to a halt at the centre of the stone circle, before a horizontal altar stone, marvelling at the writhing tendrils of ethereal energy. And then, as you stand there, listening to the mournful voices of the invisible women, those same tendrils of energy are inexorably drawn towards you. At the same time you feel yourself imbued with otherworldly strength. The Nine Maidens have chosen a champion and worked their magic upon you. (Add 1 point to both your *Initial* SKILL and STAMINA scores and then raise those scores to their new *Initial* levels. Regain 1 LUCK point and add 1 to your WILL score.

Standing just beyond the Nine Maidens, on the crest of the hill, are three stones joined to form a stone archway. Within the portal formed by these monoliths you can see a spiralling vortex forming. A gateway to another world is opening in front of you. Will you:

Pass between the stones and through
     this otherworldly portal?   Turn to **389**
Wait and see what happens?   Turn to **308**
Try to leave the stone circle?   Turn to **288**

258

Raising the skull-shaped jet amulet in your hand you feel it pulse with malignant power. The talisman is a potent evil charm and, rather than repelling the forces of darkness, actually encourages them. You know now that it was a mistake to invoke its power. Lose 1 LUCK point and 1 WILL point, record the codeword *Talisman* on your *Adventure Sheet* and turn to **132**.

⚃ ⚃

259

Back in the village square again, making sure you don't choose somewhere you've visited before, where will you go now?

The Cockcrow Inn?	Turn to **118**
The overgrown shrine?	Turn to **229**
Madame Zelda's tent?	Turn to **368**
The Burgomaster's house?	Turn to **437**
Towards the castle again?	Turn to **6**

260

The chapel, with the priest's meagre dwelling attached, is a seemingly innocuous building that stands within the bounds of a walled cemetery – complete with hummocks of earth and undulating turf – that has been used in recent decades for the burial of family members. Flickering candlelight fills the leaded panes of the stained glass windows, pouring out across the small plot of the graveyard and onto the cobbles of the courtyard beyond. It would appear that somebody is inside. Do you want to:

Enter the chapel?	Turn to **274**
Explore the graveyard behind it?	Turn to **319**
Leave this consecrated ground and explore elsewhere?	Turn to **445**

261

Giving yourself a good run up, focusing your will on the task in hand, you run towards the putrescent pool and, as your foot touches the crumbling edge of the pit, throw yourself forwards in an attempt to clear its entire width. *Test your Skill*. If you succeed, you incredibly manage to clear the stinking cesspit (turn to **421**). If you fail, you fall well short and land in the middle of the stinking mess filling the pool (turn to **222**).

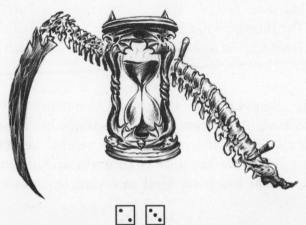

262

A horrendous stench presages the coming of the Queen's champion as a truly horrific abomination lumbers from amidst the ranks of the undead to fight you. Covered in unspeakable filth, its body decomposing and decrepit, and carrying with it the repulsive reek of the grave, the Stench Ghoul attacks.

STENCH GHOUL   SKILL 8   STAMINA 9

If you have the codeword *Host* on your *Adventure Sheet* you must reduce your Attack Strength by 2 points for the duration of this battle, so over-powering is the stomach-turning smell of the creature. Also, if you have either the codeword *Host* or *Revenant* written down, and the ghoul hits you three times, the body you are wearing will be paralysed and you will have to vacate it again.

If the Stench Ghoul destroys (or paralyses) your physical form you can fight on as a ghost but if this spectral body is destroyed too, write the number 445 on your *Adventure Sheet* and turn to **100**. If you vanquish the ghoul, it rapidly dissolves into a pool of putrescent slime on the stone-flagged floor before the Queen's throne (turn to **321**).

263

You are able to change your appearance, transforming yourself into a terrifying phantasmal horror with the power to even scare the weak-minded to death. Record the *Spectre* special ability on your *Adventure*

⚀ ⚁

Sheet and turn to the paragraph with the same number as the one that you were just instructed to write down.

264

Back where you began, choosing somewhere that you haven't been already, will you follow the passageway to your left (turn to **235**), the one directly in front of you (turn to **10**), or the one to your right (turn to **109**)? Alternatively, if you prefer, you could leave the catacombs altogether (turn to **445**).

265

'I am a ghost,' you say again and then you feel your hand sink through the stone door of the barrow. Closing your eyes, you take a step forwards – and pass right through, into the dank earth tunnel beyond. Write the number 215 on your *Adventure Sheet* and then turn to **90**.

266

With a shout of, 'Die, traitor!' you charge down the hillside and even manage to penetrate the ring of standing stones before Unthank has time to act. But before you can reach him, he turns and hurls a bolt of dark energy at you, a cruel smile on his face. You are hurled backwards by the blast and strike one of the standing stones. (Lose 3 STAMINA points and if this has reduced your STAMINA score to zero or below, write the number 132 on your *Adventure Sheet* and

⚁ ⚀

turn to **100**.) If you are still 'alive' the last thing the necromancer says to you in a gloating tone is, 'Now observe my final victory!' Turn to **132**.

267

'What in Telak's name?' Marrok exclaims as you materialise out of thin air in front of him, drawing his silver sword immediately.

'A doppelganger!' Unthank gasps. 'An evil spirit has taken the guise of our dearly departed! Oh, sir knight, banish it now before it murders us all!'

Marrok doesn't need any further encouragement and, shouting the war-cry, 'For Telak and for Valsinore!' he charges at you, his weapon raised. If you would allow the noble knight to cut you down, rather than draw your own sword against him, write the number 445 on your *Adventure Sheet* and turn to **100**. If not, you have no choice but to defend yourself.

CRUSADER   SKILL 11   STAMINA 11

Marrok's sword Deathsbane, like your own blade Nightslayer is a holy weapon and so will harm you in your undead state. In fact, for every successful strike that the crusader makes against you, roll one die and on a roll of 5–6 you lose 3 STAMINA points instead of the usual 2. If Marrok slays you, write the number 445 on your *Adventure Sheet* and turn to **100**. If you cut him down first you must lose 1 LUCK point and 1 WILL point for having to kill you battle-brother. Then turn to **348**.

268

Delighted to have found your sister safe and well you hurry over to her, calling her name. Oriana and Father Umberto turn to face you, but you are appalled to see a look of abject horror on your sister's face. 'No! No, it can't be!' she cries.

And then you see, for the first time, what it is that is laid out on the bier behind them – it is your own dead body. Seeing your corpse like this, without realising it was even here, shocks you to the core. (Add the phrase *Rest in Peace* to your *Adventure Sheet* and deduct 1 from your WILL score.)

And then Father Umberto is there, between you and your sister, the holy tome he was reading from open in his hands at a prayer for exorcism and he begins to chant. Finally, with a flourish of his free hand he shouts, 'In the name of Telak, Lord of Courage, I return thee to the hellish nether regions that spawned thee!'

There is a sudden blaze of light and you feel as if your ethereal form is being consumed by holy fire that burns with all the fury of a funeral pyre. Write the number 445 on your *Adventure Sheet*, lose 1 LUCK point and turn to **100**.

269

'Something evil is afoot here, and I wish I knew what it was. Perhaps if I were a stronger man I would have done more to find out what it is but I think things have gone too far for that now.

⚁ ⚄

'Anyway, the thing is, Unthank has called a feast, to celebrate your return. Only now you're dead and yet it's still going ahead. We're not invited. But I'm rambling.

'Thing is I have found something out but I'm not sure how important it is or what it applies to. It's a combination, I think: four-two-one. That's it. Now go, and good luck!'

Captain Cador has provided you with some valuable information and could prove a useful ally before this night is done. Regain 1 LUCK point and add the codeword *Braveheart* to your *Adventure Sheet*. Now turn to **434** as you make your way out of the barracks.

270

Sprinting through the undergrowth you take a twisting, tortuous route between the trees in an effort to confuse Baron Blood's hunting dogs. *Test your Skill* and *Test your Luck*. If you are both Lucky and successful, turn to **221**; if you fail either one of these tests, turn to **251**.

271

Climbing the twisting stone staircase, you soon find yourself at the entrance to the chamber that contains the winding gear used to raise or lower the portcullis. Slumped against one wall, an earthenware bottle held loosely in one hand, is Falstaff the castle Porter. You remember that he always liked a drink – cider mainly – but now he just looks like an utter wreck. A scraggly

⚁ ⚅

grey beard covers half his face, his skin is blotched with the spider-web patterns of purple veins and he is having trouble focusing on you. 'Halt!' he slurs. 'Who goes there?'

As he struggles to his feet, you consider the scene before you again. Looking at the capstan and considering the considerable weight of the portcullis you doubt that even with your strong will you would be able to raise it. And yet standing right before you is a man who, although drunk, has the physical strength needed to operate the mechanism successfully.

If you have the *Spectre* special ability and want to terrify the porter into helping you, turn to **247**. If you want to try to dominate his drink-addled will to make him do as you command, turn to **225**. If you would prefer to cross this chamber and continue up into the tower using the new staircase that starts at an archway on the other side of the chamber, turn to **160**. But if you would rather re-trace your steps, going back downstairs and looking elsewhere, turn to **20**.

272

As you bear down on the guardsmen your features twist and change until you become a hideous, twisted thing, utterly terrifying to behold. Hearing the howling moan issuing from your mouth as you emerge from the darkness before them – a glowing spectre, grotesque of form – the two men scream and drop their halberds. But their nightmare does not end there. Before your very eyes, the hair of one turns stark white and he runs from his post, screaming as he flees into the night. But he's the lucky one; his partner topples backwards onto the ground, as stiff as a board and dead as a doornail. You have scared him to death! He was only doing his job and had never caused you any harm. As you return to your more normal self, you are left feeling wracked with guilt. (Lose 1 LUCK point.)

But an overwhelming sense of guilt isn't the only thing you're going to have to contend with now; the castle gate is still closed and you're still stuck outside. So how are you going to get yourself inside now? If you have the *Apparition* special ability and want to use it, turn to **414**. If you have the *Poltergeist* special ability and want to use that, turn to **303**. If you have neither of these abilities, the only option left open to you is the sewer outlet (turn to **36**).

273

Roll two dice, a total of three times, to see what you manage to collect from the rubble. (If you roll a number you have rolled before, you do not find anything that turn.)

Dice roll	Treasure
2	*Potion of Skill* – if you have the codeword *Host* you can drink this to restore your host body's SKILL score to its *Initial* level.
3	*Shield* – add 1 to your SKILL score (even if this takes it above its *Initial* level).

4   *Velvet Purse* – containing 6 Gold Pieces.

5   *Potion of Strength* – if you have the code-
           word *Host* you can drink this to restore
           your host body's STAMINA score to its
           Initial level.

6   *Firestone Ruby* – worth 8 Gold Pieces.

7   *Dry provisions* – enough food for 2 Meals.

8   *Potion of Fortune* – if you have the code-
           word *Host* you can drink this to restore
           your host body's LUCK score to its *Initial*
           level.

9   *Jet Amulet* – carved to resemble a human
           skull.

10   *Battleaxe* – after a successful hit, on a roll
           of 5–6 on one die, it will cause 3 STAMINA
           points damage; however, it is not a magi-
           cal weapon.

11   *Onyx Necklace* – worth 4 Gold Pieces.

12   *Ironbane* – you find a leather pouch con-
           taining spores of this metal-eating fungus.

When you are done searching for treasure, will you
leave this chamber via the north-west spiral staircase
(turn to 294), or the north-east stair (turn to 205)?

274

The door to the chapel is closed, but not locked. If you
have the *Poltergeist* special ability or the *Apparition*
special ability you should be able to gain access (turn
to 316). If you have neither of these abilities, roll two
dice; if the total rolled is equal to or less than your

⚁ ⚀

WILL score write the number 316 on your *Adventure Sheet* and turn to **90**. If the total is greater than your WILL score, you are unable to gain entry to the chapel; you will have to look elsewhere instead. Will you go round the back of the chapel to the graveyard (turn to **319**), or leave the chapel grounds altogether (turn to **445**)?

275

You experience a sudden, weird sense of dislocation, and looking down at your body, watch as your spirit-form is expelled from the borrowed body you have been using. It is such an unnerving experience you take a sharp breath in surprise; but that shouldn't be possible either … Turn to **448**.

276

Do you have the codeword *Hellfire* on your *Adventure Sheet*? If so, turn to **122**; if not, turn to **394**.

277

You have won a mighty victory indeed and recovered a potent artefact. Regain up to 2 LUCK points and add 2 to your WILL score. All that needs to happen now is for you to return to distant Valsinore Castle where you can put the Spirit Stone to good use. If you have the *Spirit* special ability and want to fly away from here, turn to **209**. If not, you will have to cross the frozen lake on foot (turn to **252**).

⚃ ⚃

278

You are going to have to fight the Golem to get past it but as even your phantasmal blade cannot harm it, all you can hope to do is fend off its pulverising, steam-hammer blows. In the following battle calculate Attack Strengths as normal, but if you win an Attack Round you have only avoided the Golem's attack, not injured it.

HELLFIRE GOLEM   SKILL 9

If you win three Attack Rounds, you have managed to manoeuvre yourself so that you can duck past the Golem, run through the archway and over the moat-bridge (turn to 337). If the Golem destroys you before you win three Attack Rounds, write the number 337 on your *Adventure Sheet* and turn to 100.

279

'There are no second chances!' a voice like thunder rumbles across the lifeless wilderness 'You cannot conquer death!' and you find yourself before the Black Gate itself. As you gaze into the Void you feel yourself being drawn inexorably towards it. It seems inevitable now that this is it – your life and your quest really are at an end.

And then a cacophonous wailing starts up as a million lost souls plead for your release that they all might be avenged by you, the Champion of the Dead. You feel the pull of the Gate weaken and then the rushing wind is loud in your ears again and this time it is accompanied by the howling voices of the damned, all begging you to save them from their torment by seeing your quest through to its conclusion. Then darkness consumes you …

You open your eyes and look around. You are back upon the Earthly Plane. Thanks to the supplication of lost souls you have been granted one last chance to put right the wrongs that have been done to you. Raise your SKILL, STAMINA and LUCK scores to their *Initial* levels once more, add 1 to your WILL score and write the codeword *Endgame* on your *Adventure Sheet*. Now turn to the paragraph with the number you wrote down before you found yourself at the door to the afterlife.

280

Unstoppering the flask of oil you hurl it at the Necros. Viscous black fluid splashes over the repulsively rippling gelatinous body but it does nothing to slow the monster's advance. But oil is highly flammable. Grabbing a burning brand from a wall-bracket you hurl that after the oil onto the back of the Necros. The highly combustible oil bursts into flame with a satisfying roar and the undead horror emits a high-pitched scream as it begins to burn. Turn to 401.

281

'Have no fear, I mean you no harm,' you tell Madame Zelda, an imploring look on your ghostly features. 'I ask only for your aid.'

'I see dead people!' the mystic gasps, as if this is a revelation to her. 'I really can see dead people! H-How can I help?' she asks, as if suddenly remembering that you are there.

You quickly tell her of all that has befallen you since sunset and she listens intently with the same shocked expression locked on her plump face. 'Come with me,' she says when you finally finish your story.

She leads you back into the part of the tent containing the table and crystal ball. She sits down before it and starts making exaggerated hand movements over the crystal. You can see swirling clouds forming within its depths.

⚁ ⚄

'Ah, yes,' she says at last, 'the path ahead is perilous.' Her voice abruptly drops several octaves, and her eyes roll up into her head. 'Death stalks this land and soon so shall the dead,' she goes on, as if speaking now with another's voice. 'Seek out the metal-worker and the iron man. Be wary of the man who believes only in Good but seek out the court of the Liche Queen, for therein lies salvation.'

The clouds swirling within the crystal ball turn black and the table starts to shake.

'The Lord of Shadows is coming!' the mystic snarls and the crystal ball explodes, sending diamond shards of glass slicing through the sides of the tent. Incredibly both you and Madame Zelda remain unharmed. The fortune-teller shakes her head as if waking from a dream and then sees the wreckage of the crystal ball on the table in front of her. 'Oh my stars, what just happened?'

You decide that it's probably best not to tell her and so, thanking her for what she's done, you quickly vacate the tent instead. Turn to **259**.

Returning to the sanctuary of the chapel, you surprise the priest who is in holy vigil before the altar. But before Father Umberto has the chance to exorcise you from the shrine, you bring the full power of your will to bear against him in an attempt to take control of his body. Roll two dice and add 2 to the number rolled. If the final total is less than or equal to your WILL score, turn to **80**. If it is greater, the warrior-priest of Telak resists your attempts to seize control and instead attempts to banish you to the nether reaches of the Lands of the Dead. *Test your Luck.* If you are Lucky, you resist the pull of the Dead Winds and flee the chapel; turn to **13** to try another approach. If you are Unlucky, the priest manages to complete his exorcism spell; write the number 13 on your *Adventure Sheet* and turn to **100**.

283

The packed earth floor at your feet crumbles as something pushes its way up and out of the ground. It looks like a sickly yellow, mouldering skeleton, draped with the remnants of rotted clothes, and the miasma of disease and decay hangs heavy about it. A nasty buzzing fills the air around it as flies burst from the maggot-nest of its ribcage and the Decayer attacks.

DECAYER   SKILL 7   STAMINA 5

If the Decayer wounds you and you have the codeword *Revenant* on your *Adventure Sheet*, you lose 3 STAMINA points rather than the usual 2, as its corrupting touch speeds the process of decay along. If you win the battle with the Decayer but you have the codeword *Host* written down, the body you are wearing becomes infected with a horrific, flesh-eating disease. (Lose 1 SKILL point and an additional 3 STAMINA points.)

🎲 🎲

If your battle with the Decayer destroys your physical form you can fight on as a ghost but if your spectral body is destroyed too, write the number 445 on your *Adventure Sheet* and turn to **100**. If you vanquish this undead horror, it rapidly crumbles to dust as it falls victim to its own powers of putrefaction (turn to **321**).

284

You approach the door in the same manner that has got you through locked doors before, but this time it is to no avail. Powerful spells of warding cast upon the door are preventing you from gaining entry. Finding yourself powerless shakes your confidence badly. Lose 1 WILL point and turn to **264**.

285

The instant you enter the pitch black chamber beyond the Spirit Door, you feel the temperature plummet. Frost forms on the metal of your weapon and you feel your movements slow as the intense cold takes hold of your physical form. But there is worse to come.

Something is rising from the frozen floor before you,

unfolding gangly limbs as it gets to its feet. The creature looks like a horribly emaciated man, every bone visible beneath its taut, yellowed flesh, but its jaw has become distended, its mouth open wide enough to take a man's head between its jaws. But that still isn't all this horror has to offer. A horrific, discordant wailing sound rises from deep within it as the monster breathes over you, its foul breath reeking of death, and it is this discordant sound that shakes your confidence to the very core of your being.

The necromancer who summoned this diabolical undead creature, realising at last what a horror he had unleashed upon the world, trapped it behind the Spirit Door so that it couldn't get out to wreak havoc within the Keep. But now you are going to have to fight the Dirge, and defeat it, if you are ever to get out of this freezing cell again.

DIRGE   SKILL 7   STAMINA 8

For the duration of this battle you must reduce your Attack Strength by 1 point due to the intense cold. However, this penalty does not apply to your ghost-form, should you lose your physical form during the course of your battle with the Dirge. Every third Attack Round you must also lose 1 WILL point, as the horror's perpetual moaning saps your very will to live. If you somehow survive your battle with the Dirge, regain 1 LUCK point and turn to **31**. If you should 'die' facing this undead enemy, write the number 31 on your *Adventure Sheet* and turn to **100**.

⚅ ⚅

The grim gate, the entrance to the Lands of the Dead, stands before you. Beyond the gate, on every side, you can see the great rift in this dead landscape and the scudding storm clouds, but through the Gate you can see only soul-leeching darkness like you have never known. It is not merely the absence of light, it is the blackness of utter oblivion, the absence of anything whatsoever. It is the darkness of the Abyss.

And then the shadows cast by the black stones slither together and coalesce into a floating, black-shrouded figure. Beneath its hood is a fleshless skull and in its skeletal claws it grips a great black-bladed scythe.

'I am the Watcher at the Gate,' a deep voice like the slamming of crypt doors echoes from beneath the hood. 'I stand at the gate to the world beyond and cut the threads of fate when a life is done.'

The Watcher then puts a clawed hand inside its death-shroud cloak and pulls out an hourglass. You can see black sand running from the top bulb into the bottom and, judging by the amount of sand in the top bulb, it still has some time to run.

'But your life is not yet done,' it says, holding the hourglass out towards you. 'And yet you are here and no one comes to the Other Side before their time,' the sepulchral voice sounds confused. 'Then why are you here?' it asks. 'Tell me, what is it you seek?' How will you answer? Will you say that you seek revenge (turn to 256), justice (turn to 167), a second chance

⚅ ⚅

(turn to **127**), or will you attack the Watcher with your sword (turn to **102**)?

287

There is a click and the door swings open before you. The unearthly glow given off by your own ethereal form illuminates the chamber before you, reflecting from the most incredible suit of armour you have ever seen. There are no gaps anywhere, every piece – from the helmet to the leg guards – fitting with every other piece perfectly, effectively forming one unbroken piece of armour. The craftsmanship is incredible, the carefully worked steel ensorcelled with gold. The helmet is particularly striking, having been worked to give it an almost human appearance, its eye-holes set with rubies. It's only a shame that a suit of armour's no good to you in your current condition. However, should that change, it will be worth knowing of the armour's hiding place. (Add the codeword *Automaton* to your *Adventure Sheet*.)

Unable to do any more here at this time, do you want to leave the gatehouse (turn to **20**), or descend the spiral staircase to the bottom, if you haven't already done so (turn to **115**)?

288

The instant you pass beyond the boundary formed by the stones again the ethereal light fades and the otherworldly portal closes. Which way do you want to go now?

⚃

East, towards the burial mound?	Turn to **409**
North, towards the village and Valsinore Castle?	Turn to **163**
North-west, towards Wraith Wood?	Turn to **3**
North-east, towards the sea-cliffs?	Turn to **193**

289

To your right is a sturdy oak door, banded with iron. It has a suitably serious-looking lock but the key has been left in it. If you want to unlock the door and enter the room beyond, turn to **315**. If you would rather not get distracted and continue on your way deeper into the dungeons, turn to **416**.

290

And then, between the tangle of trees, the wise-woman's cottage comes into view. You can see the light of a roaring fire flickering behind the grimy windows of the tumbledown hovel, but you also notice that a dead magpie has been nailed to the door.

Some know her as Mother Toadsfoot of Wraith Wood and call on her aid when they are in need of a midwife or a cure for toothache. Others name her 'witch'. Under normal circumstances you wouldn't have any truck with witches, but these are far from normal circumstances. Still, the thought of having anything to do with the crone, after your family has avoided having anything to do with her for three generations, fills you with trepidation.

⚅ ⚀

If you want to approach the front door of her hovel, turn to **67**. If you would rather spy on her through a smeary window first, turn to **336**.

291

Although you try with all your might, you are not able to raise the portcullis by even a centimetre; it is far too heavy, and your failure leaves you feeling defeated. (Lose 1 WILL point.) You are going to have to try something else. Will you:

Use the *Apparition* special ability
(if you have it)?   Turn to **5**

Climb the staircase beyond the left
archway?   Turn to **271**

Climb the staircase through the right
archway?   Turn to **85**

Find another way into the Inner Ward? Turn to **393**

292

Wondering what else might be lurking down here in the darkness, will you climb back up out of the cave of bones to the castle's inner courtyard above (turn to **445**), or proceed along the passageway in front of you (turn to **88**)?

293

Released from the shackles of a mortal body, you are no longer bound to the ground but are able to fly high above it. Record the *Spirit* special ability on your *Adventure Sheet* and turn to the paragraph with the same number as the one that you were just instructed to write down.

294

Making your way up the winding stair you come at last to a turret room that must be at the very top of the Keep. The room is completely empty, apart from the shimmering ball of light three metres in diameter, hovering at its centre, and the object you can just about make out through the glare of the swirling surface of the spectral sphere. It would appear to be a book of some kind. Will you:

Enter the sphere of light?	Turn to **324**
Strike the shimmering sphere with your weapon?	Turn to **405**
Use the *Banish Spirit* special ability (if you have it)?	Turn to **424**
Re-trace your steps and descend the north-east stair?	Turn to **205**

⚀ ⚃

295

Leaving the sinister burial mound behind, where do you want to start looking for clues that will help you to solve the mystery of your own murder? Will you head:

North, towards the village and
    Valsinore Castle?   Turn to **163**
North-west, towards Wraith Wood?   Turn to **3**
North-east, over the moors towards
    the sea-cliffs?   Turn to **193**

296

Remembering what the Watcher told you about knowing the right time to use the hourglass you hold it up before you now and regard the motionless black sand contained within it one last time, before dashing it against a jagged rock on the ground in front of you. The glass explodes into a myriad diamond shards, the black sand briefly forming a spiralling vortex in the air in front of you before vanishing, twinkling with starlight. You watch with satisfaction as Unthank clutches at his chest and then drops to the ground in front of the altar stone, the obsidian dagger tumbling from his hand on the cold hard ground beside him. But you're not out of danger yet; your actions have been observed. Two of the three knights present break away from the circle and advance towards you, their cursed blades bared. You must fight them at the same time.

	SKILL	STAMINA
First DREAD KNIGHT	9	9
Second DREAD KNIGHT	8	9

If a knight wounds you, roll one die; on a roll of 5–6 its sword will cause you 3 STAMINA points of damage, rather than the usual 2. If the Dread Knights dispatch you, write the number 423 on your *Adventure Sheet* and turn to **100**. If you manage to defeat them, turn to **423**.

297

It does not take you long to find the gravedigger again, still at work in the plot behind the chapel. Wasting no time you attempt to merge your mind with Yorrick's and take control of his wiry form. Roll two dice and deduct two from the total. If this new total is less than or equal to your WILL score, turn to **357**. If it is greater, despite your best efforts you are unable to take control of Yorrick's body; turn back to **13** and try something, or someone, else.

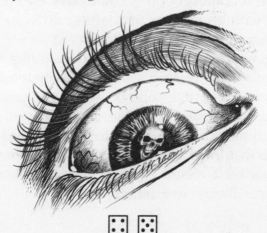

298

Unthank invites Marrok to take a seat at the top table and partake of some nourishment after his long journey, an offer he accepts willingly, although with an air of sadness. He is still hungry, no matter how much grief he feels at news of your death. But Unthank then makes his excuses and leaves the hall via a passageway half-hidden by one of the great tapestries that adorn the walls. If you want to follow the chamberlain, turn to **384**. If you would rather reveal yourself to your friend now that he is alone, turn to **329**.

299

And in a trice it's as if you weren't there at all, your ghostly form dissolving into the darkness that permeates the shadowy corners of the room. As you survey the bar, your attention is drawn to two men seated at a corner booth. The first is dressed completely in black, with a broad-brimmed hat on his head, and a velvet cape around his shoulders. He is also festooned with all manner of charms and is holding a finely-wrought, basket-hilted silvered rapier in one black-gloved hand. His companion looks like nothing less than a thug. The rogue's nose has obviously been broken on more than one occasion, the tattoo of a spider's web covers one side of his shaven head – although he still sports a bushy beard – and a contraption that looks like a silver bear-trap hangs from his waist by a chain. Approaching their table you listen in on their conversation.

⚅ ⚅

'From what I hear, the old Burgomaster up at the grand house seems to think this cesspit's crawling with lost souls,' the tattooed man whispers out of the corner of his mouth.

'Then my holy work may progress a-pace,' the darkly-dressed gentlemen mutters, a look of grim satisfaction on his face. 'My brother shall be avenged! I shall rid this Sleath of its ghosts once and for all, or my name's not Josef Van Richten.'

'And a pretty penny it'll cost 'em too,' his companion sniggers.

'Streng,' the other scolds, 'that is not why we are here.'

'No, but it helps. Cover our costs as it were. That's all I'm saying.'

'It is time I retired for the evening, to prepare for the work that awaits me here.' And with that the ghost hunter rises from his seat. Followed by his bruiser of a henchman, he makes his way upstairs; he must have taken a room at the inn.

If you think the ghost hunter could help with the search for your killer and want to follow him upstairs, turn to 331. If not, there is no point in delaying here any longer and so you depart the tavern (turn to 259).

300

With a bellow of frustrated rage you bring your scintillating ethereal blade down upon the monster and the necromantic spell animating it is savagely broken. The Golem's body bursts apart, showering you with grave dirt, human remains and rotting coffin wood. At the same time, the souls of those bound to it fly free. As they ascend into the night's sky, they call their thanks and praises to you for freeing them from their undying nightmare.

And your good deed does not go unrewarded. As they depart the Earthly Plane for good, the ghosts share a portion of their power with you. Roll one die and add 6, (giving you a total of 7–12) and regain this many STAMINA points. You may also add 1 to your WILL score and 1 to your LUCK.

The Ghosts of Sleath freed, you too are free to continue with your quest. Passing beyond the boundary wall of the cemetery at last, you find yourself on the road leading into the village. Turn to **61**.

301

Making your way back through Valsinore Castle you find a suitable subject on sentry duty on the battlements. The poor wretch's eyes widen in horror as you come at him out of the night and he is frozen to the spot. Making the most of the opportunity, you exert your will against his in an effort to take over his body. Roll two dice. If the total rolled is less than or equal to your WILL score, turn to **26**. If it is greater, the man runs from you, screaming in terror; turn back to **13** and try someone, or something, else.

302

You squeeze past the dead husk of the giant spider and eventually reach the end of the tunnel, emerging from underground again through a hole in the stone-clad shaft wall of the castle well (turn to **5**).

303

Although you are able to will latches to uncatch and handles to turn, weighing several tonnes as they do, the gates are far too heavy for you to move merely by sheer strength of will. (Lose 1 WILL point.) So that leaves you with only two options; to use the *Apparition* special ability if you have it (turn to **414**) or the culvert (turn to **36**).

You descend the staircase for what feels like hours but at last you emerge onto one of the lower levels of the tower – but it is not a place you have visited before. How can this be? There is obviously some dark magic at work here. You are standing at one end of a vast audience chamber. At the other end of the hall stands a large throne carved from a single massive block of black ice. Seated upon it is a colossal armoured warrior, his plate armour gleaming with a blue-metal sheen beneath the layers of ice covering his body.

As you enter the echoing vault, the giant stands, hefting his ice-bladed battle-axe in his armoured hands as he does so. 'Only a fool would attempt to steal the Spirit Stone from the Winter King. Now you shall pay for your crime with your soul!' the corpse king roars. You know that you have no choice but to fight the armoured giant if you are to retain the Spirit Stone, but you are going to have to get past his minions first. 'Arise, my warriors!' the Winter King bellows in a voice loud as colliding icebergs.

The spirits of those who died here remain trapped inside their frozen bodies and, at the Winter King's bidding, those same spirits re-animate the ice-locked corpses of ancient warriors present within the audience chamber. Roll one die; this is the number of Ice Ghosts that you must fight before you can get to the Winter King. If you have the *Spirit* special ability you may reduce this number by 2. Each Ice Ghost that you have to fight has the following attributes.

ICE GHOST   SKILL 7   STAMINA 6

Once you have dealt with his undead minions, you must then confront the demon-possessed Winter King himself.

WINTER KING   SKILL 11   STAMINA 14

If you defeat the Winter King in mortal combat, turn to **277**. If he should slay you, however, your soul will become his for all eternity, and you will become one of his Ice Ghosts, locked in service to him, waiting until the glaciers cover the world again and Hell itself freezes over.

305

'So be it!' the Queen of Liches declares. 'Prepare to meet your doom!' Roll one die. On a roll of 1–2, turn to **340**. On a roll of 3–4, turn to **262**. On a roll of 5–6, turn to **283**.

306

Making your way back through the castle you come to the cookhouse once again. Ingelnook the corpulent cook, quakes in fear before your unstoppable advance until the only method of defence he has left is to resist your efforts to possess him with the strength of his own mind. Roll two dice. If the total rolled is less than or equal to your WILL score, turn to **318**. If it is greater, Ingelnook resists your attempts to seize control of his bloated body to the end and you are forced to leave the kitchens in defeat. Turn back to **13** to try another approach.

307

With a roar of rage you reveal yourself and fly at the death cultist. Chamberlain Unthank steps back into the shadows to observe the battle from a safe distance. Robbed of his magic powers now that he is without his crystal ball, the Death Acolyte pulls a blade of black metal from within the folds of his robes and prepares to finish you for good.

DEATH ACOLYTE   SKILL 7   STAMINA 6

Your ethereal form is vulnerable to the Acolyte's cursed blade and a successful hit from it will cause 2 STAMINA points damage. If the Death Acolyte manages to finish what he started on the Moot Road and kills you, write the number 445 on your *Adventure Sheet* and turn to **100**. If you kill the Acolyte within 5 Attack Rounds, turn to **370**. If the battle lasts more 5 Attack Rounds, turn to **370** anyway.

308

As you watch, the swirling silvery light between the stones ripples like liquid moonlight. Something is coming through from the other side. The thing stalks through the portal in a crouch, almost walking on all fours as it knuckles towards you. It looks like a cross between a wolf and an ape. Its flat snout wrinkles in a snarl revealing knife-sharp teeth. The creature's fur sparkles silver and it has the same ethereal quality as you. This thing – this Visitation – is a creature of the Spirit World. Sensing that you are a thing of the other world too, it gives a bark and bounds towards you. It has come to claim you and drag you back with it to the Lands of the Dead by whatever means necessary. Phantom sword in hand, you prepare to defend yourself. After all, you have unfinished business in this world and are not ready to leave yet.

VISITATION   SKILL 8   STAMINA 8

Being a thing of the spirit world, like you, the Visitation's cruel claws will harm you, just as your phantasmal sword will harm it in return. If the Visitation wins two consecutive Attack Rounds, turn to **328** at once. If the Visitation reduces your STAMINA score to zero, write the number 288 on your *Adventure Sheet* and turn to **100**. If you slay the Visitation with your phantasmal sword, turn to **359**.

309

And so you step up to the forbidding gateway. Within the circle of black stone is a whirling vortex of starlight and some sixth sense tells you that your destiny lies beyond it. Taking your courage in both hands, you step through it …

You emerge on a windswept hillside overlooking a circle of nine standing stones. But that is not all you can see before you. At the end of the headland jutting out into the cold, dark Diamond Sea ahead of you, stands Valsinore Castle. The magical gateway has transported you to virtually the very spot where the drama of this night's unfolding adventure began. Not far away lies the moorland road where you were struck down by the murdering band and the cruel-hearted Death Acolyte. And here you are again, as Chamberlain Unthank prepares to bring his evil plans to fruition. But what are they exactly?

Looking out across the wind-blasted heather you can see the traitorous necromancer standing before the altar stone of the Nine Maidens. He is clad in black and holding an obsidian dagger in both hands over the body of the sacrificial victim that has been bound to the stone with glowing chains of magical power – your sister, the Lady Oriana!

Standing within the ring of standing stones, forming a second circle around the altar, are the members of Unthank's death cult. There are five black-clad acolytes, three Dread Knights of the Order of the Black Shroud, and four faceless shadow-born creatures, trailing smoky tendrils, with claws formed of impenetrable darkness. With the necromancer that makes thirteen – a full coven.

Everything about the scene before you gives the impression that the ritual being enacted here is approaching its climax. It is then that the moonlight itself fails and fades. Looking up at the cloudless heavens you see a dark shadow fall across the face of the moon, as a lunar eclipse plunges the world into

⚁ ⚅

total darkness. You can't shake the feeling that this darkness could well last longer than the duration of the eclipse if something isn't done to stop Unthank and his death cult. Do you want to rush to attack the necromancer and save your sister from certain death (turn to 266), or will you fight every instinct that tells you to do otherwise and take your time to consider your actions more carefully (turn to 241)?

310

You race towards the Sundered Oak, determined to reach the tree before the snarling dogs catch up with you. Roll three dice. If the total rolled is equal to or less than your STAMINA score, roll two dice and this time, if the total is equal to or less than your WILL score, turn to 221.

However, if the first dice roll is greater than your STAMINA score or the second dice roll is greater than your WILL score, the dogs run you down before you are even halfway to the lightning-struck tree (turn to 251).

311

You are unable to influence the stone at all. (Lose 1 WILL point.) If you want to try to go back to looking for another way into the barrow, turn to 431. If you have already tried another method, or if you would rather quit this place, turn to 295.

312

Taking to the air, you easily evade the raging Golem. But now that you have broken the bonds that keep you earthbound, will you fly towards the battlements of the Keep (turn to **214**) or land again on the other side of the moat at the end of the bridge (turn to **337**)?

313

Stepping off the track that leads over the bridge on the way to Valsinore Castle, you scramble down the bank to the river's edge. Far to your right the stream tumbles over the edge of the Sourstone headland and into the sea far below as a dramatic waterfall but you are a strong swimmer, and the river isn't particularly wide here so you see no reason why you shouldn't be able to cross safely. You're sure that the knight's ghost is bound to the bridge, so what's the worst that can happen? Besides, you're a ghost; you'll only need to wring out your shroud once you get to the other side. And so you step into the fast-flowing stream.

If feels like you have been struck by lightning as crippling pain sears through your body and you are hurled back from the river to land on the bank, your ghostly form contorted in pain. Running water is anathema to the ranks of the Undead and, no matter how much you might hate the fact, you are now one of the Undead. Roll one die, add 2 and deduct the total from your STAMINA score. If this has taken it to zero or below, write the number 6 on your *Adventure Sheet* and turn to **100**. If not, the pain begins to pass and you are able to pick yourself up again, but you are still on the wrong side of the river and so are forced to approach the bridge.

'Halt!' the knight challenges you again. 'I have sworn to guard this crossing and Valsinore Castle from evil spirits and you will not pass!' To proceed any further you are either going to have to engage the knight in battle (turn to **175**), or submit to him (turn to **391**).

314

'There's been a great deal of to-ing and fro-ing of late. No one from the village is allowed past the main gate anymore, although Bertild the Blacksmith does come out from time to time to collect supplies, but from what she's let slip it sounds like there are sinister goings on indeed. It was nearly a year ago now that the knights first appeared.'

'What knights?' you ask.

'I don't know, but the only heraldry they bore was a plain black field – no decoration whatsoever. They arrived after dark one stormy night. They're rarely seen outside the castle, but when they are, it's always during the hours of darkness.'

What is Chamberlain Unthank up to, admitting this strange order of knights into your ancestral home? Has he had to bolster the castle's defences in light of the rising numbers of restless dead in the area? Or is there another reason?

⚃ ⚀

'Do you know if anyone has seen any Death Acolytes about the place?'

'No, not to my knowledge,' the hermit confesses, and his knowledge certainly appears to be suitably in depth. 'But that doesn't mean there aren't any there. What I do know is that there's a grand feast being held at the castle tonight, to celebrate the return of ...' the old man trails off. 'Oh,' he says, 'to celebrate your return, I suppose.'

Everything Myrddin has told you makes you more desperate than ever before to discover what's going on. It is time you were on your way again.

If you have the phrase *Something Fishy* written on your *Adventure Sheet*, turn to **145**. If not, turn to **22**.

315

As soon as you open the door, the man chained to the wall on the other side of the musty cell cries out, 'No! No more, please! Not again! Why can't you just leave me alone?'

It takes you a moment – thanks to the murky shadows and the filthy state of the prisoner – but you recognise the man. It is Iago the Gaoler, not a particularly pleasant character but no villain by any means. Do you want to enter the cell and see what you can do to help the Gaoler (turn to **332**), or would you rather leave him to his fate and get on with resolving yours (turn to **77**)?

316

As you cross the threshold and enter the chapel, your ethereal form is burned by the holy wards protecting this place from the undead. (Lose 4 STAMINA points and if this has taken your STAMINA score to zero or lower, write the number 445 on your *Adventure Sheet* and turn to **100**.)

Ahead of you, at the other end of the sanctuary beneath a cast-iron candelabrum festooned with the wax of a hundred melted candles, two figures stand before a trestle bier bearing … you can't quite see what. One of the figures is Father Umberto, Valsinore's confessor. He is decked out in the robes of a priest of Telak. The other is a young woman wearing a flowing woollen dress … It is your sister, the Lady Oriana! If you want to reveal yourself now to

⚁ ⚁

the priest and your sister, turn to **268**. If you would prefer to hide yourself away in a shadowy corner and observe what they are doing for a moment first, turn to **353**.

317

Do you have any of the codewords *Bell*, *Barking*, *Barracks*, *Battlements* or *Blacksmith* recorded on your *Adventure Sheet*? If so, make a careful note of how many and turn to **347**. If you none of those words written down, turn to **366**.

318

You have succeeded in taking over the cook's physical form, while his consciousness flees to some dark corner of his being. (Add the codeword *Host* to you *Adventure Sheet*.)

Make a note of your spirit-form's current SKILL and STAMINA score, for later use, on your *Adventure Sheet*. While you are clothed in the ample flesh of the cook you must use Ingelnook's stats which are as follows: SKILL 9, STAMINA 22.

If you are injured in battle you may eat provisions to recover STAMINA points. One meal restores up to 4 STAMINA points and as you are in the castle kitchens you are able to collect provisions equal to 6 Meals. You arm yourself with a hefty cleaver, which should make an effective weapon against mortal foes at least.

If Ingelnook's STAMINA score is ever reduced to 2 STAMINA points or fewer, the cook will be knocked out, and you will be forced to leave his body. You may then keep on fighting but now in your spirit-form again, using the stats that you have written down here. Turn to **429**.

319

You hear the sound of hammer against chisel and round the corner of the chapel to see a man hunched in front of a new, clean headstone that has been set up before the open pit of a freshly-dug grave. The light cast from his lantern resting on the damp grass beside him is allowing the gravedigger to keep working into the night. Absorbed in his work, peering myopically at the letters he is engraving into the headstone, the gravedigger has not been alerted to your presence yet. Do you want to:

Approach the gravedigger?	Turn to **397**
Linger a while within the graveyard, out of sight of the man?	Turn to **349**
Return to the door of the chapel and enter the holy building (if you haven't tried to already)?	Turn to **274**
Leave the graveyard, and the chapel, and look elsewhere?	Turn to **445**

320

Before you can reach the bridge that crosses the moat that leads to the Keep you are surprised by the sound of savage barking and an armoured figure steps from

⚁ ⚁

the shadows. The knight is barely able to restrain the huge, silver-haired dog straining at the chain in his hand. Without saying a word the knight lets go of the chain and the muscular Moon Dog leaps at you. Existing half in the Ethereal Realm and half on the Earthly Plane, the Moon Dog is just as imposing a threat to a ghost like you as it would be to any mortal soul.

MOON DOG   SKILL 8   STAMINA 8

If you have the phrase *Best Friend* written on your *Adventure Sheet* you do not need to fight the Moon Dog yourself but can instead move on to deal with its handler. If you do fight the Moon Dog yourself, after three Attack Rounds the knight will join the battle too.

DREAD KNIGHT   SKILL 9   STAMINA 9

If either the savage Moon Dog or the Dread Knight 'kill' you, write the number 117 on your *Adventure Sheet* and turn to **100**. If you should overcome both the dog and its handler, you are free to go on your way again (turn to **117**).

321

'Enough of this!' the Queen shouts in anger, fixing you with her baleful black gaze. 'Now bow before me! I demand it!' Roll two dice. If the total rolled is equal to or less than your WILL score, turn to **358**; if it is greater, turn to **112**.

Making your way through the foetid hollows of the drowned village you come at last to the village's overgrown graveyard. You creep between weed-choked tombstones and crumbling tombs but age and decay have all but obliterated the names they once bore. At the centre of the cemetery stands a large stone-built crypt that appears to be largely intact. Unconsciously your wandering footsteps have brought you to this building but you stop when you find yourself standing before its broken stone doors. Red coals blaze in the darkness of the crypt and you flinch as you realise that something is in there.

You have barely put your hand to your sword when something monstrous pulls itself out of the crypt. At first glance it resembles a gigantic bat but at a second glance you can see something unsettlingly humanoid about its make-up. The creature turns its wolf-like head in your direction and opens its jaws to reveal hugely elongated canines. The monster standing before you now is a refugee from the purges perpetrated by the crusaders of Telak. It fled to this place to hide after the cleansing of Bathoria. It was once a mighty vampire lord, but forced to live off the carcasses of wild animals and its own bat-kin in this village where everyone is already dead, it has degenerated into the feral thing you see before you now. And yet despite its bestial state it is still a deadly opponent. Do you want to stand your ground and face the bat-beast (turn to 342) or would you rather flee (turn to 35)?

⚁ ⚁

323

With the dread knights disposed of, you approach the heavy portcullis that separates the Outer Ward of the castle from the Inner. Either side of the portcullis – which is down – an arched entrance leads to a spiral staircase that in turn leads up into the Barbican itself. If you think you have the means to get past the portcullis you could do so now. If not, you will have to enter the Barbican to find a way to get through. Alternatively you may simply be curious to discover what secrets the gatehouse might hold. Will you:

Use the *Poltergeist* special ability (if you have it)?	Turn to **291**
Use the *Apparition* special ability (if you have it)?	Turn to **5**
Climb the staircase beyond the left archway?	Turn to **271**
Climb the staircase through the right archway?	Turn to **85**
Find another way into the Inner Ward?	Turn to **393**

324

Do you still have one of the following codewords written on your *Adventure Sheet*: *Revenant*, *Host* or *Armoured*? If so, turn to **381**. If not, turn to **364**.

325

You creep through an empty solar, dining chamber and servants' quarters until you come to the kitchen. Lying beside the dying embers of the fire is a large wolfhound, while a cat is curled up in a rocking chair by the door. But as soon as you enter the chamber, both the cat and the dog snap awake. The cat hisses and spits at you, arching its back in fear, its fur standing on end, while the dog starts barking furiously, jaws slavering.

And now you can hear the sounds of the household waking up. This is not what you had in mind at all and decide the best thing you can do is to leave the house as quickly as possible. Lose 1 LUCK point and turn to **101**.

326

You thought your will was strong, but that of the Shadow King is of an even greater magnitude altogether. You cannot possibly resist an intelligence as incalculably old and as evil as this one. Your mind shatters and you can do nothing to resist as the dark lord forces you to kneel before him and swear fealty to him forevermore. When the Shadow King's undead army marches on the kingdom of Ruddlestone you shall lead it in your new role as Death's Champion. And when Ruddlestone has been taken the rest of the Old World shall fall before you and your vile master … Your adventure is over.

327

No matter how much you fight their pull, the Dead Winds draw you onwards, ever closer to the black gate. And then you see something else dragging itself towards you along the avenue of stones. It appears to be incorporeal like you, with a squat, ethereal, toad-like body – although this particular toad would be the size of a horse! – broad front limbs and a gaping, shark-like maw. Everywhere it goes it leaves a slimy trail of ectoplasm behind it. From the top of its head myriad eye-stalks sway like the fronds of a sea-anemone while other tendrils emerge from the side of its body.

As you are drawn towards this hideous apparition by the relentless wind you are even more horrified to see that the waving fronds of its eye-stalks are not eye-stalks at all; each one ends in a small, snapping mouth. The creature raises a slime-dripping foot and you see that that too ends in a toothed maw. The phantasmal creature is almost nothing but mouths. And then, with a croaking cry, the Sin Eater is upon you, ready to devour your soul. Restore your STAMINA score to half its *Initial* level, plus as many more STAMINA points as is equal to your current WILL score, and prepare to fight.

SIN EATER   SKILL 8   STAMINA 8

If the Sin Eater wins an Attack Round, roll one die. If you roll a 6, as well as taking the usual damage you must also reduce your SKILL by 1 point. If you defeat this ghost eater, add the codeword *Watcher* to you *Adventure Sheet* and turn to **46**. If the ectoplasmic horror wins the fight, it hurls your savaged soul even closer to the Gate (turn to **286**).

⚁ ⚁

328

The otherworldly creature grabs you with strong arms and drags you towards the magical portal. You must fight the next Attack Round with your Attack Strength reduced by 2 points. If you win that Attack Round, you break free of its grasp and can continue the battle (return to 308 and finish the fight). However, if you lose that Attack Round the Visitation bounds back through the gateway taking you with it. Write the number 288 on your *Adventure Sheet* and turn to 100.

329

'Mighty Telak!' he exclaims as you appear out of thin air in front of him, and then, in the very next moment, his own blessed blade Deathsbane is in his hand and he is ready to do battle. 'Have at you, foul fiend!' he shouts. 'That you would take on the guise of a great and noble warrior to do your evil shall be your undoing. I curse you to Hell for all eternity!'

With a shout of, 'For Telak and for Valsinore!' he charges towards you, weapon raised. If you would allow yourself to be cut down by the noble knight, write the number 445 on your *Adventure Sheet* and turn to 100. If not, you are going to have to fight, no matter how much you might loathe the very idea.

CRUSADER   SKILL 11   STAMINA 11

Marrok's sword Deathsbane, like your own blade Nightslayer is a holy weapon and so will harm you in your undead state. If fact, for every successful strike that the crusader makes against you, roll one die and on a roll of 5–6 you lose 3 STAMINA points instead of the usual 2. If Marrok slays you, write the number 445 on your *Adventure Sheet* and turn to **100**. If you cut him down first you must lose 1 LUCK point and 1 WILL point for having to kill your battle-brother. Then turn to **348**.

330

Gaining entry to the guardhouse, you make your way silently through the building in search of anyone you think might be able to help you or at least tell you what it is that has spread its foul influence over Valsinore Castle. And then at last you come to the Captain of the Guard's quarters. The door to his spartanly decorated room is ajar and through it you see Captain Cador sitting at the room's only table. He is a courageous warrior and a doughty commander. Cador was in charge here when you left to fight in foreign lands three years ago. Since that time the hair on his head has become thinner and his beard a little more streaked with grey.

He suddenly looks directly at you, some sixth sense alerting him to your presence. He jumps to his feet, sending his chair flying. 'By Siegfried's bones!' he cries, pulling his sword from the scabbard lying on the table. 'Stay back!' he shouts, pointing the tip of his blade directly at you. The lantern-light spilling from his chamber picks out the silvered sigils ensorcelled into the blade. It's your move; will you:

⚀ ⚄

Attack Captain Cador?	Turn to **380**
Attempt to engage him in conversation rather than battle?	Turn to **39**
Try to intimidate the captain by scaring him?	Turn to **402**
Flee the barracks and search elsewhere?	Turn to **360**

331

Still in your shadow form, you follow the ghost hunter and his accomplice to one of the inn's guest bedrooms. While Streng makes himself uncomfortable on a chair outside, watching the corridor for any signs of danger, you easily slip past him and follow Van Richten into the room. Having closed the door behind you both, the Ghost Hunter goes over to a table by an open window where he unrolls a velvet cloth containing the tools of his ghost-hunting trade. There is a crucifix, a flintlock pistol and silver bullets, a flask of holy water, a holy talisman, and so on and so forth. You get the feeling that you won't get a better chance to talk to him than this and so, with a single thought, you re-materialise in the room directly in front of him.

Before you can say anything, the ghost hunter leaps up knocking over his chair with a cry of, 'Gods preserve me!' He grabs the container of holy water from the table and throws it at you. Where it touches your wraith-like form it burns like acid. Roll one die and lose that many STAMINA points. (If this has finished you off, write the number 259 on your *Adventure Sheet* and turn to **100**.)

You try to explain why you are there and that you need his help but Van Richten won't listen. 'Have at you, hellish spectre!' he declares grabbing his silvered blade from the table. 'In the name of Libra I shall exorcise you from this place and banish you to the outer darkness to join your evil masters there.' And then you are fighting for your un-life once again.

JOSEF VAN RICHTEN   SKILL 10   STAMINA 9

If the ghost hunter slays you for a second time by doing away with your undead form, write the number 259 on your *Adventure Sheet* and turn **100**. If you make it to six Attack Rounds without being killed again, turn to **365** at once. If you manage to kill the ghost hunter in less than six Attack Rounds, turn to **383**.

332

'Who did this to you?' you demand of the blinking Gaoler. And then he realises that you are not his tormentors and a smile brightens his face.

'Are you here to save me?' he asks, completely ignoring your question. You decide to help him, hoping that he will return the favour. As you do what you can to free him from his shackles, Iago's tongue runs away with him.

He tells you that Chamberlain Unthank was the one

⚀ ⚁

who had him imprisoned within the dungeons and then set his undead servants to torment him. Iago also tells you that Unthank has been hiding certain arte-facts of power, which he has recovered from all cor-ners of the kingdom, within the dungeons behind spirit-warded doors. He thinks that behind one of these doors there is an artefact he once heard the chamberlain refer to as the Soul Shield.

And then Iago is free, but at that very moment a dreadful moaning fills the squalid cell. 'Oh no! Not now! There're coming back!' he screams in panic and in a blaze of black light two hideous apparitions materialise within the cell. They look like decompos-ing corpses bound in rotting bandages, great chains dangling from their wrists and ankles. And then the Gaoler's tormentors attack and you are forced to fight for your continued survival once again. (If you have the *Banish Spirit* special ability then you will be able to use this against your first opponent and will only actually have to fight the second.)

	SKILL	STAMINA
First TORMENT	8	7
Second TORMENT	7	7

If Iago's tormentors finish you off, write the number 416 on your *Adventure Sheet* and turn to **100**. If you finish them, you may add up to 7 STAMINA points to your own ghost-form's STAMINA.

Free of his tormentors and his incarceration, Iago heaps thanks upon you, asking, foolishly perhaps, if there is anything he can do in return. And there might be one thing, if you no longer have a physical form. If this is the case and you have the *Spook* special ability (and want to use it), turn to **345**. If not, you and the freed Gaoler go your separate ways as he attempts to escape the Keep altogether while you penetrate deeper into its dungeon levels (turn to **416**).

333

Taking the Spirit Stone in hand you hear the souls trapped within calling to you again and you know that it is time to grant them their freedom. Raising the crystal cage above your head you hurl it onto the stony path before you. There is an explosion of actinic light and you suddenly find yourself at the centre of a whirling soul-storm. As your eyes recover after the blinding blast, you witness the fury unleashed by your desperate actions. The spirit-forms of those bound to the Spirit Stone are unleashed in an almighty maelstrom of ethereal fury and assault the gathered members of Unthank's death-worshipping cult. While the shadow-born Tenebrae, the Death Acolytes and the Dread Knights are preoccupied with battling the vengeful ghosts, will you make the most of the opportunity and go after the Necromancer himself (turn to **367**), or would you rather see if you can free your sister first (turn to **426**)?

334

At a thought you melt into the darkness and approach the gate. As you pass between the two sentries,

⚁ ⚀

unseen, one of them shoots an anxious glance at his companion, the hairs on the back of his neck rising. 'Did you feel that?' he asks, a panicked look in his eyes.

'Feel what?' the other says, sleepily.

'I don't know,' replies the first. 'A feeling like someone just walked over your grave.'

'No,' yawns the second. 'You're imagining things.'

You have got as far as the main gate but you still need to get into the castle. If you have the *Apparition* special ability and wish to use it, turn to **414**. If you have the *Poltergeist* special ability and want to try that instead, turn to **363**. If you have neither of these abilities, the only option left open to you is the drainage culvert (turn to **36**).

335

The door to the kitchens is open and you can feel the cauldron heat of the ovens radiating from inside as smoke rises from the large chimney in the cookhouse roof. The Cook and his staff are obviously busily engaged in preparing an almighty banquet. Ingelnook was Cook here in your father's time, as well as when you left to go crusading. But what possible reason could there be for preparing such an incredible feast at this time?

Ingelnook, an obese, blubbery man, wasn't a particularly pleasant person, but there was no denying that

⚁ ⚂

he was very good at his job. You didn't get on with him in life, and you're sure that your death won't have made your relationship any easier. If you want to enter the kitchens in full view of everyone there, turn to **355**. If you have the *Shade* special ability and would like to enter the kitchens unseen, turn to **385**. If you would rather not enter the cookhouse after all, turn to **445**.

336

You creep up to a tiny window, your ghostly footfalls making no sound on the fallen autumn leaves that strew the ground outside the hovel. Cautiously you peer inside the cottage. The scene you see there is exactly how you might have imagined it. A cauldron bubbles over a fire in the hearth, while sprigs of herbs hang drying from the rafters. On a table you see a single, black-bound book bearing a curious triangular rune, while lying on a rag-rug in front of the fire is a chubby piglet.

A sudden flicker of darting movement draws your attention back to the fireplace and then something crashes against the inside of the window, clawing and scratching at the glass in frantic agitation. You jump back in surprise as the window flies open. Out jump a gang of four demonic-looking imps. They are covered in bright red fur, have lashing tails, clawed hands and stubby horns. These witch's familiars do not hesitate and attack immediately. You must fight them altogether.

⚀ ⚁

	SKILL	STAMINA
First GRIMALKIN	6	3
Second GRIMALKIN	5	3
Third GRIMALKIN	5	4
Fourth GRIMALKIN	6	4

You will soon discover that these demonic creatures, as well as being able to sense your presence can also cause you harm. Fortunately, your otherworldly blade can injure them in return. If you should die a second death under the Grimalkins' ferocious assault, write the number 9 on your *Adventure Sheet* and turn to **100**. If you manage to fight off the imps, turn to **67**.

337

And so you make it across the moat to the imposing entrance of Valsinore Castle's Keep that you once called home and yet which now feels utterly alien and unwelcoming. There is not a single light visible in any window of the solid square stronghold. But the doors leading into the Keep are not as you remember them. The metre-thick oak doors have been replaced with some sinister black wood inlaid with silver that forms unsettling runes and esoteric symbols. As you approach you feel your progress being limited by a potent magical field. The energy shield sparks violently and you are suddenly hurled backwards by a powerful burst of magical energy. The door is resisting your ethereal essence somehow and keeping your ghostly form at bay. You cannot even get close enough to touch it.

This barrier before you is a Spirit Door, a portal intended to prevent undead spirits, like you, from passing through it. There is nothing you can do to counteract the spells bound into it. The only things capable of passing through a Spirit Door are things with a physical form. But now you are a ghost, how can you possibly acquire a physical form again?

If you have the *Spook* special ability and you want to pursue this path, turn to **13**. If you have the phrase *Rest in Peace* written down on your *Adventure Sheet* and you want to pursue this path, turn to **369**. If you have the codeword *Automaton* recorded on your *Adventure Sheet* and you want to pursue this path, turn to **427**. If you have none of these things, turn to **152**.

338

It is as if you cannot help yourself! 'As you are now, so once were we,' you growl menacingly, your leering features becoming more distorted and grotesque with every word you speak. 'As I am now, so you shall be!'

The woman gives a whimpering cry and then collapses on the floor in front of you. Her glazed eyes continue to stare vacantly into space, her features locked in a grimace of unadulterated horror. She doesn't move again.

Madame Zelda is dead. You have scared her to death! She was a harmless old soul really and did not deserve such a fate. (Lose 2 LUCK points and record

⚀ ⚁

the *Spectre* special ability on your *Adventure Sheet*.) There is nothing for you here now so you have no choice but to leave the dead woman's tent. Turn to 259.

339

Returning to Toadstone's cell once more, you find the Fool still curled up in a dank corner, telling himself appalling jokes, the same haunted look in his wide, bloodshot eyes. Toadstone's mind was broken by what he witnessed within the Keep long ago and you meet not resistance as you take over his body. (Add the codeword *Host* to your *Adventure Sheet*.)

Make a note of your spirit-form's current SKILL and STAMINA score, for later use, on your *Adventure Sheet*. While you have possession of the Fool's body you must use Toadstone's feeble stats, which are as follows: SKILL 6, STAMINA 14.

If you are injured in any way, as long as you are still wearing Toadstone's feeble form, you may eat provisions to recover STAMINA points. One meal restores up to 4 STAMINA points, but Toadstone doesn't have any food with him. He does have a weapon, however, a sharp, stiletto dagger. You wonder why he never thought to use it to help him escape from his prison cell. But then his mind has been gone a long time.

If Toadstone's STAMINA is reduced to 2 STAMINA points or fewer while you are possessing him he will be knocked unconscious, forcing you to relinquish

your control of his body. However, you can still fight on in spirit-form, using the stats that you have made a note of here. Now turn to **429**.

340

A whirlwind of necromantic power fills the chamber and it is only then that you notice the summoning circle on the floor of the tomb in front of you. With a fiery roar and a burst of blazing light, an ethereal figure materialises in the chamber. It has the appearance of a burning human skeleton, its blackened bones clothed in a body of scintillating flame. Giving voice to a wild howl of pain, the Bone-Fire flies towards you, bony hands outstretched, intent on making its fate your own.

BONE-FIRE   SKILL 7   STAMINA 6

If the Bone-Fire wounds you and you have the codeword *Armoured* written on your *Adventure Sheet*, your body catches fire; for every Attack Round after this you will automatically lose 1 STAMINA point until the end of the battle when you will be able to bat the fires out.

If the Bone-Fire destroys your physical form you can fight on in your spectral form but if this too is destroyed, write the number 445 on your *Adventure Sheet* and turn to **100**. If you vanquish the Bone-Fire, its fires are snuffed out and its blackened bones fall to the floor as ash. Your spirit-form recovers up to 3 STAMINA points as it absorbs some of the fiery ghost's ethereal essence. Now turn to **321**.

⚁ ⚁

341

Pressing your incorporeal body against the stone you strain to move it, even just a smidgeon. Roll two dice. If the total rolled is less than or equal to your WILL, roll three more dice; if this second total is less than or equal to your STAMINA score, turn to **245**. If you fail either roll, turn to **311**.

342

As you prepare to join in unholy battle with the monstrous vampire you lock eyes with the bat-beast and start to feel like you are drowning in the blood-red pools of its eyes. Roll two dice and add 2 to the number rolled. If the total is less than or equal to your WILL score, turn to **361**. If it is greater, turn to **382**.

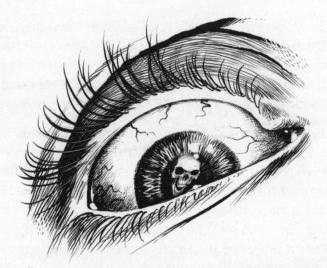

343

Sinister as it may sound, thanks to your incredible strength of will you are able to dominate the mind of another and possess them, using their body as if it were your own for a limited time. Record the *Spook* special ability on your *Adventure Sheet* and turn to the paragraph with the same number as the one that you were just instructed to write down.

344

'The Lady Oriana, you mean?' Myrddin says when you mention your sister. 'Yes, she's still there, although I hear she's made herself a virtual prisoner. Hasn't left the castle in over a year.'

'Then how do you know she's still safe and well?' you challenge the old man.

'Because I've seen her. Every day she gazes out of her apartment window, back along the road across the moors, a crucifix clutched in her hand, as if she is desperately awaiting the return of someone …' he breaks off. 'Oh, that would be you, wouldn't it?'

Everything Myrddin has told you about your sister makes you more desperate than ever to find out what's going on. It is time you were on your way again.

If you have the phrase *Something Fishy* written on your *Adventure Sheet*, turn to **145**. If not, turn to **22**.

⚁ ⚁

You force your consciousness inside the Gaoler's body, the power of your own mind too much for his own shattered sanity. (Add the codeword *Host* to you *Adventure Sheet*.)

Make a note of your spirit-form's current SKILL and STAMINA score, for later use, on your *Adventure Sheet*. While you are wearing Iago's body you must use his stats which are as follows: SKILL 8, STAMINA 18.

If you are injured in battle you may eat provisions, or consume potions if you have any, to recover STAMINA points. One meal restores up to 4 STAMINA points but, unsurprisingly, there is no food in Iago's cell. He has no weapon either, but you pull one of the lengths of chain from the wall, which should make an effective weapon. If Iago's STAMINA is reduced to 2 STAMINA points or fewer he will be knocked senseless, forcing you to vacate his body again. You may then continue fighting in your spirit-form using the stats that you have written down here.

You may well find that there are other places within Valsinore's dungeons that are still off limit to spirits. If you come to a paragraph marked with an asterisk (*), and as long as you still have your physical form, you may investigate what lies behind the door by adding 30 to the paragraph number and turning to this new reference. Now turn to **416** as you continue on your way through the castle's dungeons.

346

Although you put up a valiant defence, your weapon simply passes through the Shadow King's body as though it were nothing more than smoke. You cannot last for long against such an opponent and in the end he delivers you a series of dolorous blows. Lose 8 STAMINA points and 1 WILL point.

If you are still alive and you have something else you could use to fight the Lord of Death, such as a Spirit Stone (turn to **50**) or the *Codex Mortis* (turn to **435**), you had best use it now. If not, it is only a matter of time before you fall to the Great Undead's fell blade of night. There will be no coming back from the dead this time and your adventure, like your life, will be over ...

347

An unnerving hissing sound, coming from behind you, stops you in your tracks. You turn to see a hideous apparition rising from the very ground behind you. It looks like a human brain trailing tentacles, not unlike those of a jellyfish. It is this creature that is making the horrible hissing noise as it floats towards you, writhing tentacles reaching for you. And it is not alone.

You have perhaps been rash in how you have conducted yourself since entering the castle, perhaps not, but whatever the case, the Spirit Hunters are on to you now. Take the number you wrote down regarding the 'B' codewords before turning to this paragraph and add one. This is the number of Spirit Hunters you must fight. Each one has the following stats:

SPIRIT HUNTER   SKILL 6   STAMINA 6

You must fight theses phantasms two at a time as they try to ensnare you with their stinging tendrils. If the Spirit Hunters finish you off, write the number 366 on your *Adventure Sheet* and turn to **100**. If you defeat your spectral stalkers, turn to **366**.

348

The feast-hall is consumed by chaos as everyone sees you for what you really are. Not a single person present is not now looking in your direction. Tumblers

⚃ ⚃

flee before you – a pyramid of acrobats collapsing as those forming it all try to flee in different directions – jugglers drop their batons and fire-eaters burn their throats as they forget what they are doing for one agonising moment.

Then from out of the uproar emerge two threatening figures. Clad in suits of armour, decades old, and sinister black cloaks they are Dread Knights of the Order of the Black Shroud and formidable opponents.

	SKILL	STAMINA
First DREAD KNIGHT	9	8
Second DREAD KNIGHT	8	8

The knights are armed with swords imbued with life-stealing energy. If a knight injures you, roll one die; on a roll of 5–6 the knight's cursed blade will cause you 3 STAMINA points damage, instead of the usual 2. If the Dread Knights put an end to you, write the number 445 on your *Adventure Sheet* and turn to **100**. If you manage to defeat them both, turn to **370**.

349

As you look around you at the tombstones, you realise that you are gazing upon all that is left of your ancestors. This is your family's legacy. Only your sister now remains, and if she dies then your family line dies with her. Suddenly the desire for revenge burns bright and fierce within you again (add 1 to your WILL score).

'Here lies Agravain, Wormslayer,' one inscription reads, 'vanquisher of the Sourstone Worm. Lived his allotted span, died aged three score years and ten.'

'Rest in peace, Lydonee,' reads another. 'Three sons she bore, and daughters three. Now she sleeps eternally.'

The next headstone bears the name of one Father Ewlin, 'Who fought for justice, truth and right, and many a devil put to flight.'

Lost in thought, you have unwittingly drifted closer and closer towards the open grave and the gravedigger working away at the headstone with his chisel. *Test your Luck.* If you are Lucky, turn to **379**. If you are Unlucky, turn to **397**.

350

'It is a wise warrior who fights using knowledge as much as the sword's sharp edge,' Aramanthus says, and then goes on to school you in the art of using your ethereal powers more effectively. Add 2 to your WILL score, regain 1 LUCK point and write the number 440 on your *Adventure Sheet*. Now roll one die and turn to the paragraph indicated below.

Die roll

1	Turn to **90**
2	Turn to **120**
3	Turn to **230**
4	Turn to **263**

5	Turn to **293**
6	Turn to **343**

351

Arming yourself, you prepare to face this most appalling monstrosity.

NECROS   SKILL 10   STAMINA 12

If the Necros hits you, the acidic slime coating it will burn you whether you have a physical body or not, due to the fact that it is also one of the Undead, although like no other you have ever seen. However, if you strike the Necros, its jelly-like body will absorb much of the damage and partially heal itself when your weapon is withdrawn. As a result, you must deduct 1 point from the damage you deal it. If you manage to overcome this undead horror, turn to **401**. If the Necros ends up destroying your spirit-form, write the number 243 on your *Adventure Sheet* and turn to **100**.

352

'Please forgive Sir Calormayne for being a wits-addled old fool,' the knight says, sagging in his seat in the saddle. 'I have watched this bridge for so many centuries that I can no longer tell friend from foe.'

He suddenly looks small and pathetic. 'I am so very, very tired,' he says wearily, the exhaustion apparent in his hollow cheeks and sunken eyes. 'I have been guarding this crossing point and Valsinore these last three hundred years.'

⚁ ⚄

'Well now I am here to relieve you of that duty,' you say, 'for it is my sworn mission to cleanse this place of evil once and for all.'

The knight peers at you through rheumy eyes and he smiles weakly. 'Thank you,' he says, and promptly vanishes. But for a moment the knight's voice lingers on the wind: 'Take this my gift to you.' You suddenly feel yourself filled with new energy. Add 1 to your WILL score. Roll one die and add 2; regain up to this number of STAMINA points, and 1 LUCK point. Now turn to **6**.

353

Father Umberto finishes intoning prayers over what you can now see is a body laid out on the bier and then, having given Oriana his final blessing, departs the sanctuary, leaving her alone with the corpse ... your own dead body!

Seeing your own corpse like this, without realising it was even here, shocks you to the core. (Add the phrase *Rest in Peace* to your *Adventure Sheet* and deduct 1 from your WILL score.)

You cannot help yourself as you give a cry of shock. Oriana spins round, a look of abject horror on her face. 'No! No, it can't be!' she cries, and immediately reaches for the silver crucifix that hangs about her neck. 'Get back! Get back!' she screams.

If you want to leave your sister in peace you can either leave the way you came, through the chapel

⚅ ⚅

door (turn to **445**), or down a flight of stone steps to the right of the sanctuary that leads to the castle catacombs (turn to **88**). Alternatively you could speak to her and try to calm her down (turn to **377**).

354

In the blink of an eye you are gone … Invisible as a shadow you creep past the gate's guardians towards the portcullis-barred entrance to the Inner Ward. Only, it would appear that the knights can see you, somehow, as they move to engage you, their heavy two-handed swords raised, ready to strike. The truth of the matter is that even in your Shade form, you are still visible to those with the Second Sight and other undead and these Dread Knights are already dead like you! You have no choice but to fight them. Turn to **196**.

355

The hubbub of frantic activity consuming the kitchens is soon replaced by the screams of panicking servants and serving wenches, the harassed-looking men and women fleeing from your ghostly presence.

'Guards!' Ingelnook the cook screams. 'Guards, come quickly! We have an intruder in the kitchens! We are assailed by a terrible apparition! Save us!' Moments later, the sound of hobnailed boots pounding the passageway that leads from the kitchen to the feast hall can be heard.

Will you flee the kitchens immediately in the face of

⚁ ⚃

Ingelnook's protest (turn to **445**), or will you stand your ground and face whoever is coming for you now (turn to **198**)?

The crone mutters something in a dark tongue you do not understand, but it fills you with a sense of impending doom. (Lose 1 WILL point.) And then the spell is cast. A pack of small, be-fanged, be-horned and be-clawed apparitions suddenly pop into existence in front of you as the witch opens a door to the Spirit World, releasing these Phantasmal Fiends onto the Earthly Plane. The Fiends streak through the air towards you, screaming with elemental fury. Fight them as if they were all one creature.

PHANTASMAL FIENDS   SKILL 7   STAMINA 12

If the Fiends reduce your STAMINA score to zero, write the number 9 on you *Adventure* Sheet and turn to **100**. If you reduce your attackers' combined STAMINA score to zero, it means that you have managed to banish them from this world and return them to the Realm of the Damned. (Regain up to 6 STAMINA points.)

Mother Toadsfoot gives you a venomous look, even though you're sure she can't really see you, and hisses, 'Now return to your master and tell him I'll not be done away with so easily, or face my wrath again.' If you want to attack the witch directly, turn to **386**. If you would rather leave while you are still on this plane and capable of continuing your search for answers elsewhere, turn to **9**.

357

And then you are inside the man's mind, and Yorrick's body is yours to control. (Add the code-word *Host* to your *Adventure Sheet*.)

Make a note of your spirit-form's current SKILL and STAMINA score, for later use, on your *Adventure Sheet*. While you are wearing the body of Yorrick the gravedigger you must use his stats which are as follows: SKILL 9, STAMINA 17.

If you are injured in battle you may eat provisions to recover STAMINA points. One meal restores up to 4 STAMINA points. In Yorrick's backpack, which lies propped up against a headstone nearby, you find food enough for 3 meals. The only thing to hand that is even close to being a weapon is the gravedigger's spade which you take with you, just in case. If you make a successful strike against an opponent using the spade roll one die; on a roll of 1–2 it will cause only 1 point of STAMINA damage, rather than the usual 2. (Make a note of this on your *Adventure Sheet*.)

If Yorrick's STAMINA score is ever reduced to 2 STAMINA points or fewer, the gravedigger will be knocked out and you will be forced to leave his senseless body. Fortunately, you can keep fighting in your guise as a ghost, using the stats that you have written down here. Turn to **429**.

'It looks like I am going to have to deal with you myself!' the Queen of Liches screeches – and then the spell is broken. She is suddenly exposed as the undead nightmare she really is. She is no flesh and blood beauty but a hellish apparition. A few grey threads of hair cling to a fleshless head in the advanced stages of decomposition. Her fine robes are really rotting grave-clothes, her crown a crown of finger-bones, her own slender fingers cruel talons, and her eyes nothing but pits of darkness. With a banshee scream, the Wraith Queen flies at you.

WRAITH QUEEN   SKILL 9   STAMINA 10

If you lose an Attack Round consult the table below to see what form the Wraith Queen's attack takes. (You may use Luck to reduce any damage caused in the usual way.)

Die Roll	Attack and Damage
1–3	Clawing Talons – the Wraith Queen claws you with her broken fingernails. Lose 2 STAMINA points.
4–5	Banshee Scream – the wraith blasts you with a deafening, blood-curdling scream. You lose only 1 STAMINA point but must reduce your Attack Strength by 2 points for the duration of the next Attack Round.
6	Hell Sprites – the undead queen summons hellish imps to fight for her. For

the rest of your battle with the Wraith Queen you must also fend off these fiends. They have the following stats:

HELL SPRITES   SKILL 6   STAMINA 6

This option can happen only once; if you roll a 6 a second time, roll again.

If you manage to defeat this hellish harridan, turn to **373**. If she should destroy both your physical form and your ethereal form, write the number 445 on you *Adventure Sheet* and turn to **100**.

359

As the ghost beast dies, its body dissolving like mist before your eyes, you feel yourself absorbing some of the power of the Visitation's essence. Regain up to 4 STAMINA points. There is no reason to remain here any longer, so freed of its curious influence, you leave the stone circle. Turn to **288**.

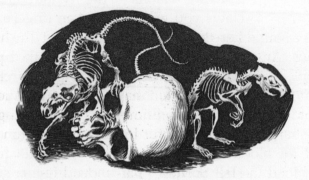

⊡ ⊡

360

Not wanting to get into a fight with the loyal Cador, you flee the barracks, but the Captain of the Guard now knows that your ghost is abroad within Valsinore Castle. Add the codeword *Barracks* to your *Adventure Sheet* and turn to **434**.

361

At the last minute you manage to drag your ethereal sword free of its ghostly scabbard and lash out at the monstrous bat-beast. The feral vampire screeches in pain and fury and then, possessed of an unthinking bestial rage, it attacks!

NOSFERATU   SKILL 11   STAMINA 14

If you manage to defeat the new vampire lord of Fetchfen, add 1 to your WILL score, and turn to **15**. However, if the bat-beast wins the battle, write the number 15 on your *Adventure Sheet* and turn to **100**.

362

With a sound like the rustling of parchment, the husk moves. Animated by the strength of your own persistent life-force, the giant spider skin goes back to behaving just as it would have in life. It quickly unfolds eight, claw-tipped limbs and then, baring its still-sharp mandibles it scuttles towards you on the hunt for blood. But seeing as how you don't have any blood to offer it, your phantasmal life-force will suffice.

SPIDER-HUSK   SKILL 7   STAMINA 6

If the husk wins an Attack Round, roll one die. On a roll of 5 or 6 it bites you with its undead fangs and sucks the residual life-force right out of you (lose 1 SKILL point as well as 2 STAMINA points and increase the Spider-Husk's STAMINA score by 2 as it absorbs your strength). If you die a second death fighting the undead husk, write the number 5 on your *Adventure Sheet* and turn to **100**. If you survive your battle with the soul-sucking spider, turn to **302**.

363

Focusing the full force of your will at the gate, you try to force them open with your mind. You are able to rattle the bolts and jangle some chains but to no avail. The gates weigh several tonnes and are far too heavy for you to move. But the eerie rattling of bolts and shaking of ironmongery has alerted the guards to your presence, even if they can't see you. Turn to **395**.

364

You find your ethereal essence easily breaches the rippling sphere of light and you see the black-bound book floating at its heart quite clearly now. You hear a susurration of whispering voices, but you can't quite make out what they are saying, and then a strange sensation comes over you. You feel your ghostly body becoming less and less cohesive, dissolving like mist which then becomes part of the luminosity of the sphere, until you share the fate of those spirits that have already been set to protect the necromancer's book of evil spells. And that shall be your fate now forevermore, until Doomsday itself. Your adventure is over.

365

The door suddenly bursts open and the ghost hunter's henchman enters the room. You must now fight the two men together. Streng's stats are as follows.

STRENG   SKILL 8   STAMINA 8

The weapons they bear are enchanted so as to be able to harm undead creatures, such as you. If both Van Richten and Streng wound you on two consecutive Attack Rounds, turn to **208**. If your ghost-form should be slain by the ghost hunter or his henchman, write the number 259 down on your *Adventure Sheet* and turn to **100**. However, if you manage to defeat both your opponents, turn to **383**.

366

If you are going to gain access to the Inner Ward of Valsinore Castle, you are going to have to go past the Barbican. As you approach the tower two dark figures melt from out of the moon-cast shadows and materialise before its imposing gates, blocking your way. They wear long black cloaks over plate mail armour of archaic, and slightly sinister, design and are an intimidating presence.

⚃ ⚃

However, having grown up in the castle and having explored practically every one of its hidey-holes and secret passageways, you also know of a tunnel that passes under the wall and into the Inner Ward beyond. Unfortunately it starts in a guard privy under the battlements in the east wall. If you want to approach the gatehouse and its sinister guardians directly, turn to **443**. If you would rather make use of the secret tunnel, turn to **393**. Alternatively, if you have the *Spirit* special ability and would prefer to fly over the gatehouse and into the Inner Ward beyond, turn to **5**.

367

Dodging first a Dread Knight and then a startled Death Acolyte as you run through the maelstrom of whirling ethereal entities, suddenly there you are, face to face with Unthank the Necromancer at last. The desire to be avenged on your betrayer burns volcano-hot within you, but the villain is ready for you, a spell of banishing already on his lips. With a roar of, 'Begone!' he hurls his arms out towards you and casts his spell. A bolt of searing necromantic energy streaks towards you; there is no way it can possibly miss. If you are carrying the Soul Shield, turn to **165**. If you are not protected by this ancient artefact, turn to **238**.

368

Slipping between canvas folds you enter the tent. The first partitioned space you enter contains a circular table draped with a blue velvet cloth, a crystal ball resting in its carved ebony cradle. Passing beyond this area into the back of the tent, you enter its owner's living quarters, or rather, at the moment, her bedroom. Tucked up in bed under a pile of knitted blankets, wearing several layers of coloured veils and shawls, is a middle-aged woman whose make-up is about as subtle as the rest of her get-up.

She suddenly sits up, eyes wide in shock, and clutches at a silver crescent moon charm hanging from her neck. 'Oh my born days,' she gasps, 'a ghost! An actual, real live spirit!'

What is that charm she is holding in her hands? And what sort of a mystic is this Madame Zelda anyway? She has a crystal ball of her own; could she be in league with the Death Acolyte who killed you? If you want to deal with Madame Zelda in a friendly manner, turn to **281**. If you want to try intimidating her, turn to **398**. If you would rather have nothing more to do with her and simply want to leave her tent, turn to **259**.

369

Leaving the Keep again, you make your way back into the Inner Ward and return to the chapel where your mortal body still lies in state. Staring down at your dead face you focus your will like never before, as you attempt to re-enter your own corpse and re-animate it again. Roll two dice and add 2. If the total is less than or equal to your WILL score, turn to **388**. If it is greater, turn to **408**.

And then Chamberlain Unthank is suddenly there before you, an expression of anger and hatred on his face. 'Why won't you just stay dead? I didn't want to have to get my hands dirty, but now it looks like I'm just going to have to deal with you myself,' he snarls.

There can be no doubt in your mind now as who your betrayer is. The blackguard that had you murdered when you were within sight of home, after three years long years away, was Unthank himself – the very man to whom you entrusted the guardianship of your ancestral lands and your sister's well-being. Never can there have been a more ruthless, vile and wholly despicable individual!

You are shocked into inaction by this realisation and in that instant Unthank casts his spell, folding reality around you while muttering something barely audible and wholly inhuman. An unearthly gale howls through the feast hall, springing up from nowhere, and it is at that moment that the traitor bellows, 'Spirit, begone!'

The screaming voice of the unnatural wind rises and spins faster and faster, creating a whirling vortex of air around you. One moment you are facing your nemesis at last, the next the veil between worlds is torn asunder and you are dragged screaming into the next world. Write the number 108 on your *Adventure Sheet* and then turn to **100**.

⚀ ⚄

371

You feel like a sweat is breaking out on your brow, from all your exertions, but how can it be? Try as you might, you are unable to pass through the stone door and into the barrow. (Lose 1 WILL point and 1 LUCK point). If you want to try to push the stone clear of the barrow entrance, turn to **341**. If you would rather quit this place, turn to **295**.

372

The voice then makes its final utterance.

> *'You shall not leave Castle Valsinore,*
> *But must remain here forevermore.'*

With that the light becomes even more intense and you feel its fiery touch upon your soul. You cannot help but cry out in pain. And then the light is gone, and so are you. All that is left is the impression of a screaming face, seemingly melted into the stone-flagged floor, joining the other screaming faces already there, trapped within the stone. Your soul is now bound to the stones of Valsinore Castle for all eternity. Your adventure is over.

373

At your killing blow, the Wraith Queen howls in frustration as her own ethereal body dissolves into smoke. At the same time a furious wind blows up from nowhere and carries the smoke away until all that is left of this Queen of the Damned is her scream

⚃ ⚀

and then that too is nothing more than a fading echo. (Recover up to 5 STAMINA points.) The Wraith Queen is truly dead at last and the blessed blade Nightslayer is yours again – or is it? If you still have a physical form, turn to **392**; if not and you are a ghost again, turn to **413**.

374

'Tell me more about this ghost hunter,' you say, intrigued.

'His name's Van ... Van-something ... Van Richten, yes, that's it. Van Richten. Apparently he's from a family of templars who have all sworn an oath to rid the world of evil, wherever it may be found. Josef Van Richten, that's his name. He's got a brother who's obsessed with vampires after one turned his bride-to-be the night before their wedding.'

You know this to be true; you heard the name Van Richten mentioned more than once during the crusade against the forces of evil in Bathoria. A man like this Josef Van Richten, with all his expertise, could be a valuable ally and may be able to help you where others cannot.

'Where would I find him?' you ask.

'At the Cockcrow in Sleath. He's taken a room there. Apparently there's been all sorts of disturbances in and around the village of late – talk of haunted houses, things hiding out in the graveyard and people suffering the worst nightmares they've ever experienced in all their born days – that's why Burgomaster Jurgen sent for Van Richten in the first place.'

Everything Myrddin has told you has left you intrigued and eager to continue with your quest. You decide it is time you were on your way again.

If you have the phrase *Something Fishy* written on your *Adventure Sheet*, turn to **145**. If not, turn to **22**.

375

'You may not fear death,' the Shadow King booms, 'but during an eternity in servitude you shall learn to fear me!' With his mighty sword of darkness in his fell grip, the Shadow King strides towards you, ready to engage you in the most titanic struggle of your life. But how can you fight one of the Great Undead and win? Will you:

Use Oil of Midnight against it (if you have such a thing)?	Turn to **233**
Use a Spirit Stone (if you have one)?	Turn to **50**
Use the *Codex Mortis* (if you have it)?	Turn to **435**

If you would rather simply face the Shadow King in hand-to-hand combat, pitting cold steel against cold night, choose the weapon you want to use carefully and turn to **249**.

As you are approaching the gatehouse that leads to the moat-bridge, you come across a scene that would make the blood in your veins run cold, if you still had any. A scaffold has been erected in the middle of the cobbled bailey and a grim execution party is now progressing towards it. At the head of the line is your sister, the Lady Oriana, her hands bound before her, flanked by two of Unthank's Dread Knights. Following her is the black-robed chamberlain himself. Already awaiting them on the scaffold, standing next to a blood-stained headsman's block, is a hulking undead monster. It is the size of an ogre but its flesh is grey and rotting. In its hands is a huge axe. There can be no mistaking what is about to happen here.

You race towards the scaffold as your sister is led to the block and forced onto her knees by her attendant knights. The voice of Chamberlain Unthank carries to you on the cold night air in time for you to hear him pronounce Oriana's fate: 'You have been found guilty of treason against the master of this house and the penalty for treason is death. Now die, traitor!'

Unthank having announced his judgement, the zombie raises its axe high above its head, ready to bring it down on your sister's neck. You cannot allow this execution to go ahead, but if you're going to stop it, it is obvious which of the villains you need to deal with first. Raging in fury, you manage to leap onto the scaffold, avoiding the Dread Knights, and come face-to-face with the hulking executioner. Moaning the zombie lumbers towards you, its slack mouth agape. Drawing your phantasmal sword you engage it in battle.

ZOMBIE EXECUTIONER   SKILL 7   STAMINA 10

Ironically, the executioner's axe being wielded by the huge zombie is bound with enchantments to ward against the undead and so can wound you. If you slay your sister's would-be executioner, turn to **91**. If the zombie kills you with its cursed axe, write the number 394 on your *Adventure Sheet* and turn to **100**.

377

'It's me,' you tell Oriana. 'It's alright, it's me. You're safe. I mean you no harm. How could I? You're my sister.'

It takes no little persuasion but gradually you are able to calm your sister down. But as the shock of seeing you again passes so the tears come. Crying your name she tries to hold you in her arms, but her desperately clutching hands simply pass straight through your ethereal essence as if you were nothing more than mist. Her tears spent, she pulls herself together enough to ask, 'What are you doing here? How can this be?'

You patiently explain to her how you have risen from the dead to seek justice for yourself, while also sharing with her all that you have learnt of what is going on in Valsinore Castle.

⚅ ⚁

'Your body was brought back to the castle after dark,' she explains, the tears threatening to come again. 'Father Umberto demanded that you be laid here, that he might bless your body that you might remain undisturbed in the ground and not suffer the Curse of the Undead that haunts this place now. In fact Father Umberto was very keen to make sure he got you into the ground this very night. He fears that a great evil has taken root here and that the doom of Valsinore Castle will come this night. He has gone to prepare for the final battle right now.'

You tell Oriana that you too have seen signs that whatever is going to happen will happen before a new day dawns. (Add the codeword *Oriana* to your Adventure Sheet.)

'Then you cannot delay here,' she says, urgently. 'What part can I play? What can I do to help?'

What Oriana has that you need is inside information. Your body lies on the bier, still clothed but, you notice, the blessed blade Nightslayer does not lie with it. Will you ask your sister whether she knows where your sword has been taken (turn to **396**), about Chamberlain Unthank (turn to **8**), or whether there is anyone else who can help you (turn to **28**)?

378

Assuming your most terrifying aspect, you swoop towards the knights, cackling insanely. Neither of them says anything or seems intimidated in any way.

⚁ ⚄

They simply raise their heavy broadswords in their gauntleted hands, ready to join with you in battle. Turn to **196**.

379

It feels as if you are being drawn to this one spot in particular, but realising this in time, you manage to break free of its morbid influence. Now will you:

Approach the gravedigger?	Turn to **397**
Return to the door of the chapel and enter the holy building (if you haven't tried to already)?	Turn to **274**
Leave the graveyard, and the chapel, and look elsewhere?	Turn to **445**

380

'Die, grave-spawn!' the guard captain shouts and lunges at you. Cador's sword is inscribed with holy wards and so is just as effective against your ghostly form as it is against corporeal opponents.

CAPTAIN OF THE GUARD   SKILL 12   STAMINA 10

If Captain Cador and his blessed blade should do for you, write the number 434 on you *Adventure Sheet* and turn to **100**. If you defeat the Captain of the Guard it is with no small measure of regret that you leave the guardhouse, knowing that you are responsible for the death of a good man. Lose 1 LUCK point and turn to **434**.

381

There is a burst of dazzling light, a sound like a hundred screaming souls, and you are thrown backwards to land in a smouldering heap on the far side of the chamber. (Lose 4 STAMINA points.) What do you want to do now? Trying something you haven't already attempted, will you:

Strike the sphere with your weapon?	Turn to **405**
Use the *Banish Spirit* special ability (if you have it)?	Turn to **424**
Re-trace your steps and descend the north-east stair?	Turn to **205**

382

Unable to tear your gaze away, you are trapped by the vampire's transfixing stare, until you no longer wish to see it dead and your own quest means nothing to you. Your will is broken, your mind no longer your own, your fate no longer yours to determine. You are now a soul in thrall to the new Lord of Fetchfen, the monstrous Nosferatu of Bathoria. Your adventure is over.

383

Hearing shouts from outside the room you realise that the noise of your battle with the ghost hunter has alerted the attention of others elsewhere in the inn. This whole exercise has been a disaster from start to finish and you don't want things getting any worse. You decide that the best course of action you can follow now is to look elsewhere for aid. Fleeing from the room and the inn you return to the village square. Turn to **259**.

384

Your suspicions aroused, you go after Unthank. From the hidden passageway behind the arras, the chamberlain unwittingly leads you to a secluded chamber at the bottom of the north-west tower. When you see who is waiting for him there, you almost give yourself away you are so shocked. It is your own cold-hearted killer, the skull-masked Death Acolyte. Chamberlain Unthank could be in danger! Will you attack the Death Acolyte immediately (turn to **307**) or will you wait and see what unfolds, just to be sure (turn to **250**)?

385

As you enter you are met by the roar of Ingelnook the cook furiously berating the servants scurrying about him, in the shadow of his blubbery, cleaver-wielding mass. His face is flushed red from shouting and his multiple chins ripple as he takes his wrath out on the unfortunate page boy whose only mistake was to be in the wrong place at the wrong time. But Ingelnook knows how things used to be before you left to fight in the Crusade against Evil and he is one of those who has been permitted to remain within the Inner Ward of the castle and so may know more about what's going on at Valsinore than others in the castle's Outer Ward. If you want to reveal yourself to the Cook, turn to **355**. If you feel that to do so would draw unwanted attention to your presence within the Inner Ward, there is nothing for it now other than to quit the kitchens (turn to **445**).

386

'I warned you!' the crone spits, and then she begins to chant. An ethereal wind rises seemingly from nowhere and starts tugging at your spectral body, making you feel as if you are about to be pulled apart as if you were nothing more than mist. 'Now leave me in peace!' the witch snarls. Roll two dice and add 3. If the total is equal to or less than your WILL score, turn to **9**. If it is greater than your WILL score, write the number 9 on your *Adventure Sheet* and turn to **100**.

387

'Stay back,' the old man shouts, 'or I shall smite you again with my magic!'

The look in the man's eyes suddenly dramatically changes from one of determined resolve to one of slack-jawed horror. It is then that you hear the splashing sounds of something wading from the breakers behind you accompanied by a croaking cry.

⚃ ⚀

'Oh no, please,' the old man cries, 'not that! Anything but that!'

You turn to see the most appalling abomination emerge from the rising tide and stalk towards you up the beach. It walks on two legs like a man and has the muscular build of an ogre, but its skin is covered with blue-grey scales. It has cruel gutting claws, its fingers are webbed and its bulbous eyes are those of a fish. A crest of spines protrudes from its head and runs all the way down its back to a long, lashing fish tail. The creature opens its mouth, revealing a maw full of shark's teeth, while the slits of gills in its neck open and close uselessly in the air.

'My tormentor comes to plague me again! Oh, woe. My doom is upon me!' the hermit cries and retreats back into his cave, leaving you to face the monster alone. The fish-beast fixes its eyes upon you and gives another croaking snarl as it continues to stalk towards you.

This is no mere creature of flesh and blood but a demon birthed from the storm-wracked sea, so the monster's cruel fish-talons will harm you just as well as if you were still a creature of flesh and blood yourself. Fortunately, your own ethereal copy of Nightslayer will also be able to injure the demon. Let battle commence!

SEA DEMON   SKILL 9   STAMINA 10

If the Sea Demon 'kills' you, record the number 145 on your *Adventure Sheet* and turn to **100** at once.

⚅ ⚅

However, if you manage to slay the demon, as its fishy carcass falls back into the sea and is washed away, the hermit suddenly runs out of his cave and down the beach towards you. Add the phrase *Something Fishy* to your *Adventure* Sheet and turn to **131**.

388

Closing your eyes, you descend upon your corpse. When you open them again you are staring up at the vaulted ceiling of the chapel through your own dead eyes. Rigor-locked joints crack into action again and you sit up. (Regain 1 LUCK point and add 1 to your WILL score.) You slowly get to your feet and stumble from the chapel, your steps unsteady at first, as if you are having to learn to walk again.

Make a note of your spirit-form's current SKILL and STAMINA score on your *Adventure Sheet* for later use. Your corpse's stats are your existing SKILL score but it has a STAMINA score equal to your *Initial* STAMINA score, minus 2. (Add the codeword *Revenant* to your *Adventure Sheet*.) You still may not eat provisions to recover STAMINA points if you are injured, but if your corpse-form should be 'killed' you may rise from it again in your spirit-form and continue fighting with the stats that you made a note of here.

But your blessed blade Nightslayer no longer lies with your body and so you are forced to look elsewhere for a suitable weapon to serve you in battle. You find a sword within an abandoned guard-post which will suffice for the time being.

⚃ ⚁

Now that you have a physical body with which you can breach the Spirit Door, you can try to enter the Keep again (turn to **276**). Alternatively, if you have the codeword *Catacombs* on your *Adventure Sheet*, there might be somewhere else you wish to visit first (turn to **11**).

389

Boldly you step forwards into the shimmering light that fills the space between the stones. You suddenly feel numb to the bone like you have never known – at least you would if you still had any bones. And then you know that, somehow, you are no longer on the Earthly Plane. Record the number 288 on your *Adventure Sheet* and then turn to **100**.

⚀ ⚃

390

'The dead of this place have been bound to its chambers, its turrets, its very stones by a greater power and cannot leave,' Aramanthus explains. 'Many are in perpetual torment. They can only be freed if the Necromancer who has bound them here is vanquished and his power broken.'

'Who is this Necromancer?' you ask, certain that the answer to that question will be the same as the one you have been seeking since you were cut down on the Moot Road. Turn to **440**.

391

Remaining precisely where you are, you call out to the ghostly knight, 'I submit!'

The knight looks somewhat taken aback. 'You what?' he splutters in bewilderment. 'You submit?'

'I submit, brave sir knight.'

'No one has ever submitted before,' he mumbles to himself. 'Then what are you doing here?' the knight asks. 'Why do you seek to cross this bridge?'

And so you relate your sorry tale to the ancient warrior, hoping that your rhetoric and noble motivations might persuade him to relent and let you pass. *Test your Skill* and if you are successful, turn to **352**. However, if you are unsuccessful, turn to **175**.

⚁ ⚁

392

With Nightslayer in your hands once more you feel now that nothing can stop you from completing your quest. It is a potent weapon indeed; it is good against demons as well as magical creatures, and against any undead creature – whether corporeal or incorporeal – it will cause 3 STAMINA points of damage on a successful strike. (Make sure that you record Nightslayer on your *Adventure Sheet*, add 1 to your WILL score and regain 2 LUCK points.)

The other undead present within the sepulchre hiss and back away from you in fear, some going so far as to clamber back into their tombs to escape your wrath. This place will need purging, in time, but for now you have more pressing matters to attend to. And so, for the time being at least, you leave the Court of the Wraith Queen and the Catacombs. Turn to **276**.

⚅ ⚅

393

Glad that you don't actually have to breathe any more and inhale the stench you clamber into the stone shaft of the garderobe and manoeuvre yourself into the cobweb-draped perpendicular shaft halfway down that leads you into the dusty passageway beyond.

The tunnel takes you down into the foundations of the wall, all manner of spiders, centipedes and other creepy crawlies being chased into dark corners by your ghostly glow. And then you come to an abrupt halt. The passageway is almost entirely blocked by the dried out husk of what must have once been a very large spider indeed. With a leg span of two metres it must have been a monster, and you're only glad you never had to face it in life.

Roll two dice and if the total is less than or equal to your current STAMINA score, turn to **362**. If it is greater, turn to **302**.

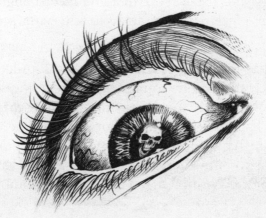

394

As you approach the shadowed archway of the gate-house at the nearside of the moat-bridge, you see two red-glowing coals in the darkness ahead of you. With a furnace roar, and a great clanking of metal, something truly monstrous rises to its full height before you, blocking your way to the bridge. Made of inter-locking plates of iron, like some goliath living suit of armour, at the joints you can see the intensity of the inferno raging within that gives it its unnatural life. The face of this engine of destruction has been fashioned to look like that of some hellish horned skull. Its huge jaw drops open and a searing blast of flame pours forth, the cobbles of the courtyard glowing red under this intense heat-blast. If you have any of the codewords *Revenant*, *Host* or *Armoured* written on your *Adventure Sheet*, turn to **194**. If not, turn to **93**.

395

Suddenly finding themselves in the presence of an undead spirit, the guards howl in terror and, falling over themselves, spring into action. 'Raise the alarm!' one of them cries, helping his companion pull back the heavy bolts holding the gate shut and heave the gate open. As soon as there is a gap wide enough for him to squeeze through, he legs it into the Outer Ward of the castle, as if the very hounds of hell were after him. The other tugs furiously at a chain-pull beside his sentry post and somewhere away within the castle a bell begins to toll. (Add the codeword *Bell* to your *Adventure Sheet*.) However, as well as raising the alarm, in their haste to pass on their dire warning the guards have also left the gate open, allowing you to slip inside. Regain 1 LUCK point and turn to **414**.

396

'Do you know what happened to the sword Nightslayer?' you ask. 'I had it with me when I was so cruelly struck down on the road to Sleath.'

'I saw the knights return with your body – carrying it on a makeshift stretcher – while I watched from my apartments in the east wall. Four carried the stretcher and another followed behind, carrying something cruciform in shape, wrapped in an oilskin. I believe that this was your blessed blade.'

'So where is it now?' you press her.

'The knight took it into the catacombs below. It lies somewhere down there even now.'

If you want to probe Oriana for more information, turn to **48**. If you would prefer to bid her farewell and be on your way, will you head down into the catacombs (turn to **88**), or leave the chapel and explore the Inner Ward further (turn to **445**)?

397

Your eyes fall on the name the gravedigger is carving into the headstone and to your horror see that it is your own. Suddenly you feel the lure of the grave like

⚃ ⚄

never before. Roll two dice. If the total rolled is equal to or less than your WILL score, turn to **195**; if it is greater, turn to **30**.

398

'Fear me, old woman!' you say as you bear down on her, your rage and frustration and desire for vengeance suddenly bubbling over. You can feel it contorting your features into a horrific, grimly-exaggerated visage.

Madame Zelda tumbles out of bed and backs away from you in panicked fear. 'You cannot escape me that easily, witch!' you snarl in a voice that is no longer quite your own, and you reach for her with one twisted, claw-like hand.

Your ghostly fingers brush the silver moon charm at her neck. You let out a cry of agony and quickly withdraw your hand. As you touched the talisman it felt like you had plucked an iron horseshoe straight from the farrier's forge. Lose 3 STAMINA points and 1 SKILL point. If this injury has reduced your STAMINA score to zero or below, write the number 259 on your *Adventure Sheet* and turn to **100**.

Once bitten, twice shy they say, but do you want to persist in your intimidation of Madame Zelda (turn to **338**), or would you rather flee her tent now. If so roll two dice. If the total rolled is less than or equal to your WILL score, turn to **259**; if it is greater, turn to **338**.

⚀ ⚁

'Mistress,' you say, 'wait! I have not come here to harm you; I come only seeking your aid.'

The crone freezes, her hands still. 'You want my help?' She sniffs the air sharply three times. 'You mean he didn't send you?'

'Nobody sent me. I have come of my own accord,' you tell her.

'But you're a ghost, I can smell it!' the witch goes on. 'And what do you mean, you want my help?'

You hurriedly relate the events of the evening so far to Mother Toadsfoot, hoping against hope that she might be able to help you in some way. When you have finished your story she looks at you, a grimace on her face, even though you're certain she can't actually see you. 'You'd best come inside,' she says and you follow her over the threshold into the cottage.

'There's certainly something afoot,' she says when you are both standing before the fire. Being blind doesn't appear to hinder her and certainly not within her own home. 'There have been signs and portents, see? Bad dreams, they're always a good sign, and people have been having a lot of them lately, a right plague of nightmares. There's been a disturbance within the Spirit World too. Something's coming; something bad.'

You press the old woman as to how she thinks she can help you.

🎲 🎲

'Well,' she says, scratching at a hairy wart on her hooked chin, 'I might have a charm in my book for bolstering your own powers on the Earthly Plane, but it'll cost you mind.' You wonder what the old woman means. It is obvious that you do not have the means to pay her for her services. 'Or I could conjure my familiar spirit to find out who's responsible for your present … condition.' Which will it be? Do you want Mother Toadsfoot to try to strengthen your own spectral powers (turn to 27), summon her familiar spirit to provide you with answers (turn to 76), or would you rather leave her hovel and not have any more to do with her, as she is obviously a witch of some power (turn to 9)?

400

And so you stand before the Gate once more, but this time, no choir of lost souls cries for you to be returned to the land of the living. Instead you hear only the screams of the dead and the damned, wailing in terror, for your failure has doomed them and you for all eternity as the Shadow King rises again. Your adventure is over.

401

In its final death-throes, the Necros' body spasms and it rises to its full height before crashing down across the stone-flagged floor on the far side of the pool, its body falling against the spiked gate with the leering demon's face. A feral voice that you realise is coming from the gate itself gurgles one word in gleeful satisfaction: 'Flesssshhh!'

⚁ ⚅

Its spikes draped with gore, the gates grinds open. Not wanting to spend another moment in this gruesome chamber, you hurry through it. Turn to **243**.

402

'You don't scare me,' Captain Cador rails, quaking in his boots as you transform into an undead horror. (Add the *Spectre* special ability to your *Adventure Sheet* if you do not already have it.) With an emboldening shout, Cador runs at you, trying to impale you with his sword. Turn to **380** to fight the Captain of the Guard but reduce his SKILL score by 1 point before you do.

403

In your physical form you may not use any of the ghostly powers you might have acquired during the course of your adventure so far. However, you are able to pick up and use physical objects. And of course, if your physical form is destroyed you can still proceed with your quest in your spirit-form, at which point you will be able to use your ghostly abilities again but will no longer be able to carry anything, unless otherwise instructed (and must immediately cross off anything you *are* carrying from your *Adventure Sheet*).

You may well find that there are other areas within the Keep that are off limit to spirits. If you come to a paragraph marked with an asterisk (*), and as long as you still have your physical form, you may investigate what is behind the door by adding 30 to the paragraph number and turning to this new reference. But for now, turn to **170**.

404

It is as you are making your way towards the road out of the village again, when you are at the heart of foetid marsh, that a semi-skeletal creature rises from the muck and slime, bogweed clinging to yellow ribs and ropes of purple-grey entrails sloshing with swampwater visible through a great rent in its stomach. As the undead horror stalks towards you, dragging its decomposing body through the swamp, more of the long-dead populace of Fetchfen emerge from where they have been lurking beneath the bog. If you are ever to leave this village of the damned you are going to have to fight the Mire-Men of Fetchfen first. Fight the slow-moving Undead one at a time.

	SKILL	STAMINA
First MIRE-MAN	7	7
Second MIRE-MAN	7	6
Third MIRE-MAN	6	7

If you have the *Spirit* special ability, once you defeat the first of your attackers you can flee the village and return to Castle Valsinore (turn to **29**). If you do not, but you defeat all of the Mire-Men anyway, you are able to escape Fetchfen at last (turn to **29**). But if the undead inhabitants of the village should win, write the number 15 on your *Adventure Sheet* and turn to **100**.

405

If you are wielding a magical weapon of some kind, turn to **424**. If not, turn to **381**.

406

Emerging from the Burgomaster's house again, through the front door, you feel relieved to be away from the place. In fact, you were lucky to escape with your soul intact and not be bound to the house for eternity. (Regain 1 LUCK point.) Now turn to **259**.

407

Although it is you who decides to take up the lyre and play, it is definitely Blondel the Bard's dextrous fingers that conjure a magical melody from its enchanted strings. The effect is almost instantaneous. As the lilting notes sing from the strings of the lyre the monster ceases its growling and a curious lethargy comes over it. It pads across the chamber towards you, then stops, swaying gently. It lies down, puts its head on its paws and closes its eyes, and within a few moments it is snoring loudly.

Now's your chance. While the dog's asleep you could try to creep past it and take the shield. If you want to do this, *Test your Skill*; if you succeed, turn to **53**, but if you fail, you disturb the dog which wakes in an instant (turn to **432**). If you would rather let sleeping dogs lie, you leave the chamber, shutting the Spirit Door behind you (turn to **182**).

408

Unable to take control of the body you had chosen, you begin to wonder whether you will ever be avenged against your enemy. (Lose 1 LUCK point and reduce your WILL by 1.) But perhaps you know of another way of acquiring a physical form.

Choosing something you haven't attempted yet, if you have the *Spook* special ability and want to use it now, turn to **13**. If you have the phrase *Rest in Peace* recorded on your *Adventure Sheet* and you want to pursue this path, turn to **369**. If you have the code-word *Automaton* written down and want to pursue this path, turn to **427**. If you have no further tricks up your sleeve, turn to **152**.

⚀ ⚄

409

The barrow has stood on this promontory since ancient times, since long before there was even a kingdom of Ruddlestone. Its ancientness reverberates deep within your soul and, at the same time, you sense that something festers within. Turf covers the man-made mound which is sealed by a large, flat stone. Despite walking the entire circumference of the barrow you cannot see another way inside. Will you:

Leave the barrow?	Turn to **295**
Try to move the stone to so that you might enter the barrow?	Turn to **341**
Persist with trying to find another way in?	Turn to **431**

410

Recalling the words of the Watcher, that you would know when the time was right to use the hourglass, you hold it up before you now and regard the motionless black sand contained within one last time, before dashing it against a jagged rock. The glass explodes into myriad diamonds shards, the black sand briefly forming a spiralling vortex in the air in front of you before vanishing, twinkling with starlight. Unthank clutches at his chest, a look of unadulterated horror entering his eyes. And then a terrible transformation occurs. As you watch, his flesh pulls taut, his skin wrinkling like a rotten piece of fruit. But the transformation doesn't stop there. His eyes melt like wax in their sockets, his black hair turns white and winds out of his head at a furious rate from his retracting scalp as the weight of years catches up with him at last and he is made to pay for all those lifetimes he stole from others – including you! And then the evil-hearted Necromancer topples face-first onto the cold hard ground at your feet, dead at last. Turn to **423**.

411

Through sheer strength of will you set the numbered tumblers to the correct combination. Subtract the combination from the number of this paragraph and then turn to this new paragraph. If the paragraph makes no sense, you have either made a mistake or you do not know the correct combination and are unable to open the door. You will either have to leave the gatehouse (turn to **20**), descend the staircase to the bottom, if you haven't already done so (turn to **115**), or if you want to and are able to use the *Apparition* special ability here, turn to **181**.

412

As you approach the statue to claim the grim blade, the Spirit Door slams shut behind you with a resounding boom. As the echo fades away a new sound reaches your ears, that of bony feet and hands scratching at the stone-flagged floor of the chamber. Spotting movement out of the corner of your eye, you snap your head round and see a tiny imp-like creature, wearing a coarse sackcloth robe and wielding a tiny scythe in its sharp-clawed hands emerge from behind the statue. It is only the first of many. If you are going to claim the Amethyst Blade as your own, or even just escape from this chamber in one piece, you are going to have to fight the invidious Deathlings.

	SKILL	STAMINA
First DEATHLING	6	3
Second DEATHLING	6	2
Third DEATHLING	5	3
Fourth DEATHLING	6	4
Fifth DEATHLING	6	3
Sixth DEATHLING	7	2

Fight the Deathlings three at a time. You will soon discover that whether you are in your ethereal form or a borrowed body, the imps' scythes are just as effective against incorporeal creatures as they are against flesh, bone or metal. If the Deathlings really are the death of you, write the number 154 on your *Adventure Sheet* and turn to **100**. If you manage to defeat them all, however, you are able to take the Amethyst Blade without further hindrance and quickly leave the room before anything else unpleasant can crawl out of the stonework and attack. Turn to 154.

413

After all that you have gone through to win back your sword, without the physical means to wield it, it is useless to you. Feeling thoroughly dejected, no longer sure if you can even see this quest through to the end, you leave the Catacombs. Lose 2 WILL points, 1 LUCK point, and turn to 276.

414

You are inside the castle at last, within the courtyard of the large Outer Ward to be precise. Overhead, the moon hangs like a silvery orb amidst the backdrop of a myriad stars, limning the buildings in its monochrome light.

You take a moment to reacquaint yourself with your castle home, having been away for so long. It appears to be as you remember it but you can sense a sinister atmosphere hanging over it like a funerary shroud. Flitting through the air above the castle is a multitude of incandescent ethereal forms, spiralling and moaning on the chill wind coming in off the Diamond Sea.

In the south-eastern corner of the courtyard is the familiar thatch-roofed structure of the smithy where you would quite happily while away hours at a time in your youth, watching the blacksmith at work, forging weapons, repairing armour and shoeing horses.

⚁ ⚄

Opposite the smithy against the western wall of the Outer Ward are the castle stables and a little further along, abutting the northern wall that divides the Outer Ward from the Inner is the sturdy stone blockhouse that is the Guard Barracks. Guarding the entrance to the Inner Ward, the Barbican is an imposing three-storey tower, more like a small keep than merely a gatehouse. Next to the Barbican, steps lead up to the battlements while below them, against the east wall, are the kennels, where the lords of Valsinore have kept their hunting hounds ever since your ancestors had the fortress constructed centuries ago.

You still have no real idea about who ordered that you be killed or where the Death Acolyte fled to, but you have an overwhelming feeling that inside the castle is where you will find the answers you so desperately seek. So, where would you like to visit first?

The smithy?	Turn to **180**
The stables?	Turn to **164**
The guard barracks?	Turn to **330**
The battlements?	Turn to **201**
The kennels?	Turn to **66**

If you would rather not delay here, you can leave the Outer Ward and make for the Inner Ward, approaching the Barbican that separates these two parts of the castle (turn to **317**).

⊞ ⊡

415

Standing directly before you is the imposing figure of a Dread Knight, but this is no mere battle-brother. Clad in ornate armour of archaic design, carrying a totally black shield and a spike-headed mace, this is the Chapter Master of the Order of the Black Shroud, an awesome opponent indeed.

DREAD CHAPTER MASTER   SKILL 12   STAMINA 12

This will be a battle to truly test your mettle, for the dark templar carries the Mace of Mabuz, a weapon as capable of battering your soul as it is your body, or even wrought armour. If your struggle against the Lord of the Dread Knights should prove too testing and the Chapter Master bests you in single combat, write the number 132 on your *Adventure Sheet* and turn to **100**. However, if it is you who is victorious, regain 1 LUCK point and turn to **132**.

416*

The passageway turns right as it wends its way through the bedrock of the Devil's Spur into which the foundations of the great keep were sunk when the first Lord of Valsinore had the castle constructed, and soon you come upon another door to your left. This too is made from black wood banded with pure silver, forming esoteric sigils all across its surface, for this too is a Spirit Door. When you are ready to move on, turn to 53.

417

'In the name of Hamaskis, begone!' the hermit suddenly shouts and, waving his hands frantically before his face, sends a bolt of searing golden light blasting into your incorporeal body. The prayer-spell burns like fire. Roll one die and lose that many STAMINA points and lose 1 WILL point too. If your STAMINA score has dropped to zero (or below), write the number 145 on your *Adventure Sheet* and turn to 100. If you are still 'alive', will you now leave the hermit in peace, and with your ghostly form intact (turn to 145), or will you persist in your questioning of the querulous old man (turn to 387)?

418

As you turn towards the front door again, it slams shut in your face! If you have the *Apparition* special ability, turn to 406. If not, but you still want to try to leave the house, roll two dice and if the total is less than or equal to your WILL score, make a note of the number of this paragraph on your *Adventure Sheet*

⚀ ⚅

and turn to **90**. If the total rolled is greater than your WILL score, or you decide to stay and explore the house of your own free will, will you start with the ground floor (turn to **325**) or the first floor (turn to **234**)?

419

'My servant failed me before,' the Shadow King agrees, his words reverberating from the ancient stones of the henge, 'but he shall not fail me again.' With that the necromancer's corpse twitches and lurches to its feet. In the short time that Unthank has been dead, his body has begun to decompose at a rate beyond all reason. Rotting hands outstretched before it, ready to throttle the life from you, Unthank the Undead lurches towards you, moaning balefully.

UNTHANK UNDEAD   SKILL 9   STAMINA 8

If the undead necromancer scores two consecutive hits against you, the shambling corpse grasps you by the neck and throttles you for an additional die of damage. If you win, turn to **375**. However, should Unthank's corpse succeed in slaying you again, there will be no coming back a second time and your adventure, like your life, will be over ...

420

'I have tried scrying to find its source but I cannot see beyond the walls of the Keep. That place is closed to me now. What I do know is that this evil is deeply

⚀ ⚁

rooted within the castle and it will take a great deal to free Valsinore from its grip.' Now turn to **440**.

421

And so you stand before the barbed iron gate, cast with a leering demon's face. It is too heavy for you to lift and is even resistant to ethereal methods of entry. There is only one thing that will cause the gate to open as it tells you with relish, in a gurgling growl of gruesome delight: 'Flesssshhh!'

If you have some Ironbane and want to try that on the gate, turn to **68**. If you have the codeword *Revenant* or *Host* recorded on your *Adventure Sheet* and you are willing to make an offering of your own flesh to the Demon Gate, turn to **438**. If you have the codeword *Armoured* written on your *Adventure Sheet* or you have one of the other two but do not want to offer up yourself to the blood-thirsty portal, turn to **24**. If you have none of these codewords currently written down, turn to **197**.

422

The stink of death hangs over Fetchfen – the sick smell of decay – and the windmill is no different. It looks like it hasn't been used for years, the mill machinery corroded into uselessness. You find nothing of interest inside. There are only the few tools of the miller's trade and mouldering sacks of mildewed grain.

⚁ ⚃

But it is as you are preparing to leave the derelict windmill again that one of the sacks tips over, spilling its contents across the floor, and something that is most definitely not grain tumbles onto the rough wooden planks. It is a human skull. 'Not going so soon, are you?' the skull asks, looking up at you from the dark pits of its empty eye-sockets. 'Not when we haven't had a chance to get to know each other yet.'

Before you can reach the half-broken-down door again, more bones rattle onto the floor from the bag, the bones flying into the air and coming together to roughly resemble the skeleton of a human being. If you are going to escape the windmill you are going to have to battle this old bag-o'-bones.

BAG-O'-BONES   SKILL 7   STAMINA 8

If the skeleton-ghost wins the fight, write the number 404 on your *Adventure Sheet* and turn to **100**. If you win this battle of the undead, regain up to 4 STAMINA points and then choose where you want to go next. To visit Fetchfen's cemetery, turn to **322**. If you would rather just leave this village of the dead, turn to **404**.

423

Unthank the Necromancer is dead! You have been avenged. (Regain 1 LUCK point and add 2 to your WILL score.) But the night is not over yet – not by a long way. Something is condensing out of the moonless night at the very centre of the stone circle. As you watch, dumfounded, a looming figure, twice as tall as

⚁ ⚄

a man, takes shape, clothing itself in the very fabric of the night. It looks like a giant wearing ancient armour forged from the metal of the night beneath a shroud of darkness, an ornate crowned helm on its head. But it is its face that stops you in your tracks – for it doesn't have one. All that lies beneath its armoured helm are two malevolently glowing coals that burn red like a pair of dying stars. And then the lunar eclipse passes and the apparition is revealed in all its malignant glory.

'The Shadow King!' the cultists gasp and fall to their knees, whimpering in fear. So this is what Unthank and his death-cult were trying to summon. Seeing the reaction of the death-cult, you suddenly feel colder than you have ever felt in your life and the hairs on the back of your neck start to rise. But that shouldn't be possible …

If you have the codeword *Revenant*, or *Host*, or *Armoured* still written on your *Adventure Sheet*, turn to 275. If not, turn to 448.

424

The Spirit Sphere disappears in an explosion of actinic light accompanied by the howling of spirit voices, as a tremendous rushing wind fills the turret room. The book that was previously suspended at the heart of the sphere drops to the floor with a bang.

It is an evil-looking thing, bound in what you hope is only black leather and bearing the image of a leering human skull on its front, along with its name: *Codex Mortis*. If you want to take this book of dark magic with you, add it to your *Adventure Sheet*. Whether you do or not, there is nothing left to do other than to leave the chamber again. Turn to **205**.

425

In your spirit-form once again, you may use all the special abilities that you will have undoubtedly acquired during the course of your adventure so far. However, you will not be able to carry any physical items with you, except in very exceptional circumstances (which will be described in the text). This includes weapons, magic or otherwise, armour and any other items you might have picked up along the way. Now turn to **170**.

426

Using the whirling maelstrom of vengeful spirits to cover your approach, you enter the ring of standing stones and hasten to your sister's side. When you are only a few metres from the altar stone, one of Unthank's death-cult steps into your path. *Test your Luck*. If you are Lucky, turn to **442**. If you are Unlucky, turn to **415**.

427

You make your way back through Valsinore Castle and enter the Barbican gatehouse again, coming at last to the room with the code-locked door and the magnificent suit of automaton armour. As you gaze

⚀ ⚅

into the ruby eyes, you imagine entering the suit and focusing your will to bring it to life. Roll two dice. If the total rolled is less than or equal to your WILL score, turn to **439**. If it is greater, turn to **408**.

428

The longed-for moment has come at last, the moment when you can be revenged against the blackguard who had you killed and who would now bring about the end of your family line by sacrificing your sister to his dark gods. There is nothing more to be said, the time for action is at hand.

NECROMANCER   SKILL 11   STAMINA 10

Unthank defends himself with the sacrificial obsidian dagger which he was about to use to spill the blood of the Lady Oriana, which is as potent against the undead as it is against the living. If you lose your battle with the evil necromancer, write the number 132 on your *Adventure Sheet* and turn to **100**. However, if it should be you who is victorious, turn to **423**.

429

Now that you have a physical body again, in which you can pass beyond the magically-warded portal of the Spirit Door, you can try to enter the Keep again (turn to **276**). Alternatively, if you have the codeword *Catacombs* written on your *Adventure Sheet*, there might be somewhere else you wish to visit first (turn to **11**).

⚀ ⚁

430

You are frozen into inaction as something truly grotesque rises from the filth of the pool. In form it is nothing more than a gigantic worm-like shape but formed entirely from a gelatinous necrotic jelly which, you soon realise, is the rendered remains of the corpses that have been festering in the pit. Suspended inside the rippling, jelly-like body are the bones of the creatures that ended up here, which give it a vague internal skeletal structure. Where you imagine its head is supposed to be is a jawless human skull. Moving with peristaltic convulsions, its body rippling like some gigantic slug, the Necros oozes towards you, leaving a trail of acidic slime in its wake.

You are going to have to face this new undead horror in battle, but how will you choose to defend yourself? If you have the Oil of Midnight with you and want to use that, turn to **280**. If you do not have this particular item then you have no choice but to draw your weapon (turn to **351**), or you could try to fight it using one of the burning brands that light the chamber (turn to **157**).

431

As you are busy searching for another way into the barrow a thought strikes you. You are no longer a corporeal being of flesh and blood; that part of you now lies dead on the road behind you. You have to stop thinking of yourself in those terms. You are a ghost now, and when have walls or doors ever been a problem for ghosts?

⚃ ⚁

Nervously you approach the stone door and place a spectral hand upon the cold stone. 'I am a ghost', you repeat, over and over to yourself. 'I am a ghost. I am a ghost.'

Roll two dice. If the total rolled is less than or equal to your WILL, turn to **265**. If it is greater, turn to **371**.

432

Weapon in hand you prepare to take on the monstrous hound. Existing half in the Ethereal Realm and half on the Earthly Plane, the Moon Dog is as effective at harming your spirit-form as it is a physical body.

MUTANT MOON DOG   SKILL 9   STAMINA 10

If the dog finishes you off, write the number 182 on your *Adventure Sheet* and turn to **100**. If you slay the monster, however, turn to **53**.

433

Taking the Spirit Stone in hand you hear the souls trapped within calling to you again and you know that it is time to grant them their freedom. Raising the crystal cage above your head you hurl it onto the stony path before you. There is an explosion of actinic light and you suddenly find yourself at the centre of a whirling soul-storm. As your eyes recover after the blinding blast, you witness the fury unleashed by your desperate actions. The spirit-forms of those bound to the Spirit Stone are unleashed in an almighty maelstrom of ethereal fury, surrounding the

Shadow King with a whirling vortex of spectral light. You watch in awe as the spirits tear the Shadow King's insubstantial form apart with their spectral talons. The Death Lord does what he can to defend himself from their relentless assault but in the end he is simply overwhelmed. Soon there is nothing left of the Shadow King but a few traces of inky darkness at the heart of the whirling spirit vortex and then, with one last howl of fury and frustration, even that is gone. Turn to 450.

434

Choosing somewhere you haven't been before, where would you like to go now, within the Outer Ward of the castle?

The smithy?	Turn to 180
The stables?	Turn to 164
The guard barracks?	Turn to 330
The battlements?	Turn to 201
The kennels?	Turn to 66

If you would rather not delay here, you can leave the Outer Ward and make for the Inner Ward, approaching the Barbican that separates these two parts of the castle (turn to 317).

435

Willing Unthank's own book of necromantic magic to provide you with what you need to defeat the Shadow King you let it fall open in your hands where it will and begin to read. But you are playing with fire

⚁ ⚃

by invoking the very powers that you seek to vanquish. Lose 2 WILL points. Now roll two dice and if the total rolled is less than or equal to your WILL score, turn to **184**, but if it is greater, turn to **326**.

436

Not much further on you come to a T-junction. Do you want to go left (turn to **289**), or right (turn to **146**)?

437

As you approach the Burgomaster's house, the imp-faced doorknocker seems to smile at you in sinister fashion. Then the great oak door swings open before you of its own accord and you enter the tile-floored hallway of the grandest residence in Sleath. The house was in darkness, but as you enter, candles mounted in candelabra on the stairs and in a chandelier above you spark into life and burn with a lambent green flame.

Before you, broad wooden stairs ascend to the first floor, while underneath them a shadowy archway leads into the rooms on the ground floor of the property. Do you want to:

Explore the ground floor of the house?   Turn to **325**
Ascend to the first floor and take a
   look around there?   Turn to **234**
Leave this apparently already
   haunted house?   Turn to **418**

438

It takes all your courage, but nonetheless you approach the gate and press a hand against one of the barbed spikes. You close your eyes and wait for the inevitable. But the sensation is not actually as bad as you were expecting. (Lose 2 STAMINA points and if this has finished you off, write the number 243 on your *Adventure Sheet* and turn to **100**.) With a grating of blood-scabbed hinges, the Demon Gate opens, gurgling happily to itself. Not wanting to spend another moment here, you hurry through. Turn to **243**.

439

Your ethereal body dissolving like mist, you ooze into the slit in the helmet that serves as a mouth, filling the armour with your essence and taking possession of it. Gazing out at the world through the crystal lenses of the armour's eyes, you test out your new iron body. It is more awkward and less agile than your own body was, but it is also significantly stronger. (Regain 1 LUCK point and add 1 to your WILL score.)

Make a note of your spirit-form's current SKILL and STAMINA score, for later use, on your *Adventure Sheet*. Your armoured body's SKILL score is equal to your *Initial* SKILL score, minus 1. However, the automaton armour has an *Initial* STAMINA score of 24! (Add the codeword *Armoured* to your *Adventure Sheet*.) You still may not eat provisions to recover STAMINA points if you are injured, but if your armoured body should be destroyed you may rise from it in your spirit-form

⚄ ⚅

and continue fighting with the stats that you made a note of here.

Although you are not armed, your new armoured fists are as effective as sledgehammers, enabling you to bludgeon your enemies into submission instead. Also, your new metal body is so tough that you may automatically reduce the damage you may suffer at the hands of your enemies by 1 point. (Regain 1 LUCK point.)

Now that you have a physical body with which you can breach the Spirit Door, you can try to enter the Keep again (turn to 276). Alternatively, if you have the codeword *Catacombs* on your *Adventure Sheet*, there might be somewhere else you wish to visit first (turn to 11).

440

A banshee wail cuts through the stillness of the tomb. 'Your presence here has been discovered!' the wizard's ghost exclaims, his features knotted in consternation. 'You must go, but take Fizzgig with you. He will be of more use than perhaps it first appears. Besides,' Aramanthus adds with what would appear to be a ghostly tear in the corner of his eye, 'I'm not much company for him anymore.'

Not questioning the wizard's decision for a second you leave the vault, the bat-winged homunculus flapping after you, burbling to itself. (Add the codeword *Banshee* and Fizzgig the Homunculus to your

⚃ ⚅

Adventure Sheet.) Fizzgig is actually a Spell Sprite, a creature imbued with great thaumaturgical potential. This manifests itself in the form of four spells, which are listed below along with their effects.

Banish Spirit – this spell will send one undead spirit back to the netherworld.

Luck Spell – this spell will raise your spirit-form's LUCK score to its *Initial* level.

Skill Spell – this spell will raise your spirit-form's SKILL score to its *Initial* level.

Strength Spell – this spell will raise your spirit-form's STAMINA score to its *Initial* level.

However, you may only call on Fizzgig's help three times; after that the creature's reservoir of magical energy will have been drained and the sprite will disappear in a puff of logic. Now turn to **264**.

441

A weather-worn signpost beside the dirt track you find yourself on reads 'Fetchfen'. You have heard of this place before. It lies on the borders of Bathoria but it is known as a village of the damned, a place of the dead. No one has lived here for over a hundred years, and yet you heard Chamberlain Unthank claim to have been born here. The village appears to have been flooded long ago and now the rotting timbers of half-collapsed buildings rise from the stagnant pools of the fen looking like the skeletal ribs of some undead creature. Only two places stand clear of the foetid marsh, a broken-sailed windmill and an overgrown cemetery. The standing water of the fen pools will prove no obstacle to your explorations, so where will you go to first?

The windmill?	Turn to **422**
The cemetery?	Turn to **322**

442

The one trying to prevent you from reaching your sister is a Death Acolyte. Armed with a dagger coated with Spectrebane, he throws himself at you.

DEATH ACOLYTE   SKILL 6   STAMINA 6

Your ethereal form is vulnerable to the Acolyte's Spectrebane-coated blade, as is your physical body. If the Death Acolyte manages to finish you off, write the number 132 on your *Adventure Sheet* and turn to **100**. If it is you who kills the Acolyte, turn to **132**.

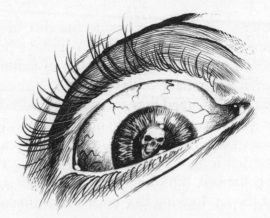

443

As you approach the gatehouse and its guardians, your ghostly blue-white glow giving your location away, you hear the clatter of swords being unsheathed as the silent warriors prepare to repel your advance. Will you:

Prepare to meet the knights in battle?   Turn to **196**

Use the *Spectre* special ability
(if you have it)?   Turn to **378**

Use the *Shade* special ability
(if you have it)?   Turn to **354**

Give up on this approach and look
for the secret tunnel instead?   Turn to **393**

444

Your mind, inside Marrok the Crusader's body will make a ruthlessly effective combination. (Add the codeword *Host* to you *Adventure Sheet*.)

Make a note of your spirit-form's current SKILL and STAMINA score, for later use, on your *Adventure Sheet*. While you are controlling Marrok's body you must use his stats, which are as follows: SKILL 11, STAMINA 22.

If you are injured in any way, for as long as you are wearing the crusader's body, you may eat provisions to recover STAMINA points. One meal restores up to 4 STAMINA points and Marrok has enough food in his backpack for 6 meals. He is armed with Deathsbane, a blessed blade not unlike your own Nightslayer, which is capable of harming undead, demons and magical creatures.

If Marrok's STAMINA is reduced to 2 STAMINA points or fewer while you are possessing him, he will be knocked unconscious, forcing you to release his body from your influence. However, you may continue fighting in your spirit-form, using the stats that you have made a note of here. Turn to 429.

445

Back in the courtyard of the Inner Ward, remembering to choose somewhere that you haven't been already, where would you like to explore next?

The kitchens?	Turn to 335
The feast hall?	Turn to 95
The chapel?	Turn to 260
The Blasted Tower?	Turn to 34
The well?	Turn to 232

If you would rather not delay here at all, you can approach the last gatehouse that guards the entrance to the sea-moat bridge (turn to 134) or, if you have the *Spirit* special ability, take to the air and try approaching the Keep directly (turn to 191).

446

Beyond the Spirit Door you find yourself at one end of a long, narrow room. It is lit by torches mounted in sconces. The flickering light is being reflected from the mirrored surface of a magnificent shield that is hanging on the wall at the far end of the chamber. But upon entering the room, you disturb the shield's guardian. Giving voice to a guttural growl, the great silver-haired beast that has been set to guard this chamber raises its head. Then a second snarling voice joins the first and a second head turns to look at you. If you want to steal the mirrored shield from this chamber you are going to have to get past the Mutant Moon Dog first. Will you:

Attack the creature?	Turn to **432**
Play it something on a lyre (if you have one)?	Turn to **407**
Slam the door again quickly before the dog can reach you?	Turn to **182**

447

'I warn you, spirit, stay back,' the old man says. 'I have a little Art of my own. Do not provoke me as I shall have no qualms about using it against you. Now, begone!'

The hermit does not seem particularly concerned by the fact that he is being visited by a ghost so perhaps he really does have some magical means of defending himself. He certainly doesn't appear to be carrying a weapon of any kind.

Do you want to continue to approach the curmudgeonly hermit (turn to **417**), or will you leave the old man in peace and return to the cliff-top (turn to **145**)?

⚃ ⚀

448

You look down at your body but you can no longer see the world through your misty form. Before your very eyes your ethereal form is becoming opaque as it solidifies and your ghost-self becomes a thing of blood, flesh and bone once more. Suddenly it all becomes clear in your mind; Unthank was living on borrowed time, your life-time in fact, and now that he is dead that life-force has been restored to you. You are alive again and a ghost no more! Restore your SKILL, STAMINA and LUCK scores to their *Initial* levels.

The monstrous night-born spectre peers down at you and a voice like thunder rolls across the wind-swept hillside. 'Bow before me, worm!' Its burning ember eyes bore into you like smouldering branding irons. Roll two dice, adding 3 to the total if you have the codeword *Talisman* written on your *Adventure* Sheet. If the final total is less than or equal to your WILL score, turn to **159**, but if it is greater, turn to **326**.

449

And so you stand before the spirit-warded entrance of the Keep once more, only this time the black wood double doors open at your touch and you enter the grand, pillared hall beyond. Now that you have gained access to the Keep at last, do you want to quit your recently-acquired physical form (turn to **425**) or would you prefer to continue on your way just as you are (turn to **403**)?

⚀ ⚁

450

You rush over to the altar stone and it is with an overwhelming sense of relief that you see that Oriana remains unharmed. But as you hold your sister close, you cannot shake the feeling that someone is watching you. You turn to see a spectral figure watching you, a look of unalloyed hatred in its eyes. You recognise the figure at once – it is Unthank the Necromancer.

With a howl of frustrated fury, the undead spirit of the necromancer flies at you. But, as they say, the night is always darkest just before the dawn. Even as

⚀ ⚁

Unthank's ghost goes for you, the first probing fingers of morning appear over the wine-dark ocean to the east as a new day dawns. With a soul-shredding scream, Unthank's undead spirit dissolves into vapour as the first rays of sunlight strike his ethereal form, sending him on his way at last to the Other Side and the Lands of the Dead where he shall be punished for all eternity. The night of the necromancer is over and it is the beginning of a new day, a day of endless possibilities ...

THE END

CHOOSE YOUR ADVENTURER

Here at your disposal are three adventurers to choose from. Over the page are the rules for Fighting Fantasy to help you on your way. However, if you wish to begin your adventure immediately, study the characters carefully, log your chosen attributes on the *Adventure Sheet* and you can begin!

Anvus Ravalan

Known to some as Nightsbane, to others as the Remorseless Hunter, Anvus earned himself a fearful reputation during the Bathorian Crusade as a warrior who was relentless in his pursuit of the forces of darkness. The first into the fray, always the last to leave the battlefield, he put many a vile Darkspawn to the sword and led the final charge at the Battle of Fang Rock.

Luck has had its part to play in Anvus's successes, as has his great strength. Serious and prone to dark moods some say that he is not that different from his enemies in his nature – but never within earshot of the humourless warrior! But it may be true, in part, as Anvus has made the study of the agents of evil his life's work that he might understand his enemies better, learn of their weaknesses and thereby put an end to them all the more ruthlessly.

Skill	8
Stamina	21
Luck	9
Will	6
Equipment	Nightslayer

Evrain Peredur

Having trained with the Knights of Telak, Evrain served for some years within the Demonkeep Outpost on Ruddlestone's border with Brice, before taking up the mantle of Lord of Valsinore, following the death of his father under suspicious circumstances. Early in his career he distinguished himself when he single-handedly thwarted the plans of the Sorcerer Belgaroth, who sought to conquer the kingdom of Ruddlestone with an army of beastmen and Chaos Knights that he was raising in the southern Banarask Hills.

During the Bathorian Crusade he added to his list of noteworthy achievements by earning himself the title Zombie Killer. A skilled swordsman and a skilled horseman too, it would seem that Evrain is blessed by the gods themselves, such is his ability in escaping from seemingly impossible predicaments at the very last minute by the skin of his teeth.

Skill	10
Stamina	17
Luck	11
Will	6
Equipment	Nightslayer

Isolde Laodegan

Isolde Laodegan, the Shield Maiden of Libra, swore her life to the service of Good following the death of her mother. She has trained at abbeys, monasteries and temples all across the Old World becoming equally proficient with the sword, bow, spear and mace. Through physical exercise and spiritual meditation she has honed her body to perfection so that she is just as adept an athlete as she is a deadly swordswoman.

However, a curse seems to hang over her family line, both her parents dying before their time and in recent years Isolde has begun to feel that some ill fate awaits her, dogging her every step, waiting until it can bring her down too and have its final, villainous victory.

Skill	12
Stamina	19
Luck	7
Will	6
Equipment	Nightslayer

RULES AND EQUIPMENT

A HERO COMES HOME

You are about to embark on a Fighting Fantasy adventure unlike any other, but before you do so you need to establish your own strengths and weaknesses. You use dice to determine your initial scores. On pages 360–361 there is an *Adventure Sheet*, which you should use to record the details of your adventure. On it you will find boxes for recording the scores of your attributes. Record your scores on the *Adventure Sheet* in pencil or make photocopies of the sheet for use in future adventures. You can also download fresh *Adventure Sheets* from www.fightingfantasy.com.

Skill, Stamina, Luck and Will

Roll one die. Add 6 to the number rolled and enter the total in the SKILL box on the *Adventure Sheet*.

Roll two dice. Add 12 to the number rolled and enter the total in the STAMINA box.

Roll one die. Add 6 to the number and enter the total in the LUCK box.

Don't roll any dice for WILL: you always start your adventure with 6 WILL points.

For reasons that will be explained below, all your scores will change during the adventure to come. You must keep an accurate record of these scores, so write small or keep an eraser handy, and never rub out your *Initial* scores. Although you may be awarded additional SKILL, STAMINA and LUCK points, their totals may never exceed their *Initial* scores, except on those occasions when the text specifically tells you so.

Your SKILL reflects your expertise in combat, your dexterity and agility. Your STAMINA score reflects how healthy and physically fit you are. Your LUCK score indicates how lucky you are.

Your WILL is a measure of your determination and strength of purpose. Your WILL score differs from your other attributes because it is not restricted by an *Initial* score. Your WILL may increase or decrease in certain situations, which will be explained in the relevant paragraphs.

Battles

During your adventure you will often encounter hostile creatures which will attack you, and you yourself may choose to attack an enemy. In some such situations you may be given special options allowing you to deal with the encounter in an unusual manner, but in most cases you will have to resolve battles as described below.

Enter your opponent's SKILL and STAMINA scores in the first vacant Encounter Box on your *Adventure Sheet*. You should also make a note of any special abilities or instructions, which are unique to that particular opponent. Then follow this sequence:

1. Roll both dice for your opponent. Add its SKILL score to the total rolled to find its Attack Strength.
2. Roll both dice for yourself, then add your current SKILL score to find your Attack Strength.
3. If your Attack Strength is higher than your opponent's, you have wounded it: proceed to step 4. If your opponent's Attack Strength is higher than yours, it has wounded you: proceed to step 5. If both Attack Strength totals are the same, you have avoided or parried each other's blows: start a new Attack Round from step 1 above.
4. You have wounded your opponent, so subtract 2 points from its STAMINA score. You may use LUCK here to do additional damage (see below).
5. Your opponent has wounded you, so subtract 2 points from your STAMINA score. You may use LUCK to reduce the loss of STAMINA (see below).
6. Begin the next Attack Round, starting again at step 1. This sequence continues until the STAMINA score of either you or your opponent reaches zero, which means death. If your opponent dies, you are free to continue with your adventure. However, if your STAMINA score is reduced to zero, your adventure may not actually be over and you should follow the instructions given at the relevant paragraph.

Fighting More Than One Opponent

In some situations you may find yourself facing more than one opponent in combat. Sometimes you will treat them as a single adversary; sometimes you will be able to fight each in turn; and at other times you will have to fight them all at the same time! If they are treated as a single opponent, the combat is resolved normally. If you have to fight your opponents one at a time, as soon as you defeat an enemy, the next steps forward to fight you! When you find yourself under attack from more than one opponent at the same time, each adversary will make a separate attack on you in the course of each Attack Round, but you can choose which one to fight. Attack your chosen target as in a normal battle. Against any additional opponents you throw for your Attack Strength in the normal way, but if it is greater than your opponent's, in this instance you will not inflict any damage. If your Attack Strength is lower than your adversary's, you will be wounded in the normal way. Of course, you will have to settle the outcome against each additional adversary separately.

Luck

At various times during your adventure, either in battles or when you come across other situations in which you could be either Lucky or Unlucky, you may use LUCK to make the outcome more favourable to you. But beware! Using LUCK is a risky business and, if you are Unlucky, the results could be disastrous.

The procedure for *Testing your Luck* works as follows: roll two dice. If the number rolled is equal to or less than your current LUCK score, you have been Lucky and the outcome will go in your favour. If the number rolled is higher than your current LUCK score, you have been Unlucky and will be penalised.

Each time you *Test your Luck*, you must subtract 1 point from your current LUCK score, so the more you rely on your LUCK, the more risky this procedure will become.

Using Luck in Battles

In certain paragraphs you will be told to *Test your Luck*, and you will then find out the consequences of being Lucky or Unlucky. However, in battles, you always have the option of using your LUCK, to inflict more serious damage on an opponent that you have wounded, or to minimise the effects of a wound you have received.

If you have just wounded an opponent, you may *Test your Luck* as described above. If you are Lucky you have inflicted a severe wound; deduct an *extra* 2 points from your opponent's STAMINA score. If you are Unlucky, however, your blow only scratches your opponent; and you deduct 1 point *less* from your opponent's STAMINA.

Whenever you yourself are wounded in combat, you may *Test your Luck* to try to minimise the wound. If you are Lucky, your opponent's blow only grazes you; deduct 1 point from the damage you sustain. If you are Unlucky, your wound is a serious one and you must deduct 1 *extra* STAMINA point than you would normally.

Remember: you must subtract 1 point from your LUCK score each time you *Test your Luck*.

More About Your Attributes

Skill

Your SKILL score may change occasionally during the course of your adventure, but it may not exceed its *Initial* value unless you are specifically instructed to the contrary.

At various times you will be told to *Test your Skill*. The procedure for *Testing your Skill* works as follows: roll two dice. If the number rolled is equal to or less than your current SKILL score, you have succeeded in your test and the result will go in your favour. If the number rolled is higher than your current SKILL score, you will have failed the test and will have to suffer the consequences. However, unlike *Testing your Luck*, do not subtract 1 point from your SKILL each time you *Test your Skill*.

Stamina

Your STAMINA score will change a great deal throughout your adventure. It will drop if you are wounded in combat, if you fall foul of traps, and after you perform any particularly arduous task. In other Fighting Fantasy gamebooks, if your STAMINA score ever falls to zero, you have been killed and should stop reading the book immediately. However, as you will soon discover, death is not necessarily the end where necromancy is concerned. Rather than having to start all over again with a new character, in this book you should follow the instructions given in the text. But if your luck should run out entirely and your adventure does indeed come to an end, if you wish to attempt your quest again, you will then have to choose a new character and start all over again.

During the course of your adventure you will find that you can restore lost STAMINA but not in the usual way, by eating meals or Provisions. But to find out more, you will just have to commence your quest.

Will

As you will soon discover, your WILL score will be very important in the adventure that lies ahead of you. You start the game with 6 WILL points. Precisely how WILL works will be revealed during your adventure: you will be instructed about this in the relevant paragraphs. However, you should note that your WILL score may never drop below 1.

Equipment

You begin your journey with some simple equipment. You are dressed in leather armour and carry a backpack. You are also the bearer of Nightslayer, a blessed blade worthy of an evil-hunting warrior such as yourself. Powerful enchantments wrought into the weapon mean that it can harm the Undead, Demons, Elementals and other magical creatures.

Alternative Dice

If you do not have a pair of dice handy, dice rolls are printed throughout the book at the bottom of the pages. Flicking rapidly through the book and stopping on a page will give you a random dice roll. If you need to roll only one die, read only the first printed die; if two, total the two dice symbols.

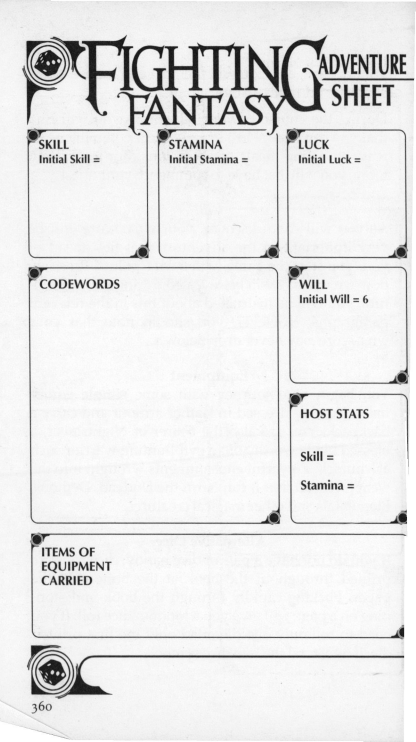

FIGHTING FANTASY ADVENTURE SHEET

SKILL
Initial Skill =

STAMINA
Initial Stamina =

LUCK
Initial Luck =

CODEWORDS

WILL
Initial Will = 6

HOST STATS

Skill =

Stamina =

ITEMS OF EQUIPMENT CARRIED

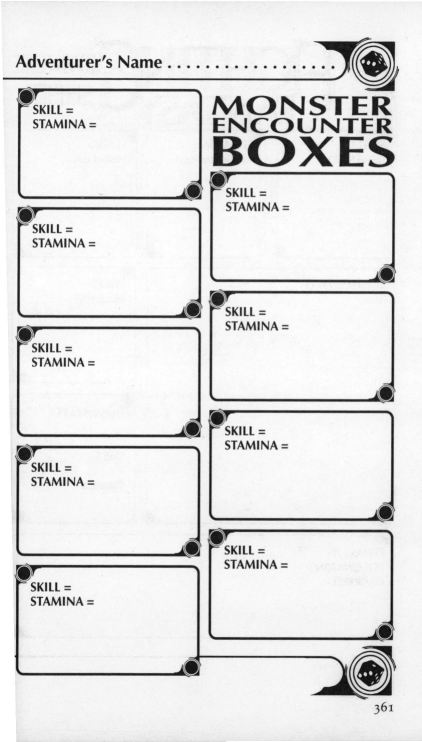

Adventurer's Name . . . .

MONSTER ENCOUNTER BOXES

SKILL =
STAMINA =

SKILL =
STAMINA =

SKILL =
STAMINA =

SKILL =
STAMINA =

SKILL =
STAMINA =

SKILL =
STAMINA =

SKILL =
STAMINA =

SKILL =
STAMINA =

SKILL =
STAMINA =

361

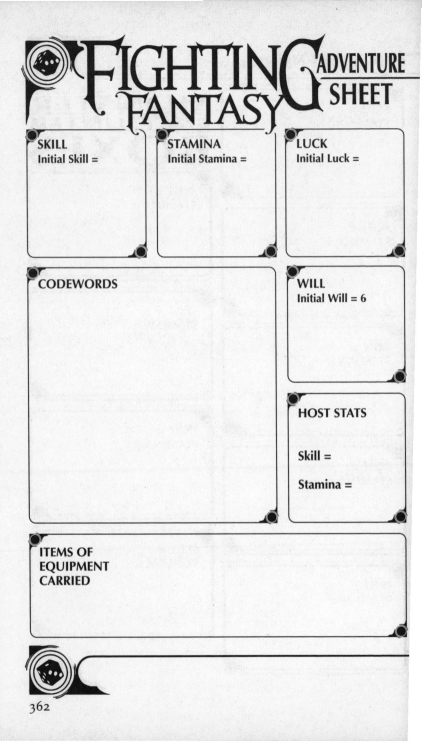

FIGHTING FANTASY — ADVENTURE SHEET

SKILL
Initial Skill =

STAMINA
Initial Stamina =

LUCK
Initial Luck =

CODEWORDS

WILL
Initial Will = 6

HOST STATS

Skill =

Stamina =

ITEMS OF EQUIPMENT CARRIED

Adventurer's Name ....

MONSTER ENCOUNTER BOXES

SKILL =
STAMINA =

SKILL =
STAMINA =

SKILL =
STAMINA =

SKILL =
STAMINA =

SKILL =
STAMINA =

SKILL =
STAMINA =

SKILL =
STAMINA =

SKILL =
STAMINA =

SKILL =
STAMINA =

FIGHTING FANTASY
ADVENTURE SHEET

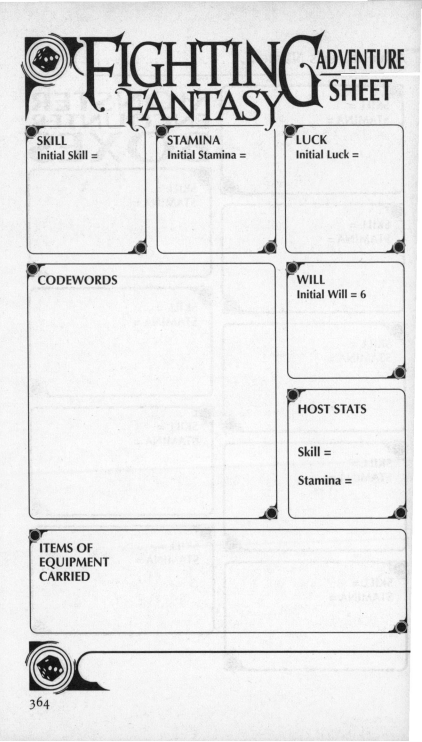

SKILL
Initial Skill =

STAMINA
Initial Stamina =

LUCK
Initial Luck =

CODEWORDS

WILL
Initial Will = 6

HOST STATS

Skill =

Stamina =

ITEMS OF EQUIPMENT CARRIED

Adventurer's Name . . . .

MONSTER ENCOUNTER BOXES

SKILL =
STAMINA =

SKILL =
STAMINA =

SKILL =
STAMINA =

SKILL =
STAMINA =

SKILL =
STAMINA =

SKILL =
STAMINA =

SKILL =
STAMINA =

SKILL =
STAMINA =

SKILL =
STAMINA =

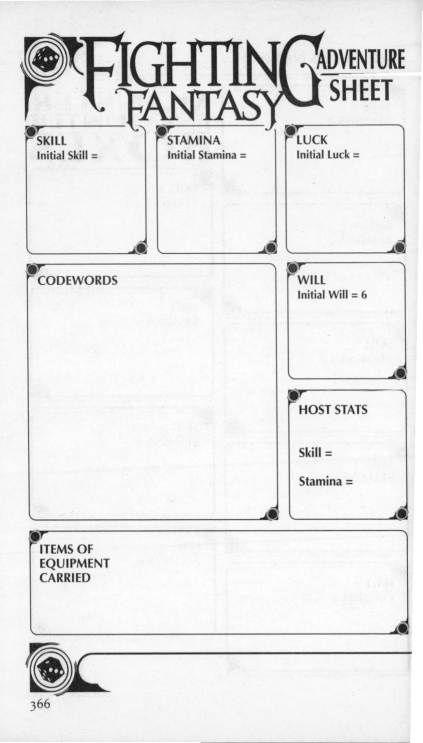

FIGHTING FANTASY
ADVENTURE SHEET

SKILL
Initial Skill =

STAMINA
Initial Stamina =

LUCK
Initial Luck =

CODEWORDS

WILL
Initial Will = 6

HOST STATS

Skill =

Stamina =

ITEMS OF EQUIPMENT CARRIED

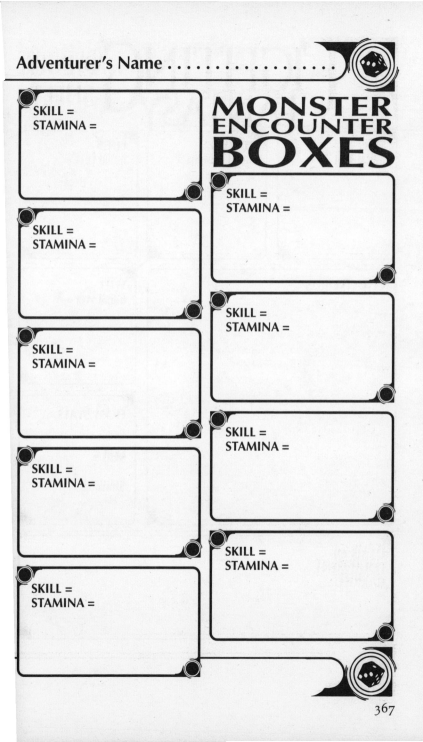

MONSTER ENCOUNTER BOXES

SKILL =
STAMINA =

SKILL =
STAMINA =

SKILL =
STAMINA =

SKILL =
STAMINA =

SKILL =
STAMINA =

SKILL =
STAMINA =

SKILL =
STAMINA =

SKILL =
STAMINA =

SKILL =
STAMINA =

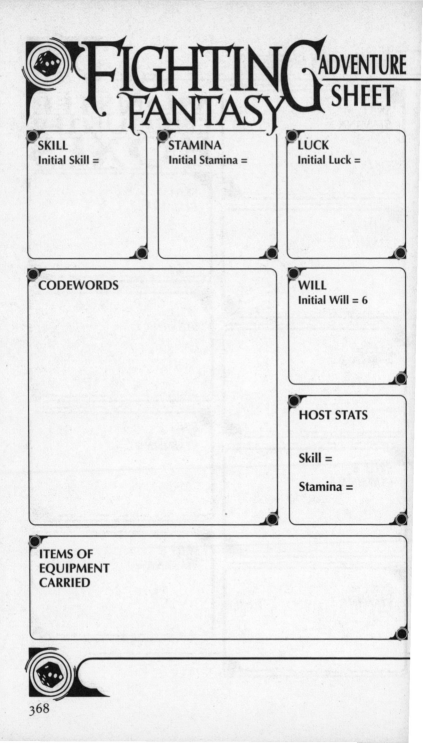

FIGHTING FANTASY — ADVENTURE SHEET

SKILL
Initial Skill =

STAMINA
Initial Stamina =

LUCK
Initial Luck =

CODEWORDS

WILL
Initial Will = 6

HOST STATS

Skill =

Stamina =

ITEMS OF EQUIPMENT CARRIED

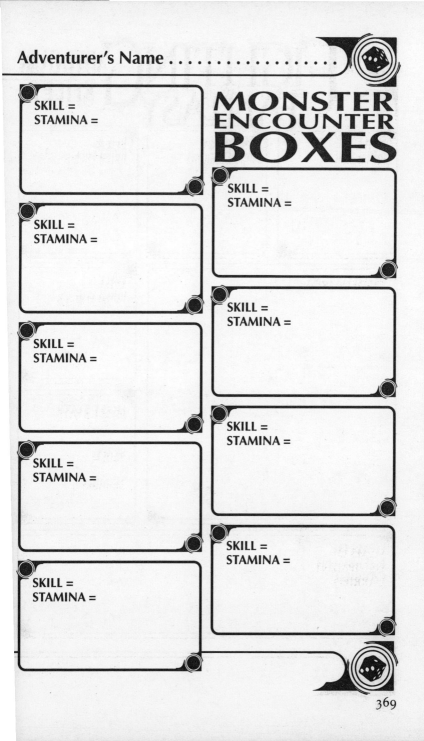

MONSTER ENCOUNTER BOXES

SKILL =
STAMINA =

SKILL =
STAMINA =

SKILL =
STAMINA =

SKILL =
STAMINA =

SKILL =
STAMINA =

SKILL =
STAMINA =

SKILL =
STAMINA =

SKILL =
STAMINA =

SKILL =
STAMINA =

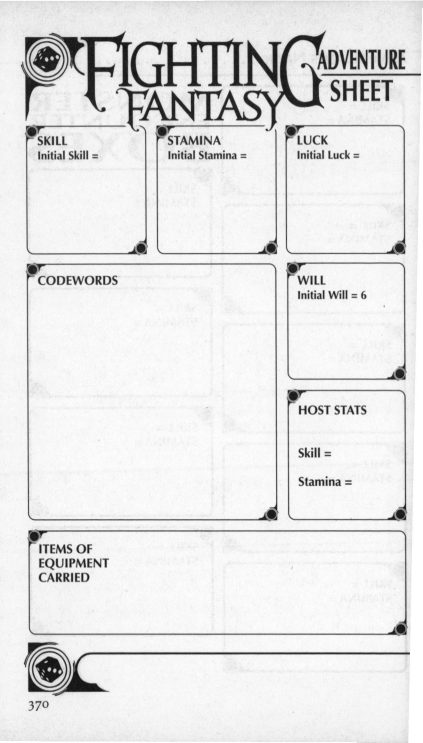

FIGHTING FANTASY
ADVENTURE SHEET

SKILL
Initial Skill =

STAMINA
Initial Stamina =

LUCK
Initial Luck =

CODEWORDS

WILL
Initial Will = 6

HOST STATS

Skill =

Stamina =

ITEMS OF EQUIPMENT CARRIED

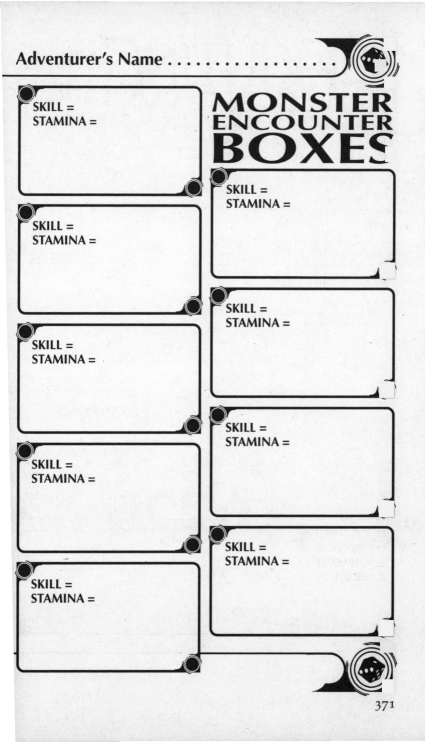

Adventurer's Name . . . .

MONSTER ENCOUNTER BOXES

SKILL =
STAMINA =

SKILL =
STAMINA =

SKILL =
STAMINA =

SKILL =
STAMINA =

SKILL =
STAMINA =

SKILL =
STAMINA =

SKILL =
STAMINA =

SKILL =
STAMINA =

SKILL =
STAMINA =

TURN OVER IF YOU DARE

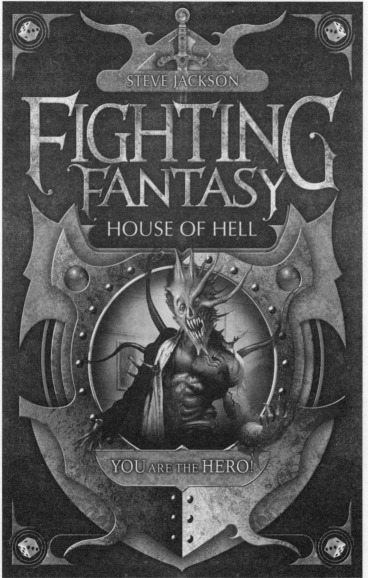

STEVE JACKSON

FIGHTING FANTASY

HOUSE OF HELL

YOU ARE THE HERO!

EXCLUSIVE EXTRACT FROM

HOUSE OF HELL

Blood-curdling terror.
Nightmarish rituals.
Can you survive a night in the House of Hell?

Stranded miles from anywhere on a dark and stormy night, your only hope of refuge is the strange, ramshackle mansion you can see in the distance. You climb out of your car; its battery is flat and there is no way you can get it started tonight. You can't afford to miss tomorrow's appointment. It is fifteen miles since you last passed a house and your only hope now is that you can telephone a garage from the foreboding dwelling up ahead.

You slam the door , turn up your collar and set off for the house. A flash of lightning lights it up clearly for you but, in your preoccupation with the rain, the warning from above is wasted on you. The house is old – even older than you thought – and in a shocking state of repair. The light in the window is flickering. Most likely an oil lamp – certainly not electric. And you don't notice a fact that might have turned you back anyway: there is no telephone line going to the house.

As you climb the steps to the front door, little do you realise what fate has in store for you.

Tonight is going to be a night to remember ...

Turn to **1**.

You climb the creaking steps up to the front door and pause to catch your breath. Even though you ran all the way up the drive from the car, you are soaked through; your feet are particularly wet. Judging by the number of puddles you stepped into in the dark, the drive needs a small fortune spending on repairs. But under the porch, you are out of the storm, and you brush the rain from your clothes before turning towards the door.

The rain is still pelting down, but an eerie silence hangs in the air. No lights are on downstairs. You step back off the porch to check the upstairs window which attracted your attention earlier. Nothing. No lights. The whole place seems to be deserted. But then you remember the time – five minutes to midnight. Everyone in the house has probably gone to bed. An owl hoots in the distance and a shiver runs down your spine. The situation is a little scary. Here you are, in the middle of nowhere, at some strange, run-down old house about to wake up whoever lives inside, at midnight. They certainly won't be too pleased. But you have no choice if you are going to make your appointment tomorrow – you must reach a telephone to call for help. You step up to the front door.

From the left-hand side of the house, a dull glow catches your attention. A light has been turned on! You breathe a sigh of relief; at least someone is awake. You consider your options: there is an elaborate knocker in the middle of the door and a bell-pull hanging down to the right. Will you rap the door with the knocker, (turn to **12**), pull the cord (turn to **8**), or creep round the house to investigate the light (turn to **9**)?

2

You sit down in a solid, carved chair and look around. The reception hall is certainly not what you would have expected from the outside. It is elegantly decorated with rich tapestries and fine oak panels. A number of portraits line the walls. A sturdy sixteenth-century table is set against one wall.

Although the house seems comfortable, luxurious almost, there is something hanging in the atmosphere that sets your nerves on edge. Something doesn't seem quite right. What will you do next if you are to have any hope of surviving the night in the House of Hell?

3

The younger man turns to the older one and angrily says, 'The Master's teachings are not for the faint-hearted. You know of his power and his promises to us all. Perhaps you are no longer strong enough to stay with us.' The older man turns away, towards the window. He is hiding the look on his face, which is one of nervousness and fear. He realizes that he has said the wrong thing. 'No,' he stammers, 'I'll be all right. Just a momentary weakness. Come, let us get on with the preparations.' Together the two men leave the kitchen, blowing out the candles on the way. You wonder what they were talking about. Now you must choose your next move. Will you try the kitchen door to see whether you can sneak inside (turn to 10) or go back round to the front and knock on the door (turn to 12)?

4

The door opens wide and the older man peers out at you before inviting you in. The two men listen as you tell them of your accident. 'Well, that *is* a stroke of bad luck,' says the older man, 'but I dare say Franklins will be able to help. Go and fetch him, Brother William.' At the mention of his name, the younger man glares at his companion, but nevertheless leaves the kitchen. You ask your host what sort of place this is and whether he and Brother William are members of a religious group. 'Something like that,' he replies. 'In fact you have arrived at an awkward time. For tonight …' he hesitates nervously, 'tonight is …' His sentence is interrupted by the arrival of Brother William and a tall man dressed in a black suit with long tails. You explain your arrival to Franklins. 'We do not welcome visitors here,' says Franklins solemnly, 'but I will introduce you to the master of the house who will decide whether we can help. Follow me.' He leads you out through the kitchen along a hallway to a reception hall and points to a seat. 'Wait here while I tell the Earl,' he orders, then he disappears through a doorway. Turn to 2.

5

You walk up to a large window which looks as though it may not be quite closed. But there are heavy bars across it. Even if you were able to open the window, you would never manage to squeeze through the bars. The house is certainly well protected from intruders! Do you want to continue round the house to see where the light is coming from (turn to 11) or return to the front door and either pull the rope (turn to 8) or use the knocker (turn to 12)?

6

'What's this?' you hear the older man ask. 'Someone knocking at the door at this time of night? Could it be one of the brethren? I thought everyone was here.' Then the two men start whispering to each other in voices too low for you to hear. You wait patiently outside in the rain until eventually, the door opens and a voice asks, 'Who is it?' Will you tell them about your predicament and ask to use the phone (turn to 4) or will you claim to be one of the brethren that you heard them talking about (turn to 7)?

7

The door opens wide and you are invited in. 'We thought everyone was here already,' says the older man. 'That's cutting it a bit fine. The others are ...' He pauses when he sees your face and the two men look at each other. 'Er, ahem ... what delayed you?' You are feeling a little uneasy about the situation and mumble some excuse about your car breaking down.

'Your car,' says the man slowly. 'What a shame – I hope it's not too bad.' From their reactions, you get the distinct impression that you have said the wrong thing. Then it dawns on you that there are no other cars around the house although, according to these two, everyone has arrived. You try desperately to think of what to say next and you do not notice that the younger man has crept round behind you. You feel a heavy blow on the back of your head, which knocks you unconscious.

Things have taken a turn for the worse adventurer,
you are now in the hands of the mysterious brethren.
Will you escape or is something much worse in store
for you? Can you survive a night of terror in
the House of Hell?

8

You grasp the rope and pull. From the depths of the house you hear a tinkling noise and the light coming from the side window goes out. Turn to **12**.

9

You walk from the porch round the side of the house. A light is indeed on, and it's shining through a window at the back of the building. Do you wish to go round to see if you can see anything at this window (turn to **11**) or will you walk up to one of the other windows along the side wall to see whether you can enter the house without anyone knowing (turn to **5**)?

10

The door is firmly locked. You will not enter the house this way. If you wish, you can knock at the door to try to attract the attention of the two men who were talking. If you decide to do this, you must Test your Luck. If you are Lucky, they will hear you and come to investigate (turn to 7). If you are Unlucky, they are out of earshot and you will not get through this way. If you decide against knocking at the door, or if you have been Unlucky, you will have to go back to the front door and either knock (turn to 12) or pull the bell-pull (turn to 8).

11

The lit window is next to a back door which leads into a kitchen. Voices are coming from the kitchen, but you cannot see anyone. Whoever is in there must be standing by the back wall, out of sight. You strain to hear what is being said. There appear to be two people in the kitchen, and they are talking excitedly. '… Master is getting ready. I'm starting to get excited. I've never been to one before. Do you really think we may be *visited*?' Another man's voice, rather more controlled, replies: 'You know, I'm having doubts about this whole affair. She is so young and she came here in all innocence. I just don't know.' The two men walk around the kitchen and you can see them more clearly. They are both dressed in white gowns. One is a good deal younger than the other. Do you wish to knock on the door to see whether they will let you in (turn to 6, ...nd listen for a little longer (turn t...

12

A few moments later, the door-handle turns slowly and the door opens. Standing in the doorway is a tall man dressed in a dark suit with tails. His long face is solemn. 'Yes?' he asks, indignantly. You smile nervously and explain your situation. Your car has broken down, you need to reach a telephone and you are soaked to the skin. The man's face remains expressionless. 'Come in,' he orders. 'The Master is expecting you. Follow me.' He leads you into a reception hall and tells you to sit down while he informs his master of your arrival. Turn to 2.

ONLINE

Stay in touch with the Fighting Fantasy community at www.fightingfantasy.com. Sign up today and receive exclusive access to:

- Fresh Adventure Sheets
- Members' forum
- Competitions
- Quizzes and polls
- Exclusive Fighting Fantasy news and updates

You can also send in your own Fighting Fantasy material, the very best of which will make it onto the website.

www.fightingfantasy.com

The website where YOU ARE THE HERO!